DEMON's DAUGHTER

Emily Book 1

By
Ashley McCook

ISBN: 978-0-9571255-0-6

Crooked
Halo
Publications

www.ashleymccook.co.uk

DEMON'S DAUGHTER

By
Ashley McCook

Published by

www.ashleymccook.co.uk

ISBN: 978-0-9571255-0-6

Graphic Design by Nigel Johnston

For Katy – my Emily
For Jack – my Seth
And for Stephen – my one and only

CHAPTER ONE

I'd made up my mind: The tall guy with the dark brown hair was an idiot.

Our history lesson was about to start and Seth (the idiot in question and, unfortunately, also my twin) was leaning over Amber Scott's desk and looking at her longingly as she texted on her phone. Occasionally she batted her eyelids in his direction and I was sure that if I got closer I would see drool leaking from the corner of his idiotic mouth.

As our teacher, Mr. Dawson came into the room, Amber leaned up and (still texting) whispered something into Seth's ear. He practically floated to his desk, grinning like the village idiot that he was. I groaned and banged my head on my desk several times to stop myself from going over there and slapping his stupid face.

My friend Dylan leaned over and whispered, "Bet she was texting Sarah." He nodded in a 'you-know-what-that-means' kind of way and moved away again.

Behind me Annie stage-whispered, "Does he seriously fancy her?"

I lifted my head off my desk and tried to concentrate on Mr. Dawson's intro to the topic of the month – Mao Tse Tung's China. All I could think about was that Seth was either going to make a major fool of himself or get his heart broken into a gazillion pieces. I wasn't sure what would be worse.

Why couldn't he have fancied Annie Poole? One of my best friends and a totally cool person with her tie-dyed t-shirts and her fringed bags. Annie was a throw-back to the sixties, a child born in the totally wrong decade. She even had the slightly eerie, breathy voice of one of the perpetually stoned, although in Annie's case it was simply that she found everything in life astonishing – every day was a gift to be investigated and then savored. Annie's like a walking encyclopaedia – okay, multi-coloured, hippie encyclopaedia, but she's a genuine memory-girl and a great friend. On my birthday she bought me a tie-dyed shirt from the local New Age shop and a cute crystal angel. The shirt

1

was purple, green and pink so I wore it to bed rather than out in public but the angel was gorgeous and came in a tiny chiffon bag with a small card inside. The card was hand printed in teeny writing. It said "This is an angel to keep my best friend safe." My angel went with me everywhere.

Or Alice? Alice Frost was a pretty girl too – in a mousy, nervous sort of way. She was the kind who walked along with her books clutched tightly to her chest and her head down in case anyone spoke to her but she had these liquid brown eyes framed with the longest, darkest lashes I'd ever seen. Why don't guys look beyond the obvious and see the true beauties sometimes?

Or even Claire Anderson – Claire was cute with a blonde chin-length bob and big blue eyes. Her skin was perfect – peaches and cream layered over mother of pearl. To me, Claire always seemed to have a kind of inner glow that formed an aura of happiness around her. Okay, so she wore a skirt that skimmed her ankles and went to church four times a week but hey! Being deeply religious doesn't make you a bad person!

Unfortunately it also doesn't make you a member of the 'it' crowd.

Amber Scott was a member of the most popular crowd in school and she was a total babe – small and curvy with a flat stomach, skin the colour of caramel and glossy auburn hair that cascaded down her back in a waterfall of loose curls. In our school she was second only to Sarah King – queen bee of Rainey High School. Sarah is a total Jordan wannabe – she's skinny with long blonde hair, big boobs and pouty lips. I've never actually heard her say anything remotely sensible but she has this throaty giggle that guys seem to go nuts for. Personally I don't get it. I mean, she's a total bitch!

Seth and I moved here from Seattle when we were twelve and Sarah's first words to us were, "Move out of the way you inbred American assholes." See what I mean? Total bitch! When she found out that our mum is a single parent, well, she really went to town on that one. I'm not going to repeat the words that she used, the names that she called us but I'm willing to bet that you can imagine.

I don't like her much. (No, really!)

Sarah dates Adam Farlow. If I didn't already detest her, then that right there would be the clincher. Adam is ...well he's...oh, he's totally gorgeous! Floppy blond hair, dark blue eyes, wide shoulders, narrow waist, cute butt... he's on the rugby team and the rowing team so you can imagine the muscles under that school uniform. Well, I can imagine every lickable inch of them anyway. He's delicious. And I get to stare at him during Biology and English Lit. Of course, so do the rest of the girls in the class.

Amber used to date Ritchie Phillips (he of the multi-millionaire Daddy and model-turned-fashion-designer mummy) but they split up about three weeks ago and, since we turned sixteen last Thursday, Seth seems to have had some kind of common-sense bypass. He asked Amber out the day after our birthday and she told him it was too soon after Ritchie "but maybe next week." So there we were – Seth following Amber around like a little puppy and Amber stringing him along with little whispers and flirty looks.

I was right, he was an idiot.

History dragged on and on. Mr. Dawson is a decent human being but he makes history as exciting as watching old wallpaper curl. Bless him! He always asks the class "How did I do?" at the end of a lesson and looks inconsolable as Dylan makes a 'poor guy' face and pats him on the back on the way out. I've tried to explain to Dylan that a little sugar coating might be better but Dylan can't tell the man a lie and he believes that constructive criticism is good for the soul.

Yes, Dylan is a nerd, but in a nice way. He knows everything there is to know about mathematics and computers. He is also loyal to his friends and completely honest, alarmingly honest sometimes. When Annie asks, "What do you think of my hair?" (She's constantly changing the colour of it), Dylan always answers truthfully – which is sometimes "Dreadful. What the hell colour IS that?" Dylan is an average height with a halo of dark curls and intense blue eyes. He kind of looks cross a lot but his brain just seems to be wired differently to everyone else – Dylan thinks about everything really deeply and doesn't cope well with minor annoyances. He will also argue about ANYTHING!

At lunch Dylan, Annie and I sat outside at the picnic tables in the quad. It was a beautiful day with the sun high in the sky and everyone in good spirits. Seth joined us for a while but soon disappeared to look for Amber because I gave him such a hard time about her.

"He thinks you don't think he's good enough for her," said Annie after Seth had left. She was nibbling on an apple, leaving tiny little bites all over it.

"I don't think that!" I sighed loudly. "*She's* not good enough for *him*."

"She's pretty 'though," mused Dylan, watching Seth's retreating back.

"Yes, thank you, Einstein," I snapped and then was instantly sorry. "I don't mean to take it out on you guys but I just think Seth's going to get hurt. She's either just playing with him to make a fool out of him or she'll use him to make Ritchie jealous and Seth'll end up getting a smack in the mouth from Ritchie." I see sawed my hands "Smack in the mouth or broken heart. Tough choice." I huffed into my cheese sandwich until the bell sounded and we trooped off to class.

The bus ride home was stifling. The driver opened some of the roof windows but there were so many bodies pressed close together that it was still too hot. Seth and I had to stand all the way to our stop, along with about twenty other little sardines. As we walked up the hill towards home, I tried to talk to my twin, to apologise for giving him the wrong impression, to caution him against his present course of action. Seth ignored it all and we walked into the house silent and tense.

Mum was waiting for us in the small living room. Her eyes were red-rimmed and she was holding a wadded up tissue. She looked up at us slowly and the only thing I could see written on her face was defeat.

Seth and I immediately forgot our fight. We dropped our bags and were beside our Mother in seconds. "What happened?" "Are you okay?" "Has something happened to Grandma?" "Or Gramps?" "Is it work?" "Did you get fired?" We were, as usual, like machine guns - question after question.

Mum held up a hand to slow us down. My heart was pounding and I looked at Seth. He looked back at me, his face strained. Bad news was coming, we could feel it.

CHAPTER TWO

Mum managed a watery smile and patted the sofa on either side of her. We sat down and she smiled at us and took a deep breath.

"I received a letter this morning," she began. "It was a letter from your…Father." She spat out the word with such venom that Seth recoiled from her a little. I gaped. Mum didn't ever talk about our dad. As far as we knew she had chosen to be alone, had chosen to have kids without a husband or partner around to help. Of course we knew that there had a to be a "Dad' somewhere in the mix (we had learned about all *that* stuff way before Miss Cafferty started teaching us about it in biology) and although I guess we'd been curious, I suppose we'd known that it was a touchy subject.

Mum swallowed, made a face, opened her mouth to speak and closed it again. She grinned at us. "I've been planning how to tell y'all this all day and it all seems much more difficult now you're sitting in front of me."

Seth took her hand and smiled at her. "Whatever you have to tell us, mum. It's okay. We're old enough to hear it now."

I looked at Seth in astonishment. He caught my gaze and looked up. *You just had your sixteenth birthday, Buster, not your thirtieth,* my look told him. He blinked and his jaw clenched; *stay out of this,* he was clearly saying, *the adults are talking about grown up stuff.* I rolled my eyes. Well, there was no grown up way to deal with him!

Mum sighed. "You remember when I told you that we were moving back to Deans Lynn?"

Seth and I nodded. "Because Gramps was ill and you wanted to make peace with him and let him know that he had grandchildren." I said.

Mum nodded slowly and chewed the inside of her cheek, her eyes watching me closely. Behind her, Seth rolled his eyes at me. I wanted to hit him. Really hard. Preferably with a high heel. Or a baseball bat.

"Well," mum began again, "It wasn't exactly like that." I raised my eyebrows at her. "I hadn't spoken to my parents for a long time. They didn't even know that you were born." She spread her hands wide. "They were always good Christian people, church goers, y'know? I felt…ashamed."

Seth was mirroring my frown. "Lots of people have children outside marriage, mum. Besides, Gramps and Grandma seem like pretty relaxed folks."

Mum smiled sadly at him. "I know, baby, I know. I was young when I had you. I had all these things fixed in my head – I forgot that, at the end of the day, they're still my parents and they love me."

A thought struck me. "Were you ashamed of us?" I asked and I was embarrassed by how small my voice sounded.

Mum turned to me immediately, her eyes shocked. "Oh, no, sweetie. Never ever. You and Seth have always been the most perfect things in my life. You're my angels." She grimaced and then smiled again, taking my hand in hers. She looked down at her hands entwined with ours. "I got word that your Father was looking for you and I panicked and …we ran."

"Is our Dad in the mafia?" Seth's eyes were wide.

I giggled and then looked fearfully at my mum. She wasn't giggling, she wasn't even smiling. She made a kind of strangled mewling sound and began to cry again. Seth dived for the box of tissues on the coffee table while I put my arm around her shoulders. She sobbed loudly, gulping for air while my brother and I sat with our arms around her and let her. We didn't look at each other, there was no need. I knew that Seth was as confused and afraid as I was.

Finally her cries got quieter and she blew her nose. She grasped our hands tightly and took a deep breath, gathering all the strength she had left. "Your Father's name is Asmodeus." She leaned over and lifted a crumpled sheet of paper from the table, shaking it at us. "He is a lord of demons and I think he wants to claim you, his children."

There was silence so loud I was certain that Seth and I could hear each others hearts pound. I wanted to laugh. More than that I wanted my mother to laugh, to tell us it was a joke, to get up from the sofa and make pancakes with honey. If she'd stood up, danced a jig and told us that she'd lost her mind and

7

needed to be committed, that would've been good too.

Instead she sat looking at the floor, her shoulders quivering and the letter in her hand.

I looked over at my brother. He was caught somewhere between laughing aloud and passing out. He slowly lifted a hand, pointed at our mum and then twirled a finger beside his right temple. I shrugged. Was she nuts? I couldn't seem to have a coherent thought – my brain was zipping through possibilities faster than I could decipher them. I opened my mouth, closed it again. My head hurt from trying to make sense of the impossible.

Mum's shoulders were shaking harder. She was crying again, quietly this time which somehow seemed more terrible. I hugged her. "Are we going to move again?" I asked.

"It's a bit late for that," said a voice from the kitchen.

Seth and I jumped to our feet as my mum said softly, "The letter was hand delivered this time."

I swear I heard Seth's chin hit the floor as a woman walked from our tiny kitchen and into the living room. She was tall with hair the colour of corn and eyes of sparkling jade. She was built like a supermodel and wearing a cat suit that left absolutely nothing to the imagination. Seth seemed incapable of doing anything other than gaping at the cheap tramp that had been hiding in our kitchen. For some reason that made me madder than hell.

"And you are?" I asked tartly.

Her sultry eyes swiveled in my direction. "Call me Rosie." she purred and Seth swallowed noisily. I looked at him in disgust and he gave me a sheepish grin without taking his eyes off her. Boys and their bloody hormones!

"So you're what? Secretary to Daddy dearest?" I folded my arms and shot her the dirtiest look I could muster.

She smiled lazily and licked her lips, causing my brother to twitch and lean a little closer to her. "Seth!" I admonished and he frowned, finally looking in my direction.

"What?!" he growled.

"She has mum in tears and you're looking at her like …I dunno, like she's a chocolate fudge sundae with extra cream." Seth looked at Rosie and back at me, his expression saying *Yeah? So? Have you looked at this woman?*

"I'm your Father's…well, you could call me his P.A." Rosie said. Her tone and expression were amused. I was not.

"So let me get this straight," I said, beginning to pace. "He loves us sooooo much that he waits twelve years to get in touch, loses track of us and then waits another four? Sorry, but he doesn't sound too keen."

Rosie tilted her head to the side and regarded me with her unnerving eyes. "Time is different for him." She said.

"Yeah, well, we've managed without him perfectly well up till now. Toddle on back and tell him that we don't need him and we don't want to meet him." I flapped my hands at her and knelt down to hug mum, dismissing Rosie with as much bravado as I could. In truth I was getting seriously wigged out. This weird woman appears in our kitchen and my mum tells us that our Dad is some demon king. My rational mind couldn't make a path through all the craziness. Reality had slipped into the twilight zone while I wasn't paying attention.

"There is no option," Rosie said, "You will come and meet him."

"Why?" Oh, good, Seth had finally found his voice.

Rosie looked at him in surprise. "Because he has decreed it." She said, sounding astonished..

I waited for Seth to argue and when he didn't I looked up at him. He was nodding slowly, his face serious, as though she'd just said something totally understandable. I was looking around for something to throw at him when mum spoke up.

"When?" she asked.

Rosie smiled at her. "Tonight. Your escorts will arrive just before eleven."

"Eleven?" I squeaked. "Not midnight?"

Rosie frowned in confusion and I suddenly found it all hilarious. I began to laugh and couldn't stop. Rosie endured it for a few minutes, her face wrinkling in disgust. With a few last instructions she left, glancing back at me several times which made me laugh harder.

After she left my laughter turned to hot, salty tears. Seth crawled across the floor to me, his eyes concerned and his face dark with his own fear and confusion. I couldn't bare it. I pulled away from his embrace and dashed upstairs to our room, slamming the door behind me and throwing myself onto my bed.

Mum let herself in a few minutes later. I felt the bed dip as she sat down on the edge of it.

"I don't know what to say, Em," she said softly. "I know how all this sounds, especially to you. You were always the practical one, the one who figured things out. Seth was always much more of a dreamer. Something weird happens? He goes with the flow until it sorts itself out." She sighed and her breath hitched. "This won't sort itself out."

I turned onto my side and propped myself up on an elbow. "You're seriously telling me that our Dad is a demon?" She nodded. "From Hell?" Another nod. "Fire- and-brimstone Hell?"

"I don't know. I...never went there with him."

I opened my mouth and closed it a few times. Laughter threatened again but I forced it away by looking at my mum's grim face. This was incomprehensible. My brain scrabbled frantically to look for an explanation. "So, er, how did you guys meet?" I asked lamely.

"At a nightclub in New York," She said, her voice totally flat.

"Riiiiight." I shook my head. The woman was nuts. "And the horns growing out the top of his head, the cloven hooves, sharp tusks and red skin didn't put you off at all?"

Mum looked at me and her eyes flashed with anger. "If he *had* looked like that then we wouldn't be in this mess!" She shouted.

"Well, how did he look then?" I shouted right back.

"Like a bloody angel!" She retorted. "Like a bloody angel," she said again, her voice quiet now, all the anger wrung out of it. She sighed, rubbed her eyes with her knuckles and looked back at me. "He looked like Brad Pitt in 'Thelma and Louise', without the Stetson and the boots."

I raised an eyebrow.

She swung away, putting her back to me as she looked out the window. "I thought he was beautiful and he made me feel so special. We met every week for about six months, sometimes at the club and sometimes at my apartment. When I found out that I was pregnant I ran away, left New York. I couldn't face him."

"Why?" I was staggered. My image of my mother as the frumpy, pancake making, brownie baking, 38 year-old was crumbling fast.

"I don't know why. Maybe because I was scared. Maybe because I knew that he wasn't the one."

"The one?" I snorted. "As in Keanu Reeves in the Matrix? Or are we venturing into chick flick territory here?"

"Hey!" Mum reached back to swat me and before I knew it we were pillow fighting and giggling like the mad people we obviously were.

Seth opened the door and stood there watching us for a minute. "Ok, so I'm confused." He announced, making mum and I stop for a moment and look at him. "Are we having a crisis or are we not having a crisis?" He gestured towards us. "Going on the evidence we're having a pillow fight."

Mum launched a pillow at him. It hit him square on the face and he made a muffled 'oomph' sound. Mum looked at me and I nodded. Giggling we both launched ourselves at Seth, battering him with my pillows until we all collapsed in a giggling heap on the floor.

We lay there breathing heavily, smiles on our faces and sweat on our brows. "So," I said, "We're demon spawn."

"Em…" mum began.

"Wow," Said Seth a note of amazement in his voice. "Does this mean we have, like, special powers and stuff?"

"Seth…" There was a note of warning in mum's voice.

"Of course we do," I said. "Mine haven't shown up yet, maybe I'm not mature enough or something. But yours have been evident for quite some time."

Seth and mum were eyeing me with suspicion.

"Okay, I'll bite," said Seth finally. "What's my special power?"

I grinned at my brother. "You can completely level a room just by farting," I told him, earning a snort of disgust from him and a bray of laughter from mum.

Chapter Three

I shifted nervously from foot to foot, fidgeted with my hair and made little popping noises with my lips. Seth nudged me and gave me a wide-eyed 'shut up' look. I rolled my eyes and turned to the guy on my right.

"Excuse me," I asked. "Is there a bathroom?"

I was vaguely aware of Seth dropping his head into his hands. The muscle bound 'escort' on my right had obviously decided that the only way to survive my company was to completely ignore me. How annoying! I stepped in front of him and waved my hands in front of his face. Nothing. I pulled a face, using my fingers to pull the corners of my mouth as far apart as I could. No reaction.

I glanced at Seth. He was watching my display of complete immaturity with a mixture of alarm and awe. It was encouraging. I turned back to Mister Muscle and did a little ghetto dancing in front of him. Zilch, nada, zero, nothing.

Dejected I moved back beside into line. Seth leaned over. "You're insane." He whispered happily.

"This is ALL insane," I whispered back. We grinned at each other.

We were standing in a large hallway in front of an ornate wooden door which was carved with a myriad of strange symbols. Mister Muscle and two similar creatures had shown up at our house about a minute after eleven. By that time our happy moods had evaporated and we were waiting in a tense little knot.

There was a dark suv waiting outside, its windows tinted. Two of the muscled escorts had slipped into the front seat, gesturing for us to take the back seat. The third guy had stayed behind. To look after the house? To rifle through our things? To make himself a coffee? Who knew?

We had driven for what felt like hours, way out of the centre of Deans Lynn and through the suburbs. I saw a sign for Cambridge as we turned onto the A14, and then we were turning to the South and the roads blurred from one to another until we turned through a pair of gates and headed down a long lane. There were a lot of trees enclosing the lane in a dark cocoon and I was just starting to get seriously claustrophobic when the trees were suddenly gone and we were in front of a large house. Lights shone in most of the windows and a beautiful mauve wisteria was growing up the left hand side of the house, clinging around a high bay window and up towards the roof.

We stepped out the car and I inhaled deeply. I could smell lavender somewhere close and the coconut scent of gorse was carried past me on the slight breeze along with the unmistakable sweet and salty tang of the ocean. I grinned. I wished it wasn't so dark – I love the ocean. We lived near it in Seattle and I missed it like crazy.

There wasn't time to dawdle though - the unsmiling, silent driver and his pal corralled us into the house and we waited.

And we waited.

And now I needed to pee.

So I wandered away from our little group and through a half open door on the right. I ignored the squeaks and muffled exclamations that mum and Seth were making behind me. I needed to pee, dammit!

The room seemed to be a dining room with a huge dark wood table and twelve chairs. There were doors set into three of the walls. I knew the one beside me led into the hall so I did eeny meeny miney mo and chose the door directly in front.

I opened the door and all the frantic activity in the room beyond stopped.

It was a kitchen – a very large, modern kitchen staffed by around 8 people who were all regarding me with wide frightened eyes. I grinned and waved.

"Um, Hi," I stammered. "Looking for the bathroom?"

They glanced fearfully at each other but no-one spoke. Maybe they were foreign?

"Can. You. Tell. Me. Where. The. Bathroom. Is?" I enunciated each word slowly and carefully.

"They aren't allowed to speak to you." The voice came from my right and I twirled to face the speaker.

The man sat sprawled in a comfortable leather chair in the corner. He was wearing a light blue denim shirt and a dark canvas jacket over jeans. His eyes were a blue so light that they almost looked silver and they regarded me with lazy amusement. He had collar-length dark hair which was tousled, as though he'd been asleep, and when he smiled I felt my toes curl up and my breath catch. He was easily the most attractive man I'd ever seen. Maybe even better looking than Adam, and he was definitely the top of my list.

"Um, ok. Can YOU tell me where the bathroom is?" I asked as he studied me from the top of my head to the tips of my toes. I felt myself blushing at his close scrutiny and his grin widened.

He pointed to a door at the far end of the kitchen. "Through there, second door on the right. Not the left. If you go to the left you'll get us both into deep....trouble."

"Right is good, left is death. Okay, yeah. Got that." I moved through the silent kitchen, past the wide-eyed and pasty faced workers, and out through the door. The noise and movement started up again as the door swung closed behind me.

I paused for a moment on the other side to catch my breath. Well, this day just kept getting weirder.

The bathroom was small but with an honest-to-God deep pile carpet on the floor and soft, thick towels on the heated rails. Once I was feeling a lot less likely to cause a flood and had washed my hands using the yummy lemon scented soap, I stood for a few moment in the corridor outside wondering which way to go. The temptation to peek into the door on the left was almost too hard to resist but just as I reached my hand out to turn the door handle, a further door at the far end of the corridor opened and Mister Muscle beckoned for me to come that way.

Mum and Seth were already seated on a beige leather sofa, cradling drinks and smiling much too widely. I raised my eyebrows at them and mum motioned for me to sit beside them. I sat down and one of the kitchen workers materialized beside me with a silver tray containing a tall glass of coke and ice.

I was thirsty and the coke was blessedly cold. I barely registered anything else in the room until I'd taken a good few gulps and then I noticed that Rosie was sitting on one of the chairs opposite us and watching me with obvious disdain. Oh, great. Her again!

Tonight Rosie was wearing a cocktail dress of deep purple silk. It was draped around her like a toga, exposing a lot of leg and shoulder. Unfortunately she looked stunning in it. I smiled gaily at her and she grinned back.

"Lovely to see you again, Emily," she drawled.

"Oh, ditto, Rosie. You wouldn't believe how much I was hoping you'd be here tonight." I trilled back, earning me a stamped toe. "Ow!" I glared at mum who gave me a 'behave yourself' stare.

Rosie wriggled in her chair, happy to have caused me pain even indirectly. She shot to her feet when a door behind us opened and her face immediately became respectfully blank.

Mum turned her head and I heard her gasp. "Oh," she whispered and stood up. Seth and I followed suit and got our first look at our Dad.

CHAPTER FOUR

Asmodeus was a tall man – maybe around 6' 4"- with a shock of artfully tousled blond hair and piercing blue eyes. He had a square jaw and a slim figure that might've looked weedy except for the fact that he absolutely exuded strength and power. He was wearing a dark grey suit with a blue shirt and no tie. I thought that he looked like an Armani model or something. Like he should be standing on a beach with a breeze tossing his hair and his steely gaze locked on the camera. Demon? I shook my head and turned my attention to Mom.

She hadn't moved. In fact she looked absolutely frozen in the middle of an attempt to form a greeting – her mouth was slightly open and her right hand was extended. I linked my arm through hers and she turned to me blinking, her lips slipped into a grateful smile.

Seth was watching the stranger cautiously. I looked between them both, noticing the similarities – the incredibly blue eyes, the strong jaw, high cheekbones, full lips – and the differences; where our father looked cold and distant, Seth had a softness to his eyes and an openness to his bearing. They looked at each other and neither smiled. Seth dropped his eyes and held out a hand and visibly relaxed when Asmodeus shook it.

I knew the moment that my father's attention turned to me. I felt his gaze as a physical weight and my head began to hum with tension. I took my time, gathered my courage and then turned to face him. Asmodeus, Prince of hell, King of demons looked into my eyes and I felt…nothing.

There was no fear, no sense of excitement. My tension drained away and I felt a smile curve my lips. My father raised an eyebrow and I opened my mouth to introduce myself.

No! You must be obeisant to him. The voice was loud and I looked around the room in shock. No-one else reacted and I frowned in confusion.

Bow your head to him

Pardon? Bow my head to him? What planet are you from, disembodied

17

voice dude? I looked around again and waited for Seth to ask 'Who said that?' or something but no-one was looking in my direction. Everyone was watching Asmodeus. I turned my attention back to my father, my brows still drawn together. He was watching me expectantly, his eyes narrowing.

I dipped my head, the barest movement, and he nodded and moved forward to take my mother's hand.

"Joanna," he said and his voice was smooth and deep. He sounded like the taste of chocolate, I thought. My mother was drinking him in with her eyes, a tense smile on her lips. He drew her hand to his lips and inhaled deeply before placing a kiss on her knuckles.

He turned to Seth and shook hands again. "Well met, my son," he said and Seth nodded, mumbling something incoherent.

And then it was my turn. I made up my mind that if he kissed the back of my hand I would vomit. As it was, he shook my hand too. His skin was very cool but dry, almost papery. "Emily," he said, elongating my name as though he was tasting it. He licked his lips and I shuddered, earning a sharp look. I did my best to look respectful.

"Father," I said softly, and dropped my eyes from his.

He stepped back. "Now, I believe there's a rather wonderful meal waiting for you in the dining room. I must change from my work clothes and then I'll join you again. It's time we got to know each other, No?"

No, no, no and again no, I wanted to say but instead I smiled sweetly and mum, Seth and I followed one of the silent servants into the huge dining room. There were four places set - according to the printed place settings Mum and Asmodeus were at opposite ends of the table. Seth and I were seated opposite each other half way down each side. And yes, the meal was incredible. The table was groaning under the weight of all the food – duck in a tangy orange sauce, sweet chili chicken, sirloin steaks, charlotte potatoes tossed in herbs and butter, pasta, rice, cous cous, an assortment of vegetables roasted, steamed, sautéed and pickled. There was a bottle of red wine at mum's end of the table and proper cherry coke for Seth and me (our favourite!).

We sat down and nervously began to eat. I put a few roast vegetables on my plate and nervously chased them around with my fork. Seth, after a slow start, demolished what amounted to half a duck, several chickens and a cow. Mum had several spoonfuls of pasta and some chicken, her eyes were still wide and she seemed to have difficulty swallowing her food.

It was weird, the three of us sitting so far apart that we'd have to shout to make ourselves heard. I thought about moving closer to mum but didn't. I also thought about going walk about again, maybe exploring the forbidden left side of the kitchen corridor. But I didn't. I was expecting to hear that weird voice again any second. Could this day get any freakier?

Asmodeus arrived in the dining room about an hour later and smiled benignly at us. "Ah, good. You've eaten. I'm sorry I took so long. Did you enjoy it?" We all made murmuring noises of assent. "Good, good. Shall we retire to more comfortable surroundings?"

"But you haven't eaten," said mum, and then blushed like a schoolgirl.

"Its fine, Joanna. I can dine later. Come let's have a chat," He led us into the living room that we'd been in before and we all sat dutifully down again.

There was an uncomfortable silence as we all regarded each other with nervous anticipation. Asmodeus finally broke the stalemate by sitting beside my mum and taking her hand in his. He had changed into a pair of camel coloured chinos and a moss green sweater that looked good on him. It didn't, however, look particularly scary or prince-of-hell-like. I wondered if that was the intention or if he just dressed like that because he liked designer gear. Maybe under the Gucci loafers were hooves instead of feet and the chinos were roomy enough to hide a scaly tail or two. I was so busy looking for signs of a hideous demon on him that I missed the start of the conversation. My brain took notice when it heard my name;

"....for Emily and Seth to be with me. I know you've been as good a mother to them as you were able under the circumstances but you have to realize that because of my position they will be in great danger until after the change. If they had come to me sooner then we could have trained them to defend themselves. Don't feel bad about that, Joanna. You were doing what you thought best and I respect that decision. You are their mother after all. However, they are 16 now and growing closer to the …" His tone was gently reproving, his eyes were kindly and his touch on my mother's hand was gentle. In short, he was doing his best to pass on bad news in a careful and considerate fashion.

Unfortunately he used the totally wrong phrase. As a single mother, mum had run the gauntlet of well-meaning folk who basically believed that she was incapable of looking after a child by herself, never mind twins. She was, therefore, a tad thin skinned when it came to her mothering capabilities. While Seth and I were silently freaking about the whole "great danger" thing and "the change", mum was on her feet and shrieking about how she was a good parent, we'd always had everything we needed, we'd never starved and how he had no right to try and take her children from her. She would fight him tooth and nail to keep us and, if she had her way, he would never see us again. This had all been a mistake and we were leaving. Right now!

The trip home was executed in complete silence. No voices spoke in the car and no voice whispered in my head, which was a relief. Seth sat between mum and me, staring ahead in stony faced confusion. I looked out my window letting my brain sort through the highlights. I knew that I should at least be considering a strait jacket and extended stay somewhere with padded cells and lots of medication but I couldn't quite manage to make myself panic and start a swift descent into insanity.

The house was exactly as we left it – whatever the dude that was left behind had been doing he hadn't left any discernible sign of damage. We changed for bed and turned off the lights.

Seth and I still shared a room which was a constant source of amusement for his more annoying friends. The fact was that we lived in a two-bed roomed semi so, short of one of us sleeping on the sofa or in a tent in the back garden, the current arrangement was likely to continue. To be honest, I wasn't bothered by it. We had a curtain that separated our halves of the room and gave us some privacy and it was kind of nice having company in the room. We'd always shared a room.

About an hour after the lights went out, Seth spoke up. "You awake?"

I snorted. "Duh!"

"What do you make of this, Em?" Seth's voice was quiet, careful.

I sighed. "Honestly? I dunno. Should we be freaking out? What was he talking about – the change? What change? And who are we in danger from?"

"You think maybe he was just exaggerating everything? "

I'd thought of that. "I'm not sure. What reason would he have?"

"He seems to want us to live with him."

"Well, yeah, but he didn't get to finish what he was saying. Maybe he wanted mum to move in with him too. Maybe he wanted to move in with us."

Seth stifled a chuckle. "Yeah, Move out of the mansion with the acres of land and into a squashed semi with a galley kitchen." He chuckled again.

I grinned into the darkness. "Good point. So how are we gonna deal with this?"

There was silence as we both thought about that one. Seth spoke up first. "Ostrich? Pretend it's not happening until we have to. Maybe now he knows that mum isn't interested in picking up where they left off..."

"Bleugh,"

"...he'll back off and leave us alone."

"Are you wishful thinking again, Seth?" I asked.

"If you're going to turn this into a conversation about Amber then I'm going to sleep," Seth turned over in his bed and huffed into the far wall.

I rolled my eyes. Who had mentioned Amber? Okay, maybe I was hoping to get onto that subject but I would've been discreet. Honest. I drifted off to sleep imagining all the ways that I could convince my brother that Amber was bad news. Strangely Asmodeus didn't feature in my dreams. Teenage love upstaged demon lords any day!

Chapter Five

There must be a loose floor board in every house that is in the perfect spot to creak whenever someone is wandering around during the night. We have one on the landing just outside mum's bedroom and for the next few months it got a real work-out. Mum wasn't sleeping, wasn't eating much either. Her skin turned dry and her cheeks hollowed. Dark circles installed themselves under her eyes and no amount of touché éclat would've disguised those babies! We were all a little more jumpy. I kept expecting to come home and find that car outside, Asmodeus and his muscle waiting for us with chains and big padlocks, and mum in tears.

Time marched on, first term melted into second, Amber and Seth actually started dating, much to my disgust. Life marched on and we slowly relaxed a little. Mum got a promotion at work which brought in more money but increased her hours so Gran and Gramps came around now and again to sit with us until she got home. Yes, we could've argued that we were old enough to look after ourselves but Seth and I both knew on some level that the whole baby-sitting thing was to make mum feel better, not that we really needed it, so we kept quiet for once and enjoyed our grandparents' company.

Just after Easter Alice Frost went missing and the town was in uproar for a few weeks. A rumor began circulating that she had been seeing a guy from Wales who had come through Dean's Lynn during the Easter break. He was rumored to be in his twenties and some people speculated that Alice had run off with him. Her distraught parents made numerous trips to Wales, to London, to her sister's place in Cambridge but Alice had disappeared.

Seth and Amber continued to date although Seth never brought her around to our house. I thought perhaps he was ashamed of our humble semi. Amber had invited him to a pool party at her house during the Easter break and Seth had come home grumpy and uncommunicative. I heard afterwards that some of the in crowd had been hard on him – making fun of his accent, his clothes, his hair – I fervently hoped that Adam hadn't been one of them. I just couldn't imagine Adam being nasty like that. Seth was tight-lipped about the whole affair though so I was left seething on his behalf.

The June exams went off without a hitch. I got straight A's and Seth managed 2 A's, 4 B's and 3 C's. Mum was thrilled and took us all out for dinner to a fancy Chinese restaurant on the river. We sat watching the sun go down, turning the river gold, red, orange and then purple, as we ate spring rolls and schewhan chili chicken. Gramps even tried dim sum for the first time and ended up snaffling seconds from everyone's plate. It was a wonderful night and I went to bed happy and stuffed full of fried rice. The following day was the last before the summer vacation and I slipped into blissful dreams of endless sunny days and lots of ice lollies.

"What are you doing tomorrow?" I asked Annie.

"Nothin'"

"What are you doing the day after tomorrow?"

"Nothin'"

"And the day after that?"

"Nothin'"

"And the day after that?"

"Nothin'"

We collapsed into giggles as Dylan rolled his eyes and muttered something about 'nerd humour'. His lips were twitching into a grin 'though. We were all a little bit giddy at the idea of eight weeks of freedom. Seth had found himself a job in an ice cream parlor downtown but I was planning on doing as little as possible for as long as possible. Seth wanted a job to earn money to take Amber out. I had no such entanglements to worry about. I glanced Adam's way. He was standing with some of the other guys, his blond hair glittering in a stray sunbeam and his smile making my heart pound just that little bit harder.

"He's pretty, Emily, but there's something not quite…right…about him," said Annie, breaking into a delicious daydream I was having involving Adam, me and a large tub of Hagen Daaz. Any flavor. I wasn't picky.

"Huh?" I said, queen of conversation that I am.

"Adam." Annie said, gesturing across the canteen.

"Shssssh." I said, pushing her hands back down to the table and tearing my gaze away. "What?"

Annie tutted. "Come back to planet earth, Emily. Step off the good ship Adam Farlow and give us mere mortals some of your attention."

I opened my mouth to retort but Dylan beat me to it. "She can't help it, Annie. It's that time of the year when teenage hormones go into overdrive. Adam is an alpha male and she can't help being attracted to him."

"Well, she's dreamy like that every time she sets eyes on him, whether it's summer or not. I think it's unhealthy. I mean she hasn't really dated anyone since Michael Thompson and that was forever ago. Since then it's just been Adam, Adam, Adam."

"I can see that, Annie. I am here too, y'know." Dylan tossed his head like the diva he was. "Anyway, like I say it's all down to genetics and hormones. Emily is looking for the most capable male who will provide for her and keep her attention. Adam is such a specimen."

"I'm not saying that I don't agree, Dylan. I'm just saying that it might help the hormone level if she were to y'know, have a dalliance with another male until the alpha male becomes available."

I looked from one to the other as they had their verbal tennis match, about me. "Excuse me," I said and they both turned to look at me. "Could you talk *to* me if you're going to talk *about* me?"

"Well, that's just the problem lately," said Annie with a sniff. "You're in cloud cuckoo land half the time."

"What?" I squawked.

Dylan nodded. "It's true. You've been distracted for months now. You hardly hear a word we say and having a conversation with you is totally hit or miss. Some days you're all Miss Chatty Pants and other days you're little Miss Single Syllables." He see-sawed his hands to emphasize the point.

I opened and closed my mouth several times and then, swallowing a torrent of tears, I grabbed my bags and stomped out of the room. *You're being a complete diva*, I told myself. I stopped for breath in the girls' toilets and, huddled into a cubicle, I had a cry. What I really wanted to do was go back to Dylan and Annie, sit down beside them and tell them everything – my dad's a demon, Seth and I may be changing into scaly skinned, baby eating monsters (yes, ok, heavy on the melodrama, I know but that's what I was scared of.) and we might also be in danger from someone, or something. I wiped my eyes with the back of my school shirt and sniffed. It all sounded like something a screwed up teenager would invent to get attention, didn't it? Damn.

I washed my face and studied it in the mirror until most of the red had gone from around my eyes and I was certain that my tear ducts had dried up for the foreseeable future. I decided that it was time to talk to Seth, to really talk to him, and maybe to mum too. If we had horns, tails or seriously bad hair in our future then I wanted to know. Taking a deep breath, I left the bathroom.

I cleared out my locker and filled my bag, looking for Seth as I wandered from corridor to corridor. There was no sign so I finally left the main school building and headed for the sports hall. Maybe he'd escaped there with Amber – it was a notorious school make-out spot at lunchtimes.

"Hello?" My voice echoed through the deserted hall. Most kids were finishing up lunch and then heading to the bus stop. There was no-one here. I retraced my steps, looping back around the school and towards the front of the buildings. I could hear noise now, people shouting and laughing as end-of-term high spirits kicked in, the low murmur of conversation and the thud, thud, thud of running footsteps as people ran to catch buses.

Buses! Damn! I checked my watch and groaned. I'd missed the bus.

Cursing Seth, and Annie, and Dylan, and life in general, and bus schedules in particular, I crossed the rapidly clearing fore-court of the school and joined the stream of kids heading through the main gate. The day was warm and most people were in regulation short-sleeved shirts with coats and bags slung carelessly over their shoulders. There was excited chatter all around;

plans were being made for parties and get togethers, for days to the coast and nights on the town. I stayed in the stream as we made our way down the road from the school and onto what passes for a high street in Dean's Lynn. Here the stream divided as some kids went to cafes, some to browse the DVDs and some to the park. I ploughed on, turning left onto Bishop's Way and then right down Dean's Avenue.

The car came out of nowhere. I heard the whump as it mounted the sidewalk, stopped in my tracks and turned towards it.

It happened fast – a blur of colours, sounds and smells. The car was far away and then it was looming over me. I could feel the heat of it; smell the heavy, hot engine oil aroma of a 5,000 pound car. I could hear screams of alarm somewhere behind me. The sunshine glinted off chrome and glass and reflected rainbows around the corner of the sidewalk. I was turning, even as my brain was registering the danger, tripping over my feet as I whirled away. There was a screech as the car scraped against the wall just behind me and then I stumbled, colliding with the wall and diving around the corner. The car engine was the sound of a monster, breathing down my neck and I squeezed my eyes shut as the sidewalk rose up to meet me. I heard my head smack against it, bursts of colour flared behind my eyeballs and a strobe of pain lanced from one side of my head to the other. There was silence.

The ground was cold, freezing against my cheek. I sat up groggily and opened my eyes. What the...? I closed my eyes again, squeezed them tight shut and counted to ten, then opened them again. I frowned. I seemed to be in a room or, given the size of the place, a warehouse. It was stacked from floor to ceiling with books in row upon row for as far as my eyes could see and everything was covered in a thick layer of ice. I crawled to the closest stack and rubbed my finger along the spine of one of the books, wincing as the ice stuck to my skin. The book seemed to be leather bound with gold writing in a language I couldn't understand and as I let my gaze drift up the stack, I realized that I couldn't see to the top. I rubbed my temples. Okay, this had to have a simple explanation. I concentrated. Aha! It was a simple enough equation;

demon blood + bang on the head = weird dream.

I sat back on my bottom, delighted with myself for figuring that one out. And then I heard a voice. A low, deep rumble coming from somewhere to my right. I clambered to my feet and walked in the general direction of the sound. The volume neither grew nor diminished but I kept walking and just when I thought I couldn't go any further in this cold, dark, damp place, I found the fireplace.

. The fireplace was made of dark marble which was carved with little figures that I couldn't quite make out and the grate was dark and empty. To the right of it there was a huge chair, old and heavily padded with a fading cover and dark cushions. It had high arms which, when I got close, seemed to be worn in paces, as though someone had sat there many times, for many hours. I shivered. The voice had stopped and silence dropped over the place again. My heart began to beat a little faster. I was scared. I looked around for a way out and, as though my mind had conjured it, I saw the door.

It was a heavy and made of wood with an old fashioned, black metal latch and hand ring. I slipped and slid my way across to it and, taking a deep breath, I grasped the ring and turned it.

The door opened and I stepped through into a garden. It was dusk but the garden was still beautiful. The ground beneath my feet, stretching off in every direction, was covered in a luxurious carpet of soft green grass. It looked like velvet and I bent down to touch it, giggling as it tickled my fingers. The whole place was awash with flowers and shrubs. I inhaled the scents of the place and I could make out coconut-thick honeysuckle and comforting lavender, roses, lilies, violets, gardenia, cherry blossom and lilac. I closed my eyes, turning this way and that as the air swirled the glorious bouquet around me. Birds were singing somewhere in the distance and I could hear shuffling, snuffling animal sounds all around. I knew that my mouth was open in astonishment. My brain tried to restructure its equation; demon blood + bang on the head = weird dream of old books and beautiful gardens? Huh. I shrugged. Why not? I opened my eyes and headed off to explore.

I slipped off my shoes and picked a flower – *hibiscus* my mind suggested as I slipped it into my hair and followed a grassy path through tall stalks of foxglove and torch lilies. It led to a stream with a little humpback bridge of red stone. On the other side I sat down and began to make a daisy chain. I felt at peace, content.

Am I dead? I wondered, threading the daisies together. Is this heaven?

There was a low rumble in the distance. Thunder? Perhaps there was a storm coming. I waited, listening intently and watching the dark sky for signs of lightning. The rumble continued, coalesced into a more recognizable pattern and I realized that I was hearing a voice. I jumped to my feet and ran in the direction of the sound.

There was a moment when the air around me seemed to vibrate, the garden shimmered and then winked out of existence. I was looking down at a man who was chained to the floor. He was filthy and cowering in front of me, his face a rictus of terror. His hands were held up in supplication and tears ran down his face, cutting a path through the grime.

"Don't hurt me again," he wailed, "I don't know anything about them. I swear. Please, please, don't hurt me."

As if in a dream, I felt my hand come down, felt the fist connect with the man's face, saw gout of blood shoot from his mouth as one of his teeth grazed my knuckle. My hand rose again and I gasped. For a split second my mind filled with confusion, then a stunned realization, and then a fierce anger which swirled around me, a maelstrom of fire. The man in front of me screeched as the fire consumed him. I could smell his flesh burn and I think I screamed in terror and disgust. Immediately I felt the sensation of my body rushing backwards – grass and trees passed at speed, the door to the warehouse opened and I catapulted through it, past the chair and the stacks of books, back, back, back into the darkness. I felt the far wall loom behind me and shut my eyes against the impact.

"I think she's coming round," said a voice.

I opened my eyes, squinting into the sunlight. There were a ring of faces above me, some of them were kids I vaguely recognized from school, and some were local shop keepers. A woman was kneeling beside me, my wrist in her hand. She looked up from her watch and smiled. "You gave us a real scare there, sweetheart."

I struggled to sit up and hands helped me. I glanced around. The car that had mounted the pavement was embedded in the corner of the building to my left. Its engine was still running. In the distance I could hear the wail of a siren. One of the kids looked around.

"Ambulance," he said.

"About time," said one of the shop keepers. "It's been almost four minutes."

"Only four minutes?" I asked but most of the people had turned their attention to the oncoming vehicle.

"Police too," said someone and a car screeched to a stop beside us.

The crowd parted and two uniformed policemen filed through followed by a cute paramedic with a large green bag and a serious expression. His face softened when he saw me sitting up and the questions began.

CHAPTER SIX

Thanks to the meds that the cute paramedic administered I pretty much floated through the whole A+E, examinations, x-rays thing. Unfortunately he wasn't around to give me anymore when mum and Seth arrived.

Predictably, mum was a wreck. She wailed that I could've been killed, she raged at the 'punk' who had been driving, she cried about the fragility of human beings and finally, exhausted, and she sat by the side of the bed and held my hand. All the while Seth stood leaning against the wall, his face serious and thoughtful. When I raised an enquiring eyebrow in his direction he nodded at mum and drew his finger in front of his lips.

I fell asleep and drifted into dreams of being chased by 'Christine'-like cars with monstrous rows of teeth interspersed by kindly nurses taking my temperature and blood pressure. I moaned in distress at constantly being woken up and felt a cool hand on my brow and a soothing murmur in my ear whispering a story of thick green grass, shady branches, peace and tranquility. I sighed and felt my body relax and I drifted again, floating in a cotton-wool sea of deep contentment.

I was aware of voices talking around me, the words slipping in and out of my head. Seth was talking to someone. I tried to open my eyes but the lids were so heavy.

"Seth..." I whispered, frowning. A hand slipped into mine, Seth's familiar drawl told me that he was there, that I probably had another fifteen minutes until the nurse came back, I should rest. "I want to go back to the garden," I told him, my voice slurring the words a little. Seth said nothing but someone-else in the room shifted position. Who else was there? Mum? I wanted to know but my body needed to rest and I fell asleep again.

When the nurse came back to wake me again, mum was gone, Seth was in the chair by my bed and the room was shadowed. I squinted up at her as she put a thermometer in my ear and a cuff on my arm. She smiled too, accomplishing her tasks with a practiced air and talking in a low voice to Seth, asking if he'd like to get some coffee, telling him that she was on hand to keep an eye on me if he'd like a break.

Seth's curt "No." made me turn to look at him in surprise. My brother may have been annoying, an idiot when it came to unsuitable girls and a complete nerd when it came to movies but he was always well mannered. Seth was watching the nurse carefully, his eyes narrowed into slits and his expression threatening. I blinked and looked again. Yep, he was definitely eyeballing the nurse. I looked back at her; she smiled at me, patted my arm and left the room.

I turned to my brother. "I know you didn't just give a nurse the evil eye." I said, glad that my voice sounded stronger now.

He looked at me glumly and sighed.

I struggled to sit up and he moved at once to help, arranging the plump hospital pillows carefully behind me. "What's wrong with you? What wouldn't you talk to me when mum was here and why were you so rude to that nurse?"

He sat back down on the chair, pulling it forward so that he was closer to me. He opened his mouth, paused and then chewed on his lower lip. I waited as patiently as I could, tapping my foot off the rail at the bottom of the bed. He looked down at it, annoyance clouding his face. "Do you have to do that? It's really annoying," he said grumpily.

"Start talking or I'll use both feet." I told him.

Seth rolled his eyes. "Okay, okay. So Dad sent someone around to check things out."

I blinked. "Excuse me? 'Dad' sent someone round to check what?"

Seth sighed and wriggled in his chair. "See, this is why I didn't want to say anything. I knew you'd be all...precious about it."

Mu mouth dropped open and I started at him in amazement. "Precious?!"

"You and mum are so predictable sometimes," he continued.

"Predictable?" I could feel the colour rise into my cheeks, a sure sign that a flash of temper wasn't far behind.

"So this guy was checking on you, making sure you were okay and stuff."

"For 'Dad'?" I couldn't help the poison in my voice.

Seth looked at me, tipping his head to the side with a don't-even-go-there look in his eyes. He swallowed a comment and leaned forward again. "They think it may have been deliberate." He said carefully, watching my face.

I made a sound somewhere between a snort and a giggle. "Deliberate? Oh, please, Seth! Some old biddy drives onto the curb and you're seeing a conspiracy here? Seriously?" I grinned at him. "And Elvis is working in a chippie in Swansea, Marilyn was murdered for shagging JFK and aliens have the technology to travel gazillions of miles to visit us but can only communicate using crop circles." I folded my arms and gave him my best don't-be-a-dork glare.

Seth sat back in the chair, shaking his head. "I told him you'd be like this," he murmured. "And by the way, Marilyn *was* shagging JFK."

"Told who? What did you tell him?" I ignored the headache that was making its presence felt just above my right eye and sat up to scrutinize my brother a little more closely.

"I just told you, Em, the guy that D…Asmodeus sent. He asked a lot of questions about the accident, about you. Like I said already." Seth rubbed his eyes with the heel of his hands and I felt a momentary stab of guilt. He'd been sitting at my bedside all day, he must be exhausted. "We had a good talk." He shrugged. "He seemed like a decent guy."

"What did he ask about me?" I asked, like I said - the guilt was momentary.

"He asked me to describe you in three words."

"Which were?"

"Smart, funny, fierce."

I grinned at him in happy surprise. "Really? You think I'm funny?"

Seth smiled. "Yes, I do. Especially now that you've got terrible bed hair and dried drool on the side of your mouth."

I narrowed my eyes at him. His smile got wider and then slid away. "Seriously, Em. There could be more to this than a simple accident."

"Why? I saw the old lady behind the wheel, she lost control. Stop making more of this than there is. You're playing right into his hands. *He* wants to make a big deal about this so he has some leverage over mum." I sat back into the pillows again and huffed.

"Emily, there was no-one in the car when the first person got to you. If there was an old lady in the car then she must've legged it at the speed of light. The car's registered to some dude from Thetford and no-one in the area saw anyone in it or running from it."

"So it was stolen. Maybe I didn't see right. Maybe it was a joy-rider in the car. He lost control and then ran off when the car crashed." I tapped my bottom lip with a finger. "He might even have bailed before the car hit the pavement which would explain why no-one saw him." I looked up, happy with my hypothesis.

"This isn't a damn movie, Em. I'm serious here. Dad has a lot of enemies and they know that we're his kids so we're automatically on the hit list. We have been since we were born." Seth looked grave; his face was dark with worry and fatigue.

"Since we were born? Well, it's just a tad convenient that nothing happens until we get to meet him and he decides to suddenly start taking his paternal duties seriously." I snapped. "We've managed perfectly well up 'till now."

"We've been lucky."

"That's bull, Seth. But I'll forgive your patheticness for the moment. You're tired and stressed. Once you've had some sleep and got your brain back into gear you'll see that this is all a big ruse to…" I paused.

"To what, Em? Explain to me what possible reason our Dad could have for wanting to protect us? Other than the fact that he's our Dad and there are some nasty things wanting to get to him by whatever means necessary."

Seth's voice was low but razor sharp.

"'By whatever means necessary'? You've been reading too much Andy McNab," I said with a snort.

Seth threw up his hands and stood up, pushing his chair back with a screech of its plastic legs on the lino. I winced at the noise and my head protested.

Mum chose that moment to come back into the room. She was smiling. "Good news, sweetie," she gushed. "The doctor says you can go home in the morning. Isn't that great?" She looked from Seth to me and we both grinned at her as she went about chatting about hospital coffee, the price of flowers in the gift shop and why the universe needed more flavors of Walker's crisps.

I looked at Seth over mum's head. *Conversation over*, his face said.

I narrowed my eyes at him. *Not by a long shot.*

CHAPTER SEVEN

Our house was busy for the next few days – I had a lot of visitors, although I suspected that some of them were just there to indulge their curiosity. Annie and Dylan called every day with Starbuck's coffee and glazed doughnuts from the corner bakery on Templeton Road. It was great to have them around and, apart from asking once on the first day they visited, the accident wasn't mentioned. I was grateful. Although I hadn't realized it at the time, my conversation with Seth had really rattled me. The 'what if' brigade were playing constantly in my head and really messing with my 'no-school-happy-happy' vibe. Was this part of what Asmodeus had been talking about – invisible men trying to run us down in cars?

By the end of that first week, mum had started to relax a little and I was allowed further than the end of the garden path (I'm not joking!). By the end of the second week after the accident, life was back to normal once again.

Or so I thought.

Annie, Dylan, Seth and I went to the cinema on Wednesday night, giggled our way through a Sandra Bullock movie, sharing a medium bucket of pop-corn and a large coke. We nipped out just before the credits started to roll so we could bag a booth at Maggie's Diner overlooking the village square.

I sat in the booth and kept the coats while Annie, Dylan and Seth argued over the menu and then stood in line (still arguing) to place the order. The square was brimming with people as it usually was at 9pm on a mild summer evening. I loved watching them all milling around; sitting on the benches, wheeling babies in strollers, sneaking a kiss on the way home from the cinema, trudging back from the football pitch. Although Dean's Lynn had grown from a small market village into a prosperous town, the village square was still its heart. The diner had chairs and tables out on the pavement now and the bakery (which had a café at the back) was open late too – I could see a lot of their hot sausage rolls doing the rounds outside. I caught a glimpse of Adam Farlow, Ritchie Phillips and a few other guys walking by on the far side of the square. They'd been to the Leisure centre by the look of things – Adam's hair was still damp and he was carrying a changing bag. Damn! We should've gone for a swim instead of the cinema then I could've seen Adam in his Speedos (hey, a girl can dream! He probably wore those long Bermuda shorts instead). Behind the group of guys came the girls and I stifled a groan. Amber looked like she'd just stepped off a Paris catwalk and, oh joy! There was Sarah too! Looking like an angel in a pair of faded blue jeans and a shirt so white I was momentarily blinded.

I was so intent on shooting evil looks at Sarah that I almost didn't see the man standing in the shadows behind them. He was at the corner where the square meets Main Street and he was looking directly at me. A jolt of alarm shot through me quickly followed by a flush of recognition.

I turned to see where Seth was. He was coming back towards our booth carrying a tray and laughing at whatever conversation he was having with Annie and Dylan. When he saw my face his smile faltered and then he was hurrying through the busy diner, bumping into people as he came.

I turned back to the square but the man was gone.

Seth slid the tray onto the table and slid in beside me, his arm going around my shoulders. "Tell me," he said gruffly. I looked for Annie and Dylan. They were caught up in a group of kids from our year at school. "Tell me NOW!" hissed Seth.

"There was a man," I whispered.

"Where?" Seth's eyes darted around the square.

"On the corner," I pointed "Over there. He was watching me, I think."

"You think?" Seth frowned at me.

"Well, I was watching Amber and Sarah and …that lot," I began, blushing furiously.

"Amber was here?" Seth strained to see around the corner of the diner.

I punched his arm. "Focus, Romeo!"

He nodded. "This man, what did he look like?" He asked.

"Well, that's just it. I recognized him." I said. "I think he was at … Dad's place the night we visited."

Seth sat back. "Ah," he said.

I stared at him. "Ah?"

Seth chewed on the inside of his lip and looked away from me. "Annie and Dylan are coming," he whispered.

"Seth? What does 'Ah' mean?!" I seethed.

"Later," said Seth, pulling away from me and lifting a plate of chips from the tray. He set them in the middle of the table and turned to Annie and Dylan, beaming.

"No, Seth, NOW!" I almost spat at him.

Annie and Dylan sat down warily, glancing from me to Seth who sighed dramatically. He turned to me, swinging his legs around on the plastic bench. "He's a friend." He said, raising his eyebrows at me meaningfully. *Not in front of Annie and Dylan*, he was clearly saying.

I looked at my friends who were watching our exchange avidly. Annie was noisily sucking diet coke through a straw. Dylan was in the process of reaching for more chips. "This is actually more entertaining than the movie," he said through a mouthful of fried potato. He twirled his fingers in a 'keep going' gesture. I glared at him and turned back to Seth.

"Are you saying that we're being *watched?*" I asked slowly.

Seth grimaced and then nodded. I mirrored him, nodding slowly. "Since when? The hospital?" I asked. Another nod. "You knew and didn't tell me?" Another hesitant nod. "Does mum know?" This time he paused and then shook his head, dropping his chin to his chest.

I took a deep breath, exhaled slowly, took another breath, exhaled. When I was certain that I wasn't going to kill my brother in the middle of the diner, I leaned forward and took a chip, eating it carefully, savoring the crisp outer skin and fluffy inside. Seth wisely said nothing.

I looked up and met Annie's eyes. She looked angry and I raised an eyebrow. I don't think I'd ever seen Annie in the midst of melt-down/volcanic anger before. She looked formidable. "So," she said in an even voice. "Who is watching you? Why are they watching you and how come you didn't tell us?" She directed this last question at Seth who shrank from her glare. Then he turned to face me.

"Now look what you've done," he accused.

CHAPTER EIGHT

Seth and I sat side by side on my bed. He had his arms folded across his chest and was glaring across the room to where Annie sat on my desk chair and Dylan lounged with his hip against the desk. Dylan was sucking coke through a straw like a five year-old and Annie was pretending not to notice. All her focus was on me.

"So?" said Annie. "'Fess up, Emily Carson. What's going on?"

Seth mumbled something about bad ideas and I ignored him. "Look Annie," I said with a sigh. "I want to tell you but, well, it's weird and it might wig you out. Either that or you won't believe me." I turned to my brother for support. "Tell her, Seth."

"Yeah, yeah. Weird and unbelievable and stuff," he mumbled, rolling his eyes. "In fact," he said, brightening up, "It's so unbelievable that I think maybe Emily made it all up just to get some attention 'cause, let's face it, that's what she does. Right?"

Annie, Dylan and I stared at Seth. My mouth had dropped open and I knew I was giving him my patented 'you-didn't-just-say-that' look, Annie tutted and turned her attention back to me, Dylan grinned. "Nice try, Seth," he sympathized.

Sighing, Seth wound his arms around himself and retreated back into his mumbling, unhappy self.

"So?" Annie said again.

"I don't know where to begin," I said, stalling. "I mean, it's all very confusing and there's so much involved and I just don't know the best place to start to help you understand and…"

"Oh, for crying out loud, Emily! Just spit it out!" Annie stood up with her hands on her hips.

I gulped. "We met our real Dad who's called Asmodeus and he's a demon and we might change into evil nasties soon and we're being chased by people who don't like demons and, well, it's all kindda scary," I said all in one breath.

Annie sat down again. "Oh," she said.

"Wow," said Dylan. "Damn! I wish we'd kept some popcorn." He nudged Annie. "I was right. This is *way* better than the flicks!"

Annie shook her head at him and then turned her attention back to Seth and me. Seth was chewing on his fingernails and watching Annie carefully. "So what kind of evil nasties are you going to turn into?" asked Annie. "Just so as I'm prepared."

I gaped.

Dylan popped the plastic lid off the top of his coke and peered inside. Sighing he reluctantly joined the conversation. "Demons, huh. What do they eat? Do they have skin like us? Where do they live?"

Seth sniggered suddenly and we all turned to look at him. He glanced up, saw us staring and began to laugh uncontrollably. We gave him a minute.

As he wiped his eyes I nipped him on the arm. "Ow!" he said, scowling. "What was that for?"

"You want to let us all in on the joke?" I asked.

Seth grinned. Well, it's just that here we are imparting the news that demons are real and our dad is one and Dylan goes all David Attenborough and wants to know their habitat and eating habits." He sniggered again.

Dylan frowned and turned to Annie. "I thought it was a perfectly acceptable question." he said, confused.

Annie cocked her head and studied Seth and me. "You're not joking are you?" she asked softly. "This isn't some elaborate twin-joke thing?"

Seth and I slowly shook our heads.

Annie nodded. "So your dad is a demon?"

We nodded again.

"So you met him?

Another nod.

"And he's not...?" she made a fluttering motion with her hands, her face contorting as she fought for the right words to use.

40

"Red, scaly and gross?" interjected Seth helpfully. "No, he looks like a regular guy."

"If the regular guy looks like an Armani model and owns a big house with lots of cars and over muscled goons." I added.

It was Annie's turn to nod, which she did with as much dignity as a panicked rabbit can muster.

"So, human skin then," said Dylan. "And a house." He looked at Seth. "And this house wasn't in 'hell', I take it?"

Seth shook his head. "It was somewhere near the ocean. Big place with a long drive and trees around it."

"Groovy," said Dylan. He looked at Annie. "What's wrong with you?"

Annie looked up at him incredulously. "Are you kidding?" she squeaked.

"We'll need proof, of course." said Dylan.

Seth and I looked at him. "You want to meet a demon?" asked Seth.

Dylan nodded. Annie nodded too, though much more half-heartedly.

Seth grinned and shook his head. "You guys are incredible." He said.

Downstairs the doorbell rang and we all looked up, startled. Seth's face drained of colour. "Oh, yeah." he muttered and started for the stairs.

I grabbed his arm as he passed. "What did you do?" I asked. Grimacing he shook off my arm and we waited in silence as he answered the door.

I looked from Annie to Dylan and shrugged. Both of them looked shell-shocked. From downstairs came the sounds of a whispered conversation and then Seth called up "Uh…guys? You want to come down here. We have a visitor."

CHAPTER NINE

We trooped downstairs, Annie and Dylan arguing in stage whispers all the way down about the endless possibilities for the universe if demons were in fact real. Thankfully we made it to the bottom before they got onto the whole evolution of the species debate. Again.

As we walked the few steps from the hall to the living room, I felt a momentary wave of dizziness and had to put a hand on the wall to steady myself. It passed quickly though and shaking my head I walked in behind Annie and Dylan.

Seth was arguing quietly with our visitor but their conversation stopped when we came in.

My eyes narrowed. The 'visitor' was the man who had been watching me at the diner. He was also the king of toilet directions from our meeting with daddy dearest. The fact that he was now in our home and conversing with my brother was not a good thing. It made me mad.

Tonight he had gone for a kind of rebel-without-a-cause look; faded blue jeans, camel desert boots, a white t and a leather jacket. A glance to my left showed me that Annie was eyeing him with wide-eyed expression of curiosity and lust. Dylan just looked pained, which was a normal look for him when he came across something he wasn't quite certain of.

I glared at both Seth and the newcomer and planted my hands firmly on my hips.

"Emily," Seth began, "this is..."

"Oh, no, no." I interrupted. "We've already met actually and I named him 'toilet guy'. Any other name is just going to confuse me." I folded my arms and waited, tilting my head to the side.

Seth closed his eyes and sighed deeply. Out of the corner of my eye I could see Annie biting her lip. When no-one else spoke I decided to break up the silence. I was on a roll. "Besides," I said, "if you insist on spilling his real name then we might have a 'Bill' moment, we would all laugh hysterically and your poor friend would feel totally unwelcome and insecure."

I smiled sweetly at toilet guy who just looked bored. His expression hadn't changed at all during my speech – how irritating.

Seth rubbed his neck – a sure sign that he was embarrassed. I grinned. Believe me, sisters live for those moments when they can embarrass the hell out of their brothers. Even brothers who are three minutes older. In fact, that makes it even sweeter.

I was reveling in my victory when toilet guy spoke. "What's a 'Bill' moment?" he asked.

Y'know…'Sookie Stackhouse', vampire 'Bill', ha ha ha?" I looked around for support. Annie and Dylan nodded vigorously.

Seth's face was a deep crimson. He was practically gnashing his teeth together. Scowling he stepped forward into my space. "You should show him some respect. He's watching out for you." He said in a frosty voice

"I never asked him to," I hissed into my brother's face (no mean feat when someone's 3 inches taller than you, believe me).

"No." Seth growled back. "*I* asked him to."

I blanched and took a step back. "What?" I asked softly.

Seth chewed on his lip for a moment. "Emily, meet Sariel." He said wearily and stood back.

I turned my attention back to our visitor. He had watched proceedings with the same expression of bored resignation. Now he pasted on a grin and stepped forward with a hand outstretched.

"Better than 'Bill'?" he asked.

Behind me, Annie giggled coquettishly and was shushed by Dylan.

I shook the offered hand and looked up into silver-blue eyes that glittered with curiosity. I smiled at him and was about to attempt an apology when I realized that Annie and Dylan were having a less than quiet discussion about our new acquaintance. Releasing Sariel's hand, I poked Annie on the shoulder. She stopped talking mid-breath and looked around sheepishly.

"Too loud?" she said.

"Just so's you'd notice. What is wrong with you two?" I hissed.

With a cautious look in Sariel's direction, Dylan leaned towards me and whispered. "We were just discussing…him."

"Uh, huh. What about him?" I whispered back.

"Well, we were just wondering…" Dylan began.

"*You* were just wondering," Annie told him, folding her arms.

Dylan rolled his eyes. "Yeah, ok. *I* was just wondering, little Miss Perfect. Honestly, can't you just help me out here?"

"Look, Dylan, I'm just making the point that you were the one who wanted to ask if the guy was a demon, not me. Okay? I'm quite happy to stand here at the back and wait to see what he says but oh, no, not you, you want to go prancing out there and start questioning people like bloody Van Helsing."

"Prancing?! Van Helsing?! He's a demon not a bloomin' vampire." Dylan complained.

"Vampires are demons you idiot!" Annie lashed back, her cheeks crimson.

Although I usually enjoy Annie and Dylan's little 'discussions', I decided that it would probably not be a good plan to allow this one to continue but as I was stepping in to break them up, Sariel stepped forward, charming grin in place and introduced himself. Eyeing him cautiously and with slightly embarrassed smiles, Annie and Dylan took turns to shake his offered hand.

He introduced himself as a 'friend of Seth's' and placed a hand on first Dylan's arm and then Annie's. Dylan seemed unperturbed as Sariel continued to chat about how they must all meet up at the diner some night and how mad the ticket prices were for the flicks. Annie frowned at his hand on her arm and was turning in my direction when I felt a wave of dizziness sweep through me. The room seemed to fade in and out of view for a fraction of a second before the world righted itself.

I shook my head and frowned, turning questioningly to Seth who didn't look as 'though anything had happened. Confused I turned back to my friends who were standing motionless, their faces blank. Still smiling, Sariel stepped away from them and back to stand beside Seth. My brother and his new pal exchanged identical dark looks and I was just opening my mouth to ask what the hell was going on when Annie and Dylan came abruptly to life making me jump and squeak like a girl.

"So anyway," Annie said brightly, "Next week it is. I honestly don't mind what we go to see. Maybe it should be Sariel's choice?" she smiled and looked at Sariel from under her lashes.

Sariel gave a little bow to her and shook hands with Dylan again who was blinking his eyes rapidly but staying quiet.

Seth pushed past me to see my friends to the door and I sat down on the sofa to think. I could feel Sariel watching me silently. "What did you do?" I asked without looking up at him.

"What makes you think I did anything?" He asked, in a voice dripping with honey.

All the connections between my brain and my voice seemed to have been severed although I think the reality was that I was so angry that I couldn't actually vocalize. Instead I imagined throwing a scream at him attached to a javelin which would imbed my glass shattering roar somewhere in his parietal lobe.

I looked up at him, imagining my scream javelin piercing his consciousness and filling his head with sound. Sariel's eyes widened and then squeezed shut in pain. He covered his ears with his hands for a moment.

Ha! That won't do you any good. I sent it right into your brain! I thought and then met his eyes as he looked up at me.

My mouth made a little 'o' of astonishment even as his voice spoke into my head.

How did you do that? He asked.

I watched his lips. They didn't even twitch.

"I have no idea," I said honestly.

You don't have to speak aloud, his voice told me and his lips once again stayed resolutely closed.

45

"Sorry," I said aloud and then clamped my hand over my mouth.

Sorry, I thought at him and he nodded, his eyes watching me carefully.

I sat down on the sofa again and put my head between my knees as my vision dipped and swirled. This was too much. I was in overload. The last thing I heard as I passed out was Sariel's voice inside my head.

You shouldn't be able to do this, he whispered.

Chapter Ten

I studied Sariel over a cup of coffee. He looked completely normal. Well, completely normal for a possible demon that could talk to me inside my head without moving his lips and had just found out that I could do the same to him.

We were sitting at the small table in our tiny kitchen with my mother fussing around making toast and chattering about her night at bingo. Seth had gone to bed shortly after she came home, making eyes at me to do the same. I'd obviously ignored him. It was heading towards midnight but I was wired on coffee and adrenaline so sleeping was a lost cause. Besides, I wanted answers and the fount of all knowledge was sitting in front of me making small talk with my mother. If I had anything to do with it he wasn't leaving until I'd had a chance to interrogate him.

For the billionth time I willed my mother to go to bed. She popped the toast and buttered it all the while rabbiting on about how many people were at the bingo and how her friend Sandra had shouted bingo when it wasn't bingo and how the oaps in the corner had tutted and what the caller had been wearing (apparently he looked like an Elvis wannabe). Sariel grinned and nodded and made the odd comment while I stewed across the table, alternately chewing my lip and taking huge gulps of coffee.

It suddenly occurred to me that perhaps we could have a conversation even with my mother there. Kicking myself for not figuring it out earlier I stared into my coffee and concentrated.

Can you hear me? I asked

Perfectly well.

I glanced up but Sariel was still focused on my mum who was now sitting down at the table and pushing a huge plate of hot buttered toast into the middle. I took a slice automatically and chewed, not really tasting.

You know I want to talk to you, I thought at him.

His gaze flicked very briefly in my direction as he lifted some toast.

Well, we are talking, he said, his voice heavy with amusement.

I ripped the corner off my slice of toast and chewed furiously.

How can you talk to me like this? I asked carefully.

It's one of my…gifts.

I thought about that for a moment. *So is it one of my gifts too?*

Silence.

Sariel? Is it one of my gifts?

More silence.

I banged my cup down onto the table, spilling some coffee. Grumbling, mum pushed her chair back and went in search of a cloth, complaining about teenagers as she went.

"Answer me!" I hissed aloud. Sariel's eyes met mine across the table and his were serious.

The children of demons do not come into their gifts until the age of eighteen. Your ability to communicate with me through a telepathic link is, I think, unrelated to your heritage.

I chewed on that and reached for some more toast as mum cleaned the table and I apologised profusely.

So you think I may just be telepathic? I asked, trying not to look as skeptical as I felt.

No, such abilities are not natural.

I frowned. *So where do they come from?*

Sariel chewed very slowly on his toast as mum went on about Asmodeus and his claim and how upset she'd been. Sariel was nodding but I could tell that, like me, he was only half listening.

True gifts like that are very, very rare.

Yes, ok but where do they come from?

Have you told anyone else about this ability?

I rolled my eyes. *I don't have this ability with anyone else. Maybe it's your fault for speaking to me like this that night we met Asmodeus.*

His eyes widened and his slice of toast paused for the barest moment on its way to his mouth. *You felt that?*

Well, duh!

Hmmm. Most people don't recognize it as a voice, or a conversation. It is like a feeling, a suggestion, or sometimes a compulsion.

A compulsion? You mean you can make people do things that they don't want to do? That's what you did to Annie and Dylan.

The barest nod.

Did it hurt them?

A slight shake.

Why did you do it? They wouldn't have told anyone.

He frowned. *It's against the rules for anyone outside of our 'family' to know about the truth of things. By telling them, you changed them, opened their minds to the realization of the existence of good and evil in their most recognizable forms.*

God and the devil?

Yes. For a human to know these things and not act on them is impossible. Faith turns an ordinary man or woman into an incredibly powerful vessel. The truth of things is even more powerful. If I hadn't removed the memory then they would've had to be…eliminated.

I stared at him and gulped. *But it was my fault and I didn't know any of this.*

Which is why I could intervene.

I sat back in my chair and thought about that.

Could you make me do something?

My mother excused herself to go to the toilet and Sariel turned his attention to me. His eerily beautiful eyes locked onto mine. "It helps to touch the other person sometimes," he said softly and placed a hand on my arm. I licked my lips and waited. There was the dizzying sensation again and a mild heat from his palm along with a light pressure in my head.

Lean across the table and kiss me, Emily. Sariel's voice whispered inside my head. The sound of it was like a caress, light and perfect, making the hairs stand up on the back of my neck.

I leaned across the table. "I don't think so," I said with a smile.

Sariel laughed softly, releasing my arm. "No, I didn't think it would work." He admitted.

"I could feel …" I began.

"Yes?" He cocked his head to the side. "No, please tell me, I've never known how it actually feels."

'Well, I felt dizzy and then there was heat from your hand. Then a feeling like someone was pressing lightly on my head and your voice…"

"Yes?"

I paused, remembering the feeling and feeling a flutter in the pit of my stomach. "Well, it didn't work." I finished lamely.

Sariel grinned. "No, it didn't." He finished his coffee. "So you haven't had any other experiences like this?"

I shook my head. "No, nothing." I lifted the mugs from the table and took them to the sink to rinse them out. "Unless really vivid dreams count." I smiled at him over my shoulder.

He shook his head. "Wouldn't have thought so. Just out of interest, though, what do you dream about?" He waggled his eyebrows and I rolled my eyes.

"A warehouse full of books and a beautiful garden that has every plant and tree you can imagine with a river and a little bridge." I stared dreamily out of the kitchen window as I thought about the garden. "It's so peaceful there. I started dreaming about it the day of the accident so maybe it's my brain taking me somewhere that I consider safe, y'know?" I set the cups on the draining board and turned to face him.

Sariel was motionless, his face pale. "A garden?"

I nodded. "Yes and a huge warehouse with stacks and stacks of books. Probably because I love books, don't you think? Although the ice everywhere is a bit confusing. I mean why would I dream of squillions of books that I can't read 'cause they're encased in ice?" I shrugged and then studied his face. "What is it?"

My mother came into the kitchen again and gave me a hug for clearing the table and rinsing the cups. She made small talk for a few minutes and then, yawning dramatically, ushered Sariel towards the door, thanking him for visiting and telling him to come again. If she noticed the atmosphere in the room she gave no indication. The front door closed.

"Bed, Emily," mum sing-songed as she flicked off the kitchen light and began to climb the stairs.

I stood in the dark for a moment confused and suddenly scared.

Sariel?

We'll talk tomorrow, Emily. Get some sleep.

But I'm scared. You looked like my dream meant something. Something terrible.

I'll explain tomorrow night.

Feeling suddenly exhausted I nodded, forgetting he couldn't see me and then rolled my eyes at my own stupidity. I checked all the doors and windows and then climbed the stairs and got ready for bed. As I slid under my duvet his voice came again.

It might be best if you didn't tell anyone about the dream.

But I already told Seth, I thought.

CHAPTER ELEVEN

Thursday was possibly the longest day in creation – not helped at all by the fact that Seth went to work and then met up with bitch face, sorry, I mean Amber. Grandpa came to stay with me (at mum and Seth's insistence) and watched with interest as I cleaned the kitchen from top to bottom, hoovered the entire upstairs of the house and then cut the grass, back and front.

I made us a cup of tea at around two o'clock and Grandpa took a few sips and then set his cup down with a decisive clink. I looked up at him in surprise.

My Gramps is a calm, quiet, sensitive man. Tall, like Seth, incredibly gentle and unfailingly kind and polite. He is the perfect anchor for the mini-whirlwind that is my Grandma and keeps the peace in our family whenever rows – differences of opinion he likes to call them – arise, which is frequently. He says that years of playing referee between my mum and grandma has made him unflappable.

"Ok, lass," he said. "What's up with you today?"

"Me? Nothing. Not a thing. I'm just feeling energetic. Y'know? School holidays, sunshine, good food. I'm just a ball of well fed teenage emotion that needs to…er…clean." I looked at him through my lashes. He had folded his arms and was smiling gently. He wasn't buying it.

"Uh, huh. You want to get out of here?" He asked shrewdly.

"Yes." I told him, surprised that I actually did.

We drove across town and climbed the hill towards the forest, pulling up outside the church that Grandma and Gramps attended. I frowned up at it and looked at Grandpa curiously.

"My turn to do the grass. Want to help?" He grinned, his gray eyes twinkling.

Bested by a pensioner.

I sat in the car for a moment until I no longer felt like taking anyone's name in vain and then joined Grandpa at the small hut where the gardening supplies were kept. It was packed with tools and pots, 2 petrol mowers and a vast array of seeds and vicious looking implements that were probably for weeding, eviscerating heathens or something. We each hauled a mower out and, after Gramps had checked them for wear and tear, off we went cutting the grass around the front of the church and then around back where the graveyard began.

It was surprisingly therapeutic, pushing the purring grass guzzling monster around. My hands and arms shuddered with the vibrations of my mini-beast and my back and shoulders ached with the unaccustomed strain of pushing the thing along but the afternoon flew as I toiled.

We were finished by four o'clock and I was tired but it was a good kind of tired – the kind you only get from doing something worthwhile. I wiped sweat from my brow with grimy hands and re-tied my pony tail, pulling wet strands from the side of my face. Gross.

"Arthur!" Called a cheery voice. "Good to see you. Great job!" We turned to see Alan Woodgate, one of the church wardens and another of those 'pillars of the community' that everyone is always going on about. Gramps introduced us and they got chatting about stuff, y'know, pensioner stuff.

I wondered off and after sitting on one of the memorial benches (for Violet Andrews, if you must know) I decided to investigate the church itself.

The front door was open and led into a blessedly cool foyer which was decorated in ornate carvings and a large stained glass window depicting the burning bush. The sun shone through the glass casting a multitude of colours around the place and lighting up the walls. There was a notice board on the far wall between a door which apparently led to the choir robing room and a staircase leading to the gallery. The board was covered with announcements about upcoming services, advertisements for local businesses, a flower rota, prayer requests, sick visit rota and a 'thought for the day' calendar. The calendar fascinated me because it was totally non-churchy. Today's thought was a quote from Mary Kay Ash – "If you think you can, you can. And if you think you can't, you're right." I nodded. Smart lady.

There was a heavy oak door on my right leading into the main part of the church and I pushed it open and let myself in quietly. I inhaled deeply and filled my lungs with holy air. That was how I imagined it anyway – exhaling all the soiled heathen fumes and inhaling the dry, prayer saturated church air. It was like a make-over which didn't involve the use of a scalpel, Botox or pain.

The church was sparsely populated. Several elderly women were dotted here and there, rosary beads in their hands. A man in a dark suit, clutching a brown leather suitcase was several rows from the front on the far side. His face shone with sweat and he stared unmoving at the statue of the Virgin in front. I closed my eyes and tried to ignore them all even as the cogs started to turn and I wondered what made them come here on this day, at this time. Were they talking to God? Asking forgiveness? Asking for a miracle? Was sweaty guy carrying a bomb in his suitcase? Was one of the old biddies an assassin for the mob? I grinned at my overactive imagination but hey! Stranger things were going on right?

I tip-toed to my right and into one of the side aisles beyond the row of immaculate stone columns. The scent of warm wax hung heavy in the air and I stopped in front of the large array of votive candles. I inhaled again, smelling the rich aromatic smoke rising from the many flickering wicks. Checking that no-one was watching I lit one and watched as the tiny ribbon of smoke rose from it and mingled with the others on their way to the cavernous ceiling. Or maybe to God himself, assuming he sat up in Heaven inhaling smoke from votive candles.

I suddenly felt very self-conscious, very aware that the rituals of this place were completely alien. I had lit a candle that was supposed to be significant in some way – was there a prayer to go with the act of lighting it?

I moved away and slid into the cool quiet of one of the shadowed pews. A few rows in front one of the women got up and made her way to the end of her pew, looking towards the front of the church she dipped into a graceful curtsy, crossing herself before turning away. She smiled gently at me as she passed and I relaxed a little.

I looked around at all the stained glass, the beautiful carvings, the candles, flowers and statues. I studied the statue of Jesus on the cross – the nails in his hands and feet, the blood eternally dripping from a gash in his side that would never heal. His expression was serene, forgiving.

I turned my attention to Mary – a beautiful woman in a blue cloak staring down with such love at the toddler at her feet, their hands reaching towards one another. The little Jesus was a chubby, curly-haired cherub with a rose-bud mouth and an expression of delight on his little round face.

I closed my eyes and let the stillness of the place seep into me and let my mind drift. I wondered what the parishioners would think if they knew the truth. Would they be overjoyed that their God was real, that their faith was well placed? If I was to stand up right now and announce to them that I knew the answers to the questions that they asked themselves in times of doubt. That I knew because my father was an honest-to-God demon king. What would they think? Would they believe me? Would they call the police? Have me taken away in a strait-jacket? If they believed me, would they appreciate the fact that the daughter of a Satan-wannabe was sitting in their church? Lighting their candles. Polluting the air with her demony breath. I opened my eyes and squinted at Little Lord Jesus. Was it my imagination or did he look a little less delighted than he had a few seconds ago? I *really* didn't belong here.

I stood up and looked around wildly for an exit. I raced to the end of the pew, banging my knee in the process. The hollow thud echoed through the church and I could sense that several people had turned to look at me. Ignoring the hot pain in my knee I made my way as fast as I dared to the door, yanking it open and running straight into the person who was trying to come in. We fell into the foyer and landed in a sprawl of arms, legs and flowing cassock. I had just knocked the priest down. Horrified I bounced to my feet and babbled about three zillion apologies, one after the other in a constant stream.

The priest clambered to his feet and smoothed his cassock. He stunned me by reaching out and pressing his finger against my lips to still my verbal diarrhea.

"I'm Father Cassidy and it's not very often someone runs from the church before I start my sermon." He grinned and released my lips, holding out his hand.

I shook his hand. "Em, Em, Emily C, Carson." I stammered. "Sorry." I added sheepishly.

"So you said," Father Cassidy told me. "About three hundred times I think."

I felt myself blush.

"So, where were you running to?" He asked softly, tilting his head to the side.

"Er..." I studied the priest, his shock of jet black hair, his eyes the colour of a stormy ocean. He looked, well, normal, not priest-like in the least. Apart from the white collar at his throat, the cassock and the enormous bible clutched in his hands of course. "My Grandpa will be looking for me, I lost track of time. We were cutting the grass and then I came in here and now I should be going." I grimaced and bit my tongue to shut my stupid babbling mouth.

Father Cassidy raised an eyebrow and narrowed his eyes for a moment. I grinned at him, putting on what I hoped was my very best 'just-a-normal-girl-not-demon-spawn' face.

"So you're Arthur Carson's grand-daughter," he said finally. "Good to meet you, Emily. Come back anytime."

I nodded and then backed away, still grinning, until I reached the door. Then I bolted through it and broke all sprinting records ever set on my way back to the car. I arrived panting and wide-eyed to find Gramps asleep in the driver's seat. I slipped in beside him and waited until my heart-rate had slowed to an acceptable level and my face was back to its usual colour before waking him.

He opened his eyes slowly. "What? Oh, there you are, Emily. I was wondering where you'd got to. I just closed my eyes for a second there to rest them." He coughed and made a big show of checking his watch. "Best get you home then, almost time for tea."

I nodded and smiled and generally behaved like a normal grand-daughter on the ride home, kissing his wrinkled cheek with true affection as he dropped me off and then raced in to have a shower and help mum cook tea.

My life wasn't getting any less complicated.

CHAPTER TWELVE

Thursday didn't improve.

Seth came home around 9, reeking of perfume and smiling like a Cheshire cat. He twirled mum around a few times in the centre of the living room before raiding the fridge for left-overs and chatting non-stop about his date with Amber. Apparently Amber just 'loves pralines and cream Hagen Daas" (well, duh. I mean, who doesn't?) and Amber just "lives to watch Bones" (Again with the duh – David Boreanaz looking all hot and gorgeous in a suit) and Amber just would "die if she didn't get her nails done once a week" (boring, boring, boring).

Just after 11pm, Rosie called to pass on a message from Sariel. Asmodeus had sent him away on business. It would be Sunday or Monday before he was back but he promised to call as soon as he was back in the country.

"That's the message?" I asked numbly.

"What were you expecting?" asked Rosie sounding totally confused. "He didn't need to send any message. He's just being polite 'cause you're the boss's kids."

I hung up on her just because that was the mood I was in and went to bed feeling angry and annoyed and much too emotional to sleep. I did 'though and Friday dawned bright and warm bringing with it an invitation form Annie and Dylan to go swimming at the mega pool in Ipswich.

They were completely themselves – arguing about the speed of the bus in comparison to the train, making up mathematical formulas to describe some of our fellow travelers – for example, a guy sitting near the front wearing a long dirty jacket with a balding head but a lush beard was 'A' minus (soap plus water) plus (hair divided by 2 equals 'B' where 'A' is a normal person and 'B' is the poor guy they picked on. I know, I know, nerd humour. You either get it or you don't.

The pool was amazing with a capital 'A'. There were four tube slides ranging from toddler friendly to 'OHMYGODI'MGOINGTODIE', a plethora of weird water games – cannons, jets, fountains to run through – and of course the pool itself which was equipped with a wave making machine and had people screaming with delight every time the over-loud siren whoop whooped through the place announcing that the waves were coming.

We fired water cannons at each other, had diving competitions, dared each other to go down the red OHMYGOD slide and ended up sharing a huge latte and a chicken and cheese melt in the café afterwards, giggling like six year olds. It was a great day and the best moment of all was when I caught Dylan looking at Annie with a 'Wow-when-did-you-get-so-hot?' expression. I wisely said nothing to either of them – coupledom would either happen or it wouldn't, nothing I said or did would change that so I preferred to let nature take its own course. I mean, the whole Seth and Amber thing was a perfect example – I hated her and yet nothing I said about her to Seth had made a difference. If the universe wants people to hook up then they will. End of story.

Or maybe it's not the universe. Maybe the hand of fate is actually the hand of God, my brain mused. I chewed that one over on the bus home as Annie and Dylan talked about the pressure of water required in one of the pool cannons to knock someone off his feet. I thought about joining in with the conversation – I mean, think how many variables there would be in THAT equation! – but I suddenly felt like an intruder in their burgeoning maybe-couple thing. A gooseberry. A fifth wheel. Deadwood. I sighed. The whole hormonal teen thing was getting old.

We parted ways on Market Street with promises to meet up on Saturday night for bowling or a movie or something. There was a club at the far end of Main Street but we figured that, since we were too young to get it, it would be a wasted journey. I watched Annie and Dylan walk away, their heads close together as they discussed some new movie that they both wanted to see and I felt suddenly alone. An outsider. I couldn't share my problems with my friends or it could get them killed. God and the Devil exist and I couldn't tell anyone. My dad was a demon and I was going to sprout horns in a couple of years. Maybe.

Adam, Sarah and Amber were sitting in Adam's Mercedes outside of our house. It looked so odd seeing a shiny sports car in the row that I gawked for several seconds before I realized who it was. My stomach fluttered and then fell into my feet.

The top was down and Amber was in the back seat, her hands combing through her hair and making it shimmer in last rays of the evening sun. Thankfully they were parked with their backs to me and I scuttled along the road as fast as I could, trying to sneak up the path before they saw me.

"Hey nerd!"

Too late.

I stopped where I was and turned around. Sarah had spoken. She smiled sweetly. "Tell your brother to move his cute ass, will you? We've been waiting for ages." She produced a fake yawn and Amber giggled. Adam was talking into his mobile, facing away from me. Typical.

I turned back and let myself into the house, tripping over a pair of trainers just inside the front door. Seth was in the living room, straightening an honest-to-God tie in front of the mirror, his face slightly flushed as though he'd been rushing.

"Sarah says to hurry up," I told him.

"Damn." He muttered. "Em, I have no shoes. Find me some shoes. I have nothing to go with this suit."

I looked at him with wide eyes. "You what?"

"Suit, no shoes, find me something." he growled.

"Where are you going that you need a suit?" I asked looking him over.

"Um, the club. Don't tell mum." he whispered.

"The club?! You'll never get into the club, Seth. You're all only sixteen." I rolled my eyes.

"Well, Adam's seventeen and so's Amber. Besides, Sarah's Dad owns the place so we can get in no problem. Dammit!" He undid the tie and started again.

I opened my mouth to argue and then thought about Annie and Dylan. Ok, so I was never going to like Amber but she was Seth's choice and if that's what he wanted then I would have to help him. I sighed. "Go take off the suit, Seth."

He twisted around to look at me. "Huh?"

I shook my head. "You don't need to wear a suit. C'mon. We'd better hurry."

Less than ten minutes later Seth left the house to cat calls and woof whistles from his new friends. He was wearing a pale blue shirt over camel coloured chinos. We'd decided not to tuck it in so it hung down a little under his dark brown leather jacket. He was wearing his camel Dockers and was walking with a swagger that said 'Yes, I know I look good in this'.

I watched until their car turned the corner at the end of the road and then I started tea.

Mum was late home on a Friday so we had a late tea of grilled chicken and pasta, chatting about the pool in Ipswich (totally cool slides), the piles of work waiting on her desk (there just aren't enough hours in the day), the new cute guy who brought the sandwiches at lunch (Alan, or Adam or something like that) and the fact that Sariel seemed ok. (For a demon.)

"We don't actually know that he's a demon," I said through a mouthful of pasta.

"Don't talk with your mouth full, Emily. Of course he's a demon. He's with...Asmodeus, isn't he?" My mother grimaced with distaste at my father's name.

"Well, yeah, but he might just be like a human employee," I suggested (*with the ability to wipe memories and talk to people telepathically?* asked my brain sarcastically).

Mum shook her head and wiped her mouth with a napkin. "No, he's a demon."

"So why'd you let him in the house?" I asked. "Why be nice to him?"

Mum sighed. "Your father seems to think that you and Seth are in some kind of danger. From his enemies. He seems to want to protect you and he's assigned people to do that. If this Sariel is one of those people then I need to be nice to him so that he looks after my babies." She reached out and touched my cheek. "You're growing up so fast, Emily. You and Seth both." She shook her head wistfully. "I don't know where the time's gone."

I smiled at her. "This is all pretty weird, huh?" I asked.

She smiled and then blinked her eyes furiously and turned to get up from the table.

"Mum?" I gripped her arm and turned her back around. "What's the matter?"

"I did this to you and Seth, Emily. All these things, all the stuff you have to deal with now. I know it's not easy for either of you and I wish with all my heart that I could take the burden from you but I can't. I can't and I'm so, so sorry." Tears were spilling down both our cheeks as I pulled my mother into a hug.

"It's not your fault mum and everything will be okay," I told her, only half believing it myself.

CHAPTER THIRTEEN

That night I dreamed about hell.

'The fiery pit' in my dream was more like a maze of rooms, each containing a torture more horrible than the last. I ran along corridors dripping with blood and gore, my feet slipping on the slimy ground as I screamed for my mother, for Seth, for Annie, for Dylan. There was booming laughter all around and the thwack and swish of weapons as they broke bones and severed limbs. Voices screamed and groaned in agony behind the doors that I ran past. Several of them screamed for help too but I kept running, sweat stinging my eyes and running down my back as I searched for a way out. Oh, and that phrase, 'hotter than hell'? I get it now. It was furnace hot with a sky that seemed to be ablaze and no hope of anyone switching on the air conditioning anytime soon.

A door opened and my father emerged, wearing robes of red and black. He saw me and cocked his head to the side a smile playing on his lips. "Come to join the family business?" he asked, reaching a hand out to me. The hand was bloody, it gleamed in the flickering light from the fiery sky and I lurched away from it and back down the corridor, his laughter following me.

I ran until my lungs were screaming for relief and my legs were too painful to keep me up any longer. Crying, I collapsed in the middle of another corridor, my sobs barely registering through the cacophony of anguish and terror all around. I curled myself into a fetal position and closed my eyes tight shut, my sobs making my body shudder.

I knew as soon as it happened that I was in the garden. The breeze was beautiful, gliding over my burning skin. My sobs became whimpers and finally my tears dried. I sighed and melted into the soft grass, relaxing enough for my aching shoulders to creak with release. The smells were sweet and seductive; tonight I could smell oranges, roses, the sweet, mossy tang of trees. It was heaven as far as I was concerned. And I was not there alone.

Sariel's cool hand brushed hair from my forehead as he spoke in hushed tones. The language was musical, beautiful and I opened my eyes to look up at him. "You're here," I said, my voice hoarse from screaming, and he nodded. I knew that there were questions that I should be asking but I couldn't find the energy to ask them. "I was in hell," I told him.

"No, you were dreaming," he told me with a gentle smile that didn't quite reach his eyes. "You were dreaming and I heard your screams and came."

"He was there," I said, my words slurred with fatigue.

"Who?"

"Asmodeus. He was there and he was wearing a robe and he held out his hand and it was all blood and I could hear screaming, people pleading and I was so scared." My barely-there voice turned into a whine as tears threatened again.

"Hush, Emily, hush. You're safe here in my garden. Sleep now," Sariel whispered, pulling me into his arms. His breath tickled my forehead a few seconds before I felt his lips brush a soft kiss there. I wanted to open my eyes, to look at him, to ask if I was awake now, but instead I slept without dreaming.

CHAPTER FOURTEEN

"You're pathetic," Annie told Dylan as we trudged to the diner. She had her arms folded and her face was all scrunched up in mega-frown mode.

Dylan sighed and kicked a stone along the footpath in front of him. He had his hands in his pockets and his head down, looking as miserable and dejected as a sixteen year old could look.

"Give him a break, Annie." I hissed. "He can't help being sick at the sight of buckets of blood. I mean that movie didn't get the ad-line "Slasher-tastic" for nothing. It was pretty gross."

Annie sighed and glanced at Dylan. She chewed on her lip for a while. "Okay, okay, okay." she said glumly as we trooped into the diner.

As always I grabbed a table while they ordered and I watched as Annie tentatively made peace with Dylan, noting that her hand stayed on his arm for a few seconds longer than was absolutely necessary and his face flushed with delight when she nudged him playfully with her hip. I sighed and slumped back in my seat, grabbing the menu to study just to have something to do with my hands and my brain.

There was a noise over by the door as it opened and the jolly four-some of Adam, Sarah, Amber and Seth clattered in. I growled deep in my throat and attempted to hide behind the menu.

A hand pulled it down from my face and I looked up to find Amber grinning at me with Seth trying to look happy to see me and failing miserably. I pasted on a smile.

"Hi, Emily," drawled Amber in her incredibly irritating false-happy voice.

"Hi, Amber," I mimicked and then, catching a dark look from Seth I asked. "So, where have you guys been?"

"Oh, we were at the cinema, watching 'A Blood Red Moon." said Amber, her eyes travelling over my face like she was trying to find something interesting.

"Really? We went to see that too. It was awful. Really gory," I said.

"Oh totally," Amber said, her eyes widening in mock-horror. "I just LOVE horror movies. Give me a chance to snuggle close to Seth's totally hot body," She giggled shrilly and caught Seth's face in her hands, kissing him soundly for much longer than my stomach was able to handle. I mean, first she calls my brother hot and then she snogs him right in front of my face.

"Would you like me to give you two some privacy?" I asked.

Amber allowed a shocked, embarrassed and delighted Seth to come up for air. She pressed a hand to her heart. "Oh, I'm sorry, Emily, I just can't resist my Sethy-wethy, he's just so…hot." She poked him in the chest and he managed a weak grin, rubbing the back of his neck.

"Yeah, so you said," I growled.

Amber stood up and waved across the now-crowded diner. "Look, they've got a table. C'mon Seth." Grabbing his hand she launched herself out of the booth, pausing long enough to trill, "Lovely to see you, Emily" and blow me a kiss, before dragging him through the crowd to the far side of the diner.

Dylan and Annie sat down in the seats that Amber and Seth had just vacated. Annie raised an eyebrow, "Do I even want to know what that was all about?" she asked.

"No you most certainly do not. If I ever have to hear anyone call my brother 'hot' and then stick their tongue down his throat in front of me again, I'll totally lose it." I told her.

Dylan made a face. "Ewww. Sharing spittle is completely unhygienic. I mean, do you know how many bacteria are in the average mouth?"

"Forty thousand," Annie and I answered.

"I don't think people are thinking about germs when they're kissing, Dylan," I said carefully, forcing myself NOT to look at Annie.

"Well, I know THAT," he answered. "But, well, think of all the possible infections and diseases that can be passed on by the sharing of bodily fluids? It's absolutely mind-blowing."

I risked a quick glance at Annie. She had her head down and was stirring her tomato sauce into her mayonnaise with rapt concentration. I widened my eyes at Dylan, nodded my head in Annie's direction and then made violent throat-cutting motions with my hand. Dylan watched me, frowning and chewing slowly on a chip. He looked at Annie, looked back at me, shrugged, looked at Annie, back at me and mouthed 'What? I don't get it.'

I closed my eyes and took a breath to stifle my first impulse which was to strangle him. "Well, not everyone feels that way, Dylan," I said loudly, nodding furiously at Annie.

Dylan frowned again in deep concentration. "Oh," he said, looking at Annie again. He looked back at me and shook his head. I thought I might cry with frustration. Dylan had an IQ of 138 for crying out loud. He was practically a genius! And yet he couldn't figure out simple sign language?

I tried again. I nodded at him and then at Annie.

He frowned and cocked his head to the side.

I pouted and closed my eyes, mimicking a kiss (I thought).

I opened my eyes to find Dylan as far back in his seat as he could get with a look of complete horror on his face. (Okay, great boost to my ego there. Not.)

I shook my head and concentrated on eating a few chips while Dylan studied the table without really seeing it.

Sighing, Annie stood up. "I'm just making a trip to the ladies," she announced, "Want to come along?"

Aha! A chance to talk to Dylan. "Er, no thanks, Annie, I'm fine." I said.

"I could do with a wee," said Dylan mournfully, starting to get up. I kicked him under the table. "Ow!" he said, looking at me with a confused and wounded expression.

"What?" said Annie. "What happened?"

I raised an eyebrow in Dylan's direction. "Er, um, I, er, I knocked my ankle on the table as I was getting up," he said, watching me carefully for signs that I might attack again.

"Oh," said Annie in a couldn't-care-less voice. "Well, are you going to go with me then?"

"Um…no, actually, I think I'll stay here and finish my fries," Dylan said, looking at me for confirmation that this was the right thing to do. I nodded.

"Okay then, back in a mo," said Annie heading off into the throng.

"You kicked me!" Dylan accused once Annie was out of ear-shot.

"You're damn right I did," I hissed, leaning across the table. "What is wrong with you? I was trying to tell you that talking about how many germs you might get from kissing Annie isn't going to improve your chances." I sat back and folded my arms, watching the display of emotions flit across Dylan's face.

"How did you…?" he began and then closed his mouth again. "Do you think that I…? Do you think that she…?" Hid hands fluttered away from his fries for a while and then settled down again. He licked his lips and tried again. "How did you know?" he asked.

I smiled at him. "It's not difficult, Dylan. You look at her sometimes like she's the most beautiful thing you've ever seen."

He pressed his lips together. "Well, she is." He said finally, "I mean, not that I don't think that you're…y'know. But she's just…" He grimaced.

I giggled at him and reached across the table to lay my hand on his arms. "It's ok, Dylan. I look at Seth and see my annoying older brother. Amber sees some kind of hot stud." I shivered at that. "I look at Annie and see one of my best friends. You look at Annie and see a beautiful girl that you want to be more than friends with. Wouldn't the world be incredibly boring if we all liked the same things and the same people?"

Dylan smiled his soft, happy, Dylan-smile and covered my hand with his own. "Thanks, Emily." He leaned over. "So how do you suggest that I…"

There was a startled gasp at the end of our table. Dylan and I looked up to find Annie standing there, her eyes glued to our hands and her face a mask of misery. We jumped apart, looking as guilty as hell and I began to stand up, reaching towards her and muttering "It's not what you think, Annie."

Annie lifted her eyes to mine and there were tears brimming there. She opened her mouth to say something and then whirled away and out of the diner.

I turned to Dylan. "Well, at least you know now."

"Know what?" he squeaked. "That I just lost any chance I might've had?"

"No, idiot. Now you know that she likes you back. Go after her." I told him, pointing the way she'd gone.

Dylan gulped. "But what will I say? How will I convince her?"

"Find her first, Dylan. The words will come and if they don't, well, you could always kiss her."

"That would work?" Dylan looked unconvinced.

"It'd work for me," I told him. "Now go!"

Grinning, Dylan gave me a quick hug and then shoved his way through the diner and out after Annie. I watched him go with a contented, maternal smile on my face and then went to pay the bill.

Leaving the diner, I saw the Amber and Seth still sitting in their booth. Sarah and Adam must've left already. I could hear Seth laughing loudly. Amber's shrill giggles followed me out into the square and I swear I could still hear her clear across Market Street and down to the end of Dean's Avenue. What did he see in her?

I was musing the possible attributes that, although deeply hidden, might make Amber a person worthy of my idiot brother's affections, when I became vaguely aware that someone was walking behind me. To be honest, it didn't cause any alarm. I mean I was being guarded from harm by demons for goodness sake. I started thinking about Annie and Dylan. Had he caught up with her? Were they talking now? Kissing? I grimaced. Thinking about your two best friends kissing was not normal. I gave myself a mental shake and pulled my jacket a little closer. It was getting cold now that August had arrived. I quickened my pace, thinking about home and sliding under my warm duvet.

The footsteps behind me quickened too and I felt the first stirrings of fear. I hurried past Dean's Crescent and over past the Primary School. Home was in sight when an arm encircled my waist from behind and a hand covered my mouth. I could taste something faintly alcoholic.

"There you are," snarled a voice. "I've been looking everywhere for you."

The hand left my mouth and I drew in a breath to scream. I never made it. Strong fingers went to the pressure point on my shoulder and gripped hard, freezing the muscle and trapping the nerves. I made a choking sound and pitched backwards into blackness.

CHAPTER FIFTEEN

I became aware of the smell first.

It was a heavy, thick, coppery smell, so pungent that I could almost taste it. I thought about opening my eyes, bit back a wave of nausea and tried to clear my head. What had happened? Where was I? All I knew was that somewhere close by there was a lot of blood. Memories of the slasher movie surfaced and I groaned. The blood might even be mine!

With that thought, I concentrated on how my body was feeling. My head was pounding and my top lip felt swollen. My left arm was numb but I could flex my fingers which was a good sign. It was the burning across my abdomen that was the biggest cause for concern. I moved a fraction of a millimeter and the whole area lit up with pain. I moaned and bit my lip.

Something moved nearby and I froze. My heart was thumping wildly in my chest, adrenaline causing goose bumps to come to life down my arms. I lay motionless, listening. The sound came again. A low scrape, like the scuffing of a shoe against concrete, or maybe the sharpening of a long, gleaming, wickedly curved talon? I swallowed the lump of fear that seemed lodged in my throat. I suddenly began to feel surrounded, like the crash survivors on 'Pitch Black' as they race towards their new space ship followed by thousands of hungry, sharp toothed alien monsters. Bloody movies!

There was nothing else for it – I would have to open my eyes.

Biting my lip against a hysterical bout of tears and trying to calm down for fear that my galloping heart would burst from my chest, I slowly opened first one eye and then the other. I frowned in confusion.

I was lying on my back on a table in the school cafeteria.

I knew exactly where I was because of the crappy ceiling panels stained with flung food and the weird, recently installed lights which looked like something out of Star Trek with their futuristic, conical shape and burnished steel covers. And there was that noise again.

This time, I turned in the direction of the sound, hissing as my belly stung and my pounding head swam. My mouth dropped open.

Chained to one of the other bolted down tables was Adam Farlow. Adam's normally perfect blond hair was matted with a dark brown substance which might have been dried blood. One of his utterly gorgeous dark blue eyes was swollen shut and bruised alarmingly in various shades of blue and black. He was wearing his usual expensive-looking suede jacket although it was now dirty and ripped in places. His heavy cotton trousers hadn't faired any better.

"Bloody hell," I said. My voice echoed around the cavernous room and Adam looked up at me.

"Pardon?" He said, his voice sounded even more huskier than usual.

"Well," I said, frowning. "If this is a dream then it's a very odd one. Normally you're not tied to a cafeteria table in my dreams. Or wearing your… um…jacket." I paused, embarrassed.

"Uh, I see," said Adam, managing to look smug and uncomfortable at the same time. A tough expression to pull off when you're having the worst possible hair day and you only have one good eye.

I sighed and turned my attention to my stomach, pulling my pale green shirt up. There was a shallow cut from the right side of my belly button to just above the second belt loop of my cream cord skirt. My skirt and shirt were both red and the wound was still oozing. I felt nauseous again. I shivered.

"You're hurt?" asked Adam, straining to see from his position on the floor.

"I have a…well, it's like a long cut which is bleeding. It looks like a knife wound." I sounded, even to my own ears, amazed.

Adam snorted. "Still think you're dreaming?" He asked sarcastically.

"I think you're chained to a table, Adam. Not exactly the best position to be an asshole." I flung back at him.

Adam opened and closed his mouth a few times and then studied his knees. I looked around. The cafeteria was dark with shadows of inky blackness stretching out from every corner. There were a few chinks of light where the heavy blinds hadn't been closed properly and long shards of silver sliced into the room and illuminated parts of the floor.

Adam was watching me with narrowed eyes. "They hurt your head too," he said.

"Really?" I lifted my eyebrows. "Where?"

"Just above your right eye, I think…" he leaned over slightly to see better and I shifted around so he could see my back, gasping at the pain in my belly. "…no, it's at the back. The blood must've dripped over your head when they were carrying you in or something."

"Who's they?" I asked, swiveling around to face him again. "Who did this?"

Adam shrugged. "Didn't see any faces. Just caught a glimpse of two of them walking away after they dumped me here and did this…" he shook one of his hands and the chain clinked and jangled against the table that he was tied to.

"Why you?" I asked. I shook my head and then bit my lip a little as all kinds of pain signals flashed to my brain. Once I could open my eyes again without seeing stars I said. "Scratch that. You're the most popular guy in school. Why me?"

"Because we need a virgin," boomed a voice from the door. Adam and I both jumped, Adam swore as he hit his head on the table he was chained to. I turned around as someone walked into a patch of light.

He was wearing a nondescript jacket, jeans and plain black sneakers. He looked, well, average. From his average length brown hair, to his average face with a small scattering of acne to his average slim lips and average blue eyes. He grinned at me.

"Hello little virgin," he sneered in a voice that made my skin crawl.

More figures filed silently into the room, forming a loose circle around me, Adam and the newcomer. I pretended not to notice them, I was concentrating all my efforts on trying to figure out who mister average was as he began to bark orders to the others.

"David Blakely!" I exclaimed and all faces turned to look at me. Mister average grinned again.

"Clever girl." he said and turned back to watch his friends as they moved a number of items into the centre of the room.

"How do you know that she is?" asked Adam, his voice stronger than before.

David looked back at him. "How do I know what, maggot?'

"That she's a virgin."

David laughed. "She's one of the nerd squad, loser. You really think any of them have time to date never mind screw? They're too busy getting turned on by additional maths and the laws of physics. Ain't that right, nerd?"

I blinked at him and said nothing. I had a feeling that all the smart answers in my head would be a really bad idea. Instead I turned to Adam. "Any other stupid questions to ask?"

Adam attempted to flip me the finger but his chains wouldn't reach far enough and he only succeeded in having them dig further into his wrist. He grimaced.

I shook my head. "Juvenile." I whispered and turned my attention to what was going on around us.

Two of the David wannabes were walking around the room with what looked like sacks of sugar, tipping the stuff out in a neat line around the perimeter of the two central tables where Adam and I were. Three others were positioning something around the far reaches of the room. I strained to see what was going on until another figure began to go around lighting them.

"Candles," I said and frowned. This was too weird to be a birthday party.

"Are you in any of my classes?" Adam asked.

I turned to look at him. "What? Yes two of them. English lit and Biology. I sit behind you in Biology so I get to hear all the really funny jokes that you and Ritchie Phillips make up. It's just wonderful." I rolled my eyes. *Oh, and I love you,* my brain wanted to add. "My brother Seth is dating Amber." I added reluctantly.

Adam looked at me carefully. "Do you always have your hair up?"

"Yes."

"And do you go to any of Sarah's parties?"

"No."

"And you always wear…" Adam pointed at my clothes.

"Yes!" I yelled at him, exasperated. "Look, don't go getting your boxers in a twist, Adam. You don't notice girls like me when there are wonders like Sarah and Amber around. It's okay. That's how it is and I've dealt with it, a long time ago. Now get over it and help me figure out what's going on here." I shook my head and watched the figures flitting through the hall.

David walked back into view wearing a long black robe with a hood which was currently pooled behind his head. He was carrying a knife and a tattered old book with a hideous sallow coloured cover. He laid them down on a table just outside the circle of sugar. The table had been covered with a black cloth and held a collection of candles in various shades – red, black, green, blue and brown.

"Is this like a hazing?" I asked no-one in particular. "What the hell do they need the sugar for? Are we going to have to go around on all fours licking it up?"

"Sugar?! Lick it up?!" Adam was looking at me with an expression that I was all too familiar with. It was a combination of embarrassment and anger and I saw it every day in every class as I answered or asked question after question. The average kids in the class would look at me, Annie and Dylan with that same expression, usually just before calling us 'dork', 'nerd' or some other wonderful name. I'd never seen a popular kid do it though – normally they were together in a little huddle just doing their own thing and ignoring everyone whose parents didn't own a Mercedes or have a couple of million in the bank.

Adam was looking around the room and I saw him pale in the flickering light of the candles. "Shit." he mouthed.

"What?" I asked. "What?!" I squeaked again when Adam didn't answer.

"It's not a hazing. We're in trouble. Big trouble. That's salt. They're using it to create a protective circle. See?"

I looked around, nodding, but not really understanding. My insides, however, were fluttering with fear.

"Looks like David and his buds are going to attempt a summoning." Adam said, his jaw tight and his eyes wide.

I chewed on my lip again. David had drawn the hood of his robe over his head. It almost obscured his face. He had opened the book and was chanting something in a low musical voice. The words sounded like vaguely rhyming nonsense but I felt myself shiver as I listened.

I closed my eyes and concentrated. *Sariel?*

Nothing

CHAPTER SIXTEEN

I tried again, putting all my will into it. *Are you there, Sariel?*

Emily? His voice seemed faint, as though he was far away.

Oh, thank G...goodness. I think I'm in major trouble.

Damn right you are! You've been missing almost 24 hours. Your mother's frantic. Asmodeus is ...um, upset with your guards. They changed shifts quite irresponsibly. I could hear the tightness in his voice, the anger. *Where are you?*

School cafeteria. What's a summoning?

There was silence.

Sariel?

What makes you ask? What do you know about a summoning?

Well, I don't know anything but Adam's here, chained to a table and he says that there's a salt circle and this weird guy, David, is reading something from a book in a weird language.

Uh, huh. Is there a pentagram on the floor?

I looked around.

"What is it?" hissed Adam.

"Don't they need a...a...thingy on the floor to have a protective circle?" I asked.

"A thingy? You mean a pentagram? Usually, yes. Unless..." he stopped and a nerve twitched in his jaw. He was looking at me sadly. Almost apologetically.

"Unless what?! Jesus can't you just finish a sentence?" I wriggled in annoyance and then cried out as the pain in my abdomen flared again. I lay back on the table and pulled up my t-shirt. The wound gaped horribly and blood seeped from the ragged edges. "Which one of you shits did this to me?!" I yelled. No-one paused what they were doing and no-one answered. I felt a hot tear slide down my cheek. I brushed it away angrily and pulled myself back into a sitting position. "Well?" I hissed at Adam.

Are you hurt? Sariel said in my head.

Um, yes, a little.

Define 'little'.

My lip's swollen, the back of my head's cut and I have a long cut on my stomach that's bleeding a lot.

Sariel growled. *I'm coming.*

Adam was looking towards the table where David was still standing with his book, chanting that weird rhyme and swaying a little. Back and forward, back and forward, as though keeping time.

"Adam!" I yelled.

Adam didn't look at me. His attention was riveted on a bundle that two of our captors were carrying towards the circle. They were struggling a little with the shape and weight of it as they finally hoisted it over the salt and threw it forward towards the centre of the circle. Whatever it was landed with a muffled thump and slid a little way past my table.

I struggled to sit up and get a better look at the bundle as Adam moaned and turned his head away.

I peered over the edge of my table, holding my arm across the wound in my stomach. The bundle had become partially unwrapped as it had been thrown and I found myself staring into the open eyes of a young woman. For a moment, I simply stared and took in the pale grey colour of the skin, the glassy blankness of the once beautiful brown eyes, the almost-white lips, the long, slim arms bent at an impossible angle. My brain fought to stay in control as my mouth opened to scream.

Instead of a scream, however, I heard my voice say a name. "Alice Frost."

"You know her?" asked Adam, his face was even paler now, his good eye wide and afraid.

I nodded. "Yes, we were in the same history class. She went missing months ago." I slowly shook my head, unable to tear my eyes away from Alice Frost's body. "Everyone thought she'd run off with a boy." I said sadly. I looked sharply at Adam. "They killed her didn't they?"

Adam nodded and squeezed both his eyes shut.

"Why? I don't understand…" My voice trailed off as I realized that I was tasting salty tears.

You're crying? Sariel sounded closer now and I took heart, wiping my tears with the back of my hand and wincing at the pull on my stomach wound.

There's a dead girl and I know her…knew her.

"They needed the blood," Adam whispered.

"For what?" I managed to cough out between sobs.

"You don't want to know." Adam turned away from me, sliding his knees up to his chest and bending his head over them.

I opened my mouth to argue and quickly shut it again. Maybe I didn't want to know. I took a last glance at Alice and then scooted back on the table again. I looked around. The hall was now lit by a couple of hundred candles set at intervals all around. They made odd and terrifying shadows dance around the walls and bounce backward and forwards in drafts from around the windows and the doors. The cafeteria had always been draughty. In the middle of winter, it had been strangely soothing to sit in here with a bowl of hot soup and listen to the wind howl outside as it tried to slip through all the nooks and crannies in the room.

Most of the wannabes had departed, probably to stir a cauldron somewhere, I thought wryly, leaving David chanting his weird poetry over at the table.

"Is that where you're going to slit my throat?" I asked loudly and pointed at the table. David's voice faltered for a moment and then he continued, glaring at me. I grinned.

"Are you insane?" hissed Adam. "You're making him mad."

"Oh, so what? If he's going to kill me then I'm not going to be bloomin' nice to him!" I rolled my eyes and was surprised to hear Adam laugh.

"You're witty…for a nerd." He said and guffawed even louder.

"Oh, very good. Instead of cracking up at your own jokes could you perhaps figure out a way to rescue me?" I yelled indignantly.

"Beg your pardon?" Adam's good eye blinked at me as his swollen eye twitched in what I supposed might be astonishment.

"Well, here I am – damsel in distress and you're the big tough guy that most of the school is swooning over. So go on then! Get off your ass, break free from the chains and rescue me."

"Er…I can't." Adam said softly, blushing furiously.

"Why not?" I asked angrily.

"It's hard to explain."

"I'll try to keep up."

"He can't help you because the chains are made of silver." said David from across the room. I looked at him in surprise. I had been so caught up with being cross at Adam that I hadn't realized that David's annoying chanting had stopped. I glared at him.

"Silver?" I asked. "Well, great. You buy *him* jewellery and cut *me* with a knife. That's totally unfair."

Both David and Adam stared at me in astonishment. I looked from one to the other. "Cat got your tongue?" I asked.

David pressed his lips together and began to pace just beyond the circle of salt. From time to time he mumbled to himself. I sighed and tried to fold my arms but the wound in my belly was too painful and I couldn't manage it. At least the bleeding seemed to have stopped. I looked at Adam who was watching me nervously, his even white teeth nibbling his bottom lip. If he hadn't been chained to a cafeteria table, covered in blood and bruises, he'd have looked adorable.

"Bloody hormones," I whispered to myself, dragging my gaze away from Adam long enough to scowl at David. He was still pacing. I dragged myself to the edge of my table again and peered over at poor Alice. I tried very hard to study her compassionately, like on CSI. Forget that the vic is a person and look at the evidence.

I pursed my lips and concentrated. Okay, numero uno, Alice...no, the vic, was dead. Numero dos, the vic was naked, well what could be seen of her was. Numero tres, she was pale, even for a dead girl. I thought about that for a moment, let my brain lead me in the right direction. I turned back to Adam.

"It's about blood, isn't it?" I asked.

Adam gaped at me.

"Like you said?"

I gestured towards Alice, "Her, I mean. They used her blood for something."

"Er..." Adam's eyes darted around the room, trying to avoid me.

"Oh, spit it out, Adam. I'm trying to understand here, and if you know something then you need to tell me." I was exasperated. I punched the table for effect and grimaced at the pain in my knuckles, head, stomach and several other places that had started to complain, and the thud that echoed around the hall. I hated that I couldn't work it out by myself.

Adam frowned at me, colour returning to his cheeks for a moment as he obviously fought the urge to drag the table across the hall and throttle me. "Okay, smart girl, I'll tell you if you're so hell bent on knowing. They had to drain the blood from her and drink it. While she was still alive. They kept her alive for a very, very long time, living off her blood. It's the best way to purify their bodies for the..." he gestured around the room, "...for the ritual."

I took a deep breath and closed my eyes for a moment as panic threatened.

They drank her blood. They kept her alive and drank her blood. Oh, Alice I'm so, so, sorry.

When I opened my eyes again, I was clear headed and calm. Adam was still frowning. "Okay, so they spend a few months drinking some poor girl's blood and then they take over the school cafeteria, deck it out with candles, kidnap the school rugby captain and a nerd. Have I got it so far?"

Adam nodded, a corner of his mouth threatening to turn up in a smile.

"You're making it sound stupid," growled David. He had stopped pacing and was now staring angrily at me.

I turned slightly to face him. "Those are the facts, David. So, are you going to tell me what you're doing here? Trying to channel the spirit of Groucho Marx?"

David looked at me blankly.

I raised my eyebrows. "Elvis?"

David looked at Adam who was slowly turning purple as hysterical laughter threatened to escape the hand that was currently clamped over his mouth.

"Are you laughing at me, half-breed?" asked David, his voice horribly calm. Adam's head snapped up and he paled again, glancing quickly at me and then back at David.

"What did you call him?" I asked, keeping my eyes on Adam.

David grinned. "I called him a half-breed 'cause that's what he is. Betcha didn't know that Mr. All star rugby captain and chick magnet Adam Farlow is part 'Other'." He grinned at me and spat in Adam's direction.

Can demons or part demons be restrained by silver? I asked Sariel.

No, he replied reluctantly.

What's 'other'?

Um…

Sariel? C'mon! I need to know what I'm dealing with here!

Restrained by silver would be, um, Were.

CHAPTER SEVENTEEN

Adam Farlow is part Werewolf?

I looked carefully at Adam, my heart pounding. Adam studied his knees. My brain stuttered for a moment and then spluttered back into life. Adam Farlow sprouts hair all over his body, howls at the moon and eats people? No, my brain went back into retreat for a second.

I went back to basics.

Weres are real? Yep, okay. It seemed that I could deal with that. I grinned to myself. Demons are real so why not Weres?

Sariel was silent, letting me work through it myself. Weres were real. What next? Vampires? Ghosts?

"Were," I said softly. "You're part were. That's why you can't get out of the silver chains."

Adam looked up at me. He looked miserable. Well, even more miserable. I cocked my head to the side and studied him. This time he didn't look away but held my gaze. I encouraged my brain to call up every possible thing I'd ever enjoyed reading about Weres. Thank God for Kelly Armstrong! "Helps with the sports I would imagine – Were genes, I mean. Speed, power, agility. No wonder you're captain of everything in school. And the pheromones help to attract all the females." I grinned. "Although the looks help too."

David cleared his throat. "Look, nerd, as much as I'm sure you'd just love to start dissecting Mr. Farlow here to find out what makes him tick. And, although, I truly wouldn't mind watching that, we do have a schedule to stick to." He checked his watch and walked back to the table, taking a small plastic bag from behind it. He rummaged in the bag for a moment and then threw something towards me. It landed just beside me on the table and I jumped away from it, wary now of anything that David might throw at me.

"Put that on," ordered David. "I'll get the others and we'll get started."

I lifted up the item that David had thrown and my mouth twisted into a sarcastic half-smile. "You have GOT to be kidding me." I shouted at David's retreating back. "You want me to wear this flimsy white dress? Could you build any more clichés into this ritual?"

I held the dress up in front of me and turned her eyes to Adam who was eyeing it with a look of confused appreciation. "I'm not wearing it." I told him.

Adam raised an eyebrow.

"Don't look at me like that," I snapped. "If I'm going to get gobbled up by some Were or other then I can surely choose how I'm dressed. Besides, there's not much they can do about it unless they want to come into the circle." I grinned smugly.

Adam sighed. "It's up to you, I suppose. I just don't know that it's a good idea to keep pissing David off. Wait a minute…" he looked at me sharply. "…you think I'm going to eat you?!"

I squinted at him. "Well, that IS why you're here isn't it?"

Adam frowned as though in deep thought. He shook his head. "You've lost me. You think I'm going to eat you and then what?"

"Well, I don't know. Then the whatever they're hoping to summon from wherever it is it is eats you? How should I know? You obviously know more about this stuff than I do. What do YOU think is supposed to happen next?"

Adam stared at me for a moment and then smiled. "You don't like it when someone knows more than you, do you?" he asked.

"Quit smirking." I said and gingerly slid forward off the table. "Now what do you know?"

Adam pressed his lips together into a thin line and chewed at the bottom one again for a few seconds. "Well, the ritual purification that they've been doing with…" he gestured towards Alice. "Well, that's pretty big. Few people have the will, the patience or the resources to do that. You have to be bloody dedicated to kidnap and torture someone for months."

"And drink their blood," I said. "Yuck." I grimaced.

Adam cleared his throat. "Er, yes. Exactly. Also, the kidnapping of a virgin and an 'other' takes a lot of planning." He shook his head. "I don't know how they figured it out."

"What? That I'm a virgin?" I looked at him incredulously.

"Er…no. That I'm part Were. I mean, I don't exactly go around with a sign painted on my forehead. And I haven't managed a change yet. My dad thinks the genes might be too diluted now. All I have going for me is the strength and agility. It's why I go for all the sports."

"Huh." I frowned. "So what's the point in grabbing you then?"

"My blood will still work for their purposes and I'm not as dangerous as a full breed. Silver keeps me from using any strength to overpower them," he jangled his chains and smiled sadly. "I think they're trying to raise a full blood demon. And if they do it will drink my blood for strength and, well, it'll either drain you too or…use you for something else." He blushed and looked away.

I laughed; a short burst of angry scorn. "So a demon is let loose from hell and the first thing, no sorry, the second thing it wants to do is screw a virgin?!"

Sariel? I'm in big, major, enormous, huge poop here!

Adam shrugged. "Well, it's just a guess."

I leaned back against my table and rolled my t-shirt up a little. The long thin cut had finally stopped bleeding but I knew that any sudden movements would rip it open again. I looked up at Adam. "Did you just lick your lips?" I asked, my voice high and reedy.

Adam opened and closed his mouth several times, his eyes wide and unblinking in an attempt at innocence. Then he sighed and nodded sadly. "Your blood smells really good. I've never wanted to…eat someone before but you really do smell good."

I dropped my top and closed my eyes, shaking my head. "Well, that's great. I'm either going to be fed on or used by a hell beast but hey that's okay 'cause the most popular guy in school thinks I smell good enough to EAT!" I spat the last word at Adam, my eyes flashing. Adam opened his mouth to say something and then looked past me.

I followed his gaze and stiffened. David was leading a crowd into the cafeteria. All of them were wearing robes now, the hoods over their heads. Their feet were bare and their arms were folded in front of them, their hands concealed in the deep folds of the robes. They were all chanting as they filed in and moved to stand around the circle. I counted quickly, my head whipping around to follow them all. There were 26 of them in total. I wondered if there was any significance in the number.

Any significance to the number 26?

It's two times 13?

Well, I know that! Hello? Maths nerd here! I was thinking more of the whole demon summoning thing.

Well, it could be the gate of hell they want to open.

There are 26 gates in hell?

No, many, many more.

Great. So what joys are behind gate 26?

I'm not sure.

Well, that's just terrific.

David pulled the cowl off his head and pulled his hands out of his voluminous sleeves. He was holding a short knife which flashed gold in the candlelight. The handle was oddly shaped and ended in a wicked looking claw. The blade gleamed. Still chanting, David closed his eyes and held the knife aloft, then he brought it sharply down, slashing across his open palm.

I winced and Adam made a small noise of fear. Or hunger.

Okay, David the chanting guy just cut himself with a weird knife-slash-claw thing. Ewwww. Did he cut me with that?

A claw? Is the handle made of gold?

Yes! Yes! What is it?

How the hell did he get that?

Sariel?!

Making a fist with his injured hand, David held it over the circle and

86

squeezed. As three drops of his blood dripped onto the floor just inside the ring of salt he chanted even louder, finishing his frenzied warbling with the words, "Hear me, Azrael."

Does the name 'Azrael' mean anything to you?

Azrael? They want to call up Azrael? Okay, I'm going to tell you what to do but when it happens you must show no fear and you must do and say exactly as I tell you. Now are you listening…?

Chapter Eighteen

I listened with my mouth open in astonishment. I knew that I was very scared, shaking like a leaf. I also knew that it would be a miracle if I got out of the school cafeteria alive. Although I told myself that was a risk you took with school cafeterias generally. Ta da! Gallows humour.

Sariel finished his instructions. *Be brave,* he said softly. *You can do this.*

I looked at David who was wide-eyed with excitement. "Oh, God" I whispered as the first wave of power slipped around the room.

David and his followers sank to their knees and began to sway from side to side in a kind of fanatical dance of supplication. Once again they began to chant, their voices unmelodious and sinister, echoing around the hall. Inside the circle the air began to shimmer with heat.

I pushed myself away from my table and across to where Adam sat. Wincing I reached under my t-shirt and scraped at my wound, biting my lip at the pain. Then I brought my hand out and reached out to Adam who shrank away.

I sighed. "Look, we're in a bit of a pickle here, Adam. You'll have to be a man about it and trust the poor little nerd in distress to protect your ass. Ok?"

Adam nodded mutely and watched my hand as I pressed it to his forehead, leaving a smear of my blood there. His eyes when he looked back at me were full of questions.

I slid down to sit beside him on the floor, pressing my hand to my stomach where the blood was oozing out again. Around the circle the keening of the David wannabes was reaching a crescendo. I saw David look up at me, triumph in his cruel eyes. As the chant ended, I winked at him. David's face crumpled and took on an almost comical mask of utter bewilderment.

Neither of us had time to react further as a sound like enormous thunder rattled through the hall. All at once there was a sharp smell of sulphur and the roof of the cafeteria began to cave in. Adam dragged me back under his table as debris and dust fell around us, putting all the candles out. A voice roared in the sudden darkness and there was a flash of energy at the centre of the circle. I closed my eyes at the brilliant light and when I opened them, the hall was quiet and the dust was settling. There was now only one small section of ceiling left above us.

In the centre of the circle stood a demon almost seven feet tall. His skin was a deep red and he stood on two enormously muscled legs. His arms were wrapped around his torso as he surveyed the wreckage of the hall with cat shaped yellow eyes. He opened a mouth of razor-sharp teeth and roared again, making more debris fall from the roof. Laughing manically he surveyed the room.

Now! Sariel yelled inside my head and I slipped forward out of my hiding place.

"Emily!" shouted Adam. "Get back."

Hearing Adam, the demon swung around to fully face us. He opened his mouth to roar again, his eyes narrowing when I stood up in front of him, my hands on my hips and my head cocked to the side. My heart had gone beyond pounding and I was almost certain that a cardiac arrest was imminent. My legs were like jelly and I had to concentrate to stay on my feet. Scared? Nope, totally, completely and utterly terrified. I only hoped that I looked braver than I felt. Adam's mouth was open and his mouth was working but all he seemed capable of producing was a kind of squeak.

On the far side of the room, David and his followers were immobile with fear. David still had the old book open across his palms but the chanting was over and, although his mouth was open, he seemed to have caught Adam's illness as no sound was coming out.

All eyes were on the demon and me.

I pretended to look at an unfiled fingernail and then yawned in mock boredom. I held up my hand still covered in my own blood and tried to look totally nonchalant as the demon lowered its head and took a sniff. It sighed and then a rough tongue slid from its mouth and licked my palm.

"Mmmmmm." It said. I shivered but forced my mouth into a smile.

Adam, David and the others in the room gulped audibly.

The demon sighed. "Might've known something would spoil a good human scaring," it grumbled and I saw Adam wince. The thing's voice was deep and loud but had the same effect on our ears as a nail down a chalk board.

"Oh, pipe down, Az. I didn't plan to be here." I walked pertly forward until I was a few steps away. I folded my arms. "What's this all about?" I asked, my brows lowering.

The demon made an annoyed, tutting sound. "I could ask you the same thing. If you didn't plan to be here then how did you get here?" it asked.

I gestured behind me to Adam, "Well, Adam and I got kidnapped by..." I paused, my heart's rhythm stopping altogether, as the demon lowered it's head close to Adam and sniffed loudly.

"Mmmm. Were,' it breathed. "Tasty." It frowned. "You blooded it." It folded its arms and pouted. "I can't eat it."

My heart bounced back into mere panic-mode.

I grinned. "As I was explaining. Adam and I got kidnapped by these guys," I pointed around the room. "Apparently I was the virgin sacrifice and Adam was the half-breed."

The demon looked incredulous and then it began to laugh – a loud throaty gurgling giggle that erupted between its devilishly sharp teeth. "You!" it spluttered. "You? A Virgin sacrifice?!" It laughed until it had to sit down, denting the floor of the cafeteria in the process.

I turned towards Adam. "Sorry about this," I said, my cheeks heating with embarrassment.

"You know this…thing?" asked Adam, his voice barely a whisper.

I puffed out my cheeks and sighed. "Well, yes, although I don't like to advertise the fact. He's apparently kind of almost nearly like my sort of half-brother. More or less."

Adam lifted his eyebrows and managed to make a "huh" sound. He was obviously thrilled that he wasn't squeaking any longer. In fact, it seemed that he was suddenly starting to feel much better. He lifted his face to where David was standing with his eyes as big as school dinner plates. Adam grinned and sat back.

The demon had finally stopped laughing and was wiping its eyes. I waited.

"So," it said, standing up again. "These guys kidnapped you to be their virgin sacrifice," its voice wobbled as laughter threatened again but, looking at the dark anger on my face it rapidly pulled itself back together again. "Dog-boy was to be the half-breed appetizer and bobs your uncle, here I am." It grinned, difficult to do when your mouth is a half-moon slash of flesh full of razor-sharp teeth.

I smiled. "Yes. There's a slight problem, though."

The Demon frowned. "Explain," it said, all traces of mirth gone.

I began to pace, my hands clasped behind my back and Sariel's voice whispering instructions in my head. "As I understand it, these guys used a blood sacrifice to facilitate the ritual. Their method of purification."

The demon was still frowning but his mouth had dropped open at the word 'facilitate'. I was fairly certain that it was confused, although demonic expressions of confusion and anger looked pretty much the same.

I looked at it. "Yes?" The demon nodded.

"Okay. So for the ritual to be completed then you would have to eat Adam and...well, do whatever you were going to do to me. Am I correct?"

The demon shivered, its shoulders undulating like huge snakes. "Yuck." it managed.

I smiled. "No offence taken, brother dearest." I turned and looked around the hall. "Stalemate, folks." I called in a loud cheerful voice.

Adam held up a hand and I looked at him. "Er...I'm sure I don't want to know this but why is it stalemate?"

I held up a finger, delighted to finally be able to answer a question. "Good question, Adam. This is stalemate because Azrael here can't eat me or do anything else for that matter – Daddy would not be a happy bunny..."

Azrael looked fearfully around. "Are you nuts?" he asked. "Don't call him a bunny!"

Across the hall David barked a laugh, earning him a dirty look from everyone else.

"As I was saying," I said, "Adam can't be eaten 'cause I've marked him with my blood – therefore he's under my protection. Therefore," I paused dramatically, "The ritual cannot be completed and Azrael cannot leave the circle." I clapped my hands and smiled. "Home time, I reckon."

Azrael folded his arms across his thick chest and frowned. "I want something." he said, his thunderclap voice petulant.

I sighed and the breezy smile slid from my face. I turned to face my new brother. "Like what?" I asked.

"Eh?" Azrael gaped and I chewed down the comment that even big, red, scary demons could be incredibly stupid.

"Well, what is it that you want?" I asked, exasperated.

"I want...I want...I want..."

"Yes, yes, spit it out, Az. I have a wound that mum needs to have a look at, two friends to check up on - y'know the whole have-they-haven't-they thing - and I'd really, really, really like to get some sleep sometime soon. Hurry up!" I was tapping one foot with impatience, a bravado that I wasn't going to be able to maintain for much longer.

"I want a snack!" roared Azrael and the final chunk of the cafeteria ceiling fell down, covering us all in dust and tiny stone fragments once again. Coughing, I surveyed the damage, sighing at the sight of one of the fancy new lights protruding from the rubble like a trapped, stainless steel spider.

"You can't," I said slowly, as though talking to a stubborn five year old. "The ritual wasn't completed, the first course is under my protection and you're sure as hell not eating me. Go home."

"No. I want one of the humans who did this and messed up." Azrael turned his attention to the outside of the circle, grinning malevolently.

Oh, God. Oh, God. Oh, God. What do I do? What do I do?

CHAPTER NINETEEN

I faced the demon Azrael across the wreckage of our school cafeteria.

"You know I can't condone you eating a human." I said.

Azrael bellowed a laugh. "I don't need your permission, daughter of the dark one. I just need you and your little Were boyfriend to make yourselves scarce." He looked around, licking his lips in eager anticipation of a tasty morsel of human flesh.

Sariel? Can he do that?

I listened as Sariel explained and my heart sank.

"Can he do that?" Adam asked tentatively.

I nodded sadly and knelt down beside him, wincing as my wound opened once again. "Apparently the rules are many and complicated, Adam, but the simple truth is that once a person turns themselves over to evil, once he or she commits a crime in the pursuit of greater evil, then...well, Azrael or any demon like him can take what's theirs, what the human has already agreed to give him. Taking the flesh releases the soul and evil souls are black and nasty. Heaven doesn't open its gates for their kind."

Adam shook his head. "But, but they're just school kids like us," he said softly, looking around at the frightened faces ducking through the settling debris.

I nodded. "I know. But they killed a girl, Adam. They drank her blood. They invited a demon to cross over from hell. Azrael owns them now." I wanted to cry and scream and pound on the demon with my bare hands. If Sariel hadn't been whispering calming words in my head I might have done it.

Adam looked shocked, scared and sick. "Do you think they knew that?"

"No, I think most of them thought it was a weird, twisted game, Seems to me that the whole, drinking someone's blood thing would've been a clue that they weren't playing though."

Sariel. How do we get out of here? I can't do this anymore. I just can't.

I listened and then I stood up. "Azrael, release the Were and then release us from the circle." I said wearily. "Then do what you will."

Azrael leered once more at the figures trying desperately to escape from the hall and then he leaned towards Adam who shrank away as far as his silver chains would allow. Azrael held his gaze for a few seconds during which Adam most likely concentrated very hard on a) not appearing TOO scared and b) not soiling himself. Then Azrael blew on the chains which slid apart with what sounded like a sigh of relief, something that Adam echoed. Standing up on shaky legs, he rubbed his wrists and headed towards the closest pile of salt not buried by chunks of ceiling.

I reached out and stopped him. "No. We have to be released. The ritual was incomplete which means that the circle belongs to Azrael. If we leave without his permission then he will track us down and…well, best we don't go any further."

Adam nodded. "He wouldn't do anything to you though, would he?"

I smiled and shook my head. "No, I'm safe this time although it doesn't make me any less scared to be honest. Older brothers can be tricky buggers. And I think that for you it's best to be safer than sorry."

Adam nodded and gulped. "All those things you asked me about the ritual, you already knew them, didn't you?"

I shook my head "No, I didn't. But now I do know and there's always room inside a nerd's head for more info. Isn't life weird? You never know who you're going to end up chained to a table beside." I turned back to Azrael. "Any time you feel the need, Az."

Azrael sighed, closed his eyes, muttered a few words and reached out one of his hands to touch Adam and I on the head. Azrael's one palm covered both our heads with room to spare. Adam looked up at it through his brows, struggling not to squeak with fear again.

And then I was leading him away from the centre of the room as Azrael began to mutter again and several kids stood up at their hiding places and walked past us in a daze. Some of the others had escaped or were far enough away for the incantation to have little or no effect. I felt the pull of it as I stumbled along in front of Adam, I tightened my grip on his hand.

"Keep walking, don't look back," I instructed. I was looking at the faces of the kids walking past us. "I don't know any of these people." I felt instant relief followed by a mountain of guilt at my relief.

David passed us, his eyes glassy but scared. "I didn't know," he gibbered, spittle dribbling down his chin, "You just look like a skinny little bookworm."

"Rule number one in the nerd's rulebook, David," I said as I led Adam away from David's stumbling form, "Never judge a book by its cover."

Adam giggled hysterically and I pulled him on out over the rubble and into the school grounds. A noise to my right made me jump and then smile with delight as Sariel appeared from the darkness. I made to go to him but he held up a hand, shook his head and motioned to me to go on. Stung, I did as I was told, looking back to see him climbing over the remains of the cafeteria and heading towards Azrael.

We walked down the back road from the school, down past Taylor's Row and on past the cinema without saying a word. I was shaking with cold and adrenaline. The heat from Adam's hand was keeping me anchored and I was certain that some day soon I would be able to do a little dance and be thrilled that I had held hands with Adam Farlow but just now I was just concentrating on staying sane and glad not to be demon chow.

We stopped walking at the football pitch and Adam dropped my hand self-consciously. "Um, so, Emily, I think we need to talk about the whole Were thing," he said and coughed.

"Okay. What do you want to talk about?" I asked, too tired and too sore everywhere to think about being nice.

He coughed into his hand. "Well, the pack doesn't take too kindly to people knowing about us." He looked up at me meaningfully.

Pack? There's more of them? My brain chewed on that little tidbit. I sighed and rubbed my eyes, wincing. "Are you threatening me?"

Adam made a face. "Um, well, no. Not really. It's just that if anyone outside of…well, if anyone else found out then…um."

I looked at him. "I'm part demon, Adam. I know the score. Demons kill people who find out about them." I waited.

Adam's eyes widened for a moment and then he grimaced and studied his hands. "Well, we kind of know that demons exist and stuff and I'm sure that when the pack finds out that you saved my life, there won't be any need for any retribution." He looked me in the eye and waited.

Stand tall, Emily. They value bravery and strength, Sariel told me.

I pulled myself up and moved to within an inch of him. "Well, they know where I am if they ever want to say thank you." I said.

Adam laughed, leaned forward and hugged me. "Thank you, Emily. I know that's not enough for what you did but I won't forget it and neither will the pack. Do you want me to walk you the rest of the way home?"

I shook my head and turned to go.

"Um, Emily?"

I turned back. Adam looked nervous, bouncing from foot to foot.

"Spit it out Adam, it's been a long day."

"Yeah, sorry. It's just that, well, I wanted to make sure you knew that, um, at school and stuff, um…"

I sighed. "I'm very aware that I'm a nerd, you're one of the it crowd and never the two shall meet, Adam. I'm also very aware that even saving your life doesn't change the fact that I'm not pretty or rich or whatever criteria you guys use to decide whether people are good enough to join your little club. I'm not expecting us to suddenly be friends or anything and yes, I will pretend none of this happened if I ever see you again."

I turned around and walked away, leaving him standing there looking bloody, beaten and adorable with a look of shock on his truly gorgeous face.

Bloody hormones.

CHAPTER TWENTY

One of the goons fell into step beside me a few minutes after I left Adam. He spoke softly and rapidly into a radio mike at his wrist and took my arm, steadying my slightly wobbly steps. I scowled at him. I didn't want to think about what it might say about my mental state when the sight of a heavily muscled demon guard made me feel safe.

My reunion with mum and Seth was predictably emotional – hugs, kisses, tears, more hugs. I clung to my brother for a while and tried to shut out the fact that our little home seemed far too over-populated. As well as mum and Seth, Asmodeus and Rosie were there with an impressive array of goons and a small Mexican looking girl who seemed to be serving tea and sandwiches. That blew my mind for a few minutes as I watched her weave among all the big men with her little tray. Weirdness on top of weirdness.

The questions began as soon as mum's tears dried up and I realized two very important things; number one – Sariel hadn't filled them in on anything and number two – he was no-where to be seen. Interesting.

I answered all the questions as honestly as I could, bigging up Adam's role in everything and minimizing my own. I excused my ability to reason with Azrael as simple nerd/library/brainpower stuff although I saw Asmodeus narrow his eyes a little. Mum squeaked as I described the ritual and even Rosie paled a little when I told them about the draining of Alice Frost. She exchanged a significant look with Asmodeus when I mentioned the clawed knife too. He quietly dispatched a goon to retrieve it and Rosie pulled out her cell phone and headed to the kitchen.

Once I had the gathered crowd up to speed on mad demon summoners and Were packs and Alice Frost's place in our town and every other little detail that they could prise out of me, I pleaded to be allowed to go to bed. Asmodeus stood up and took my hand. I managed to quell an inner shudder of revulsion at his papery touch and bowed my head – which truly wasn't difficult this time; I was almost asleep on my feet.

"I must apologise to you Emily," he said, his smooth, caramel voice gliding over my senses. I wondered if he was trying some kind of mojo on me.

"You have no need to apologise, Sir." I told him. "I was in the wrong place at the wrong time."

Asmodeus smiled but shook his head. "Like your mother, you are incredibly kind, Emily." He smiled in my mum's direction and then turned his attention back to me. "I'm afraid that I must take some of the blame for this. I sent Sariel away on business which, although urgent at the time, could quite easily have been concluded by someone else. Leaving my children in the care of those whose...abilities do not match Sariel's was a mistake. If anything had happened to you, or to Seth, I would never have forgiven myself. I'm sorry." He pressed his other hand on top of mine and I swallowed bile. How had my mother let this man touch her?

I cleared my throat. "Your apology is, of course, accepted. Although I didn't ever hold you responsible in any way, Sir." I told him carefully. They were pretty words, delivered in a voice of careful reverence but I was almost certain that if I didn't get away from him in the next few seconds I would vomit all over his Gucci loafers.

"And now we shall let you rest, my dear," he told me, finally releasing my hands. "I will, if you don't mind, discuss security measures with your mother and Seth for a brief time."

I nodded and made my escape upstairs, pausing on the landing to hear Rosie tell her employer that the damage to the school canteen had been 'taken care of' and David Blakely would become the victim of a nasty car crash on the notorious accident black spot of Vale Road. The others involved were mainly runaways that David had found and seduced with promises of wealth and fame or something. No-one was unaccounted for, young malleable minds had been scrubbed clean of any kind of demon knowledge. The situation had been 'managed'. Yadda, yadda, yadda.

I stumbled into my room, closing my bedroom door behind me very quietly even as I bit my hand to stop from screaming. My tears fell and I slid down the back of my door, re-opening the cut on my stomach. I moaned and clutched at it, feeling completely overwhelmed as the final dregs of my adrenaline fuelled energy bled away and all the aches and pains made themselves felt.

I thought of crawling to my bed, thought of crawling to the shower, thought of just staying curled at the door until the world managed to right itself and the past year rewound, leaving me a normal, boring little nerd who never got kidnapped by mad school kids, never knew about demons and certainly didn't have one for a father.

I waited for maybe ten minutes but the universe refused to rewind and so I began to crawl to my bed. It was agonizing and I whimpered with pain and exhaustion. The few metres between the door and my bed suddenly seemed like miles.

Sariel was suddenly there and kneeling beside me. "You can stop fighting now, Emily. I'm here. Let me do this now."

I gave in gladly, closing my eyes and letting him carry, drag, float me to my bed. Whatever he did, it didn't hurt and once my head lowered onto my pillow I sighed with relief and satisfaction. I swore I would never again call my pillow lumpy, my duvet pathetic or my bed too small.

"Where does it hurt," he asked softly.

I pressed my hand onto my belly, my lips trembling.

"I'll be gentle," he promised and carefully pulled my shirt up a little. There was a moment of silence and then he growled deep in his throat, an animal noise of anger and distress.

I opened my eyes a little and his face was dark with outrage. He turned his eyes to me and they had darkened from their usual silver blue to a deep violet. I blinked and time slipped away from me for a moment. When I came back he was whispering to me about healing. Or perhaps he was whispering to himself. I was too exhausted to know the difference.

"Unless it's asked for, bargained for, I can't heal this. But it needs healed. It can't be left like this. There's a lot of blood lost and it needs to heal now. Dammit! If it was caused by one of us, then could I heal it? Wait! It was indirectly caused by one of us – it was torture inflicted in the course of a summoning so surely that counts." He looked at me, his eyes lightening and his gaze softening. "Eravate così coraggioso, dolce uno."

I smiled. "Sweet talker." He grinned. "What did you say?"

"I said that you were very brave, Emily. I'm going to heal this for you."

I swallowed. "Will it hurt?" I was ashamed that my face tightened and my eyes filled with tears at the thought of more pain.

Sariel cradled my face in his hands and looked into my eyes. "I promise not to hurt you, Emily. I promise." I nodded and closed my eyes, waiting.

Sariel's fingers were cool, his touch so light I might not have felt it if I hadn't been so hypersensitive already. His caress danced along the ragged edges of the wound in my belly as he whispered words that I didn't recognise. I felt his breath on my belly and sucked in a ragged breath.

"Did I hurt you?" he asked in surprise.

"Er…no." I told him, blushing furiously.

He went back to his work on my stomach, my head and then my lips. I floated somewhere between wakefulness and sleep, hearing his murmurs, feeling his light touch but unable to fully open my eyes.

Finally he brushed a gentle kiss on my forehead. "They're coming to bed, quello cara. I must go." I whimpered and reached for him. "I won't go far, Emily but I can't be found here tonight. Do you understand?" I nodded mutely, not understanding at all, and felt the air stir beside me.

Seth opened the door to our room and, after covering me with my duvet, slipped quietly into his bed. I slept.

CHAPTER TWENTY-ONE

I woke to the sound of mum and Seth arguing and the smell of bacon crisping in the pan. My mouth watered and I rolled over in bed, trying to open my crusted-together eyes. I stopped dead.

Sariel was asleep on my desk chair. He looked rumpled and slightly unkempt in a long taupe jacket and jeans. His head was on his left shoulder and his hair had, for once, escaped the leather strip that he kept it bound with, covering the left side of his face in an unruly screen. His perfect lips pouted beneath it and I thought about how he'd brushed a gentle kiss on my forehead the night before, how his breath had felt on my belly, the gentle touch of his fingers. I wondered what he would do if I went over there and pressed my lips to his, pulled his hair back from his face, sat down on his lap and wrapped my arms around him.

Sariel opened his eyes with a snap and we regarded each other, both of us wide eyed.

Seth opened the door, carrying a plate of toast, bacon and beans. Mum was behind him carrying two cups of tea.

"You're awake!" announced Seth, still king of the obvious. I grinned at him and gladly accepted the plate. Mum kissed me on the cheek and deposited one of the cups of tea beside my bed, handing the other to Sariel.

"When did you get here?" I asked him, through a mouthful of beans.

"Sariel's been here since really early this morning," mum answered, making Sariel grin into his mug. "His flight got in around 3 and he came straight here. You need some sleep, Sariel, you look dreadful."

Sariel looked up from his tea with an expression of astonishment that made me laugh and choke so Seth pounded me so hard on the back that I was certain he'd broken a rib and Sariel would need to do some more healing (wishful thinking?).

We talked about nothing and everything for a few minutes and then I set down my fork and looked from face to face. Everyone stilled under my scrutiny and I took a deep breath.

"So," I began, "What was decided in the pow wow you all had last night?"

Mum chewed on her lip and glanced at Seth who made a face and looked towards Sariel. Rolling his eyes, Sariel set down his mug and faced me.

"Asmodeus has decided that I am to be your personal guard from now on, Emily," he said. "Arkron will attend Seth. You are both to be guarded at all times."

I chewed my top lip. "At all times?"

Sariel nodded.

I turned to Seth. "And what do you think about this?"

Seth shrugged. "Last week I would've said it was a waste of time."

"And what changed?" I asked, keeping control of my simmering temper with difficulty.

Seth frowned and shook his head at me. "You got kidnapped, Emily. You got slapped around and almost fed to a damn demon."

"But not because I was Asmodeus' daughter, Seth. Because I was a little virgin who happened to be in the wrong place at the wrong time." I turned to appeal to our mother. "Mum? You're agreeing with him on this?"

Mum looked from me to Seth and then flicked a glance at Sariel. "Don't look at them, mum. Look at me. Sariel does what he's told, no matter what he thinks. Seth's a wuss, obviously. I want to know what you think."

"I'm a wuss now?" Seth stood up and glared at me.

"If you seriously just *accepted* the fact that someone's going to be watching you every hour of every day from now on for no good reason then yes, you're a wuss." I slid my legs out of bed and stood to face him, hands on my hips.

"It's no different to what's been in place for almost a year anyway, Emily," Seth said through tight lips.

That stopped me. "What?"

"I told you that Sariel has been watching out for you. Asmodeus offered it and mum and I agreed it would be a good idea. Arkron's been my shadow, Sariel's been yours. There are people out there who want nothing more than to eradicate our kind from the face of the earth. They think we're an abomination, evil." Seth glanced at mum. "We didn't tell you 'cause we knew this was how you'd react. It's always your way or nothing, whether you're right or not. Well, this time you're wrong. Be grown up enough to admit for once that you don't know everything."

I felt tears prick at my eyes — tears of anger, embarrassment, hurt? I wasn't sure but I was damn sure that I wasn't going to cry in front of Seth at that moment. I nodded. "I see. So it's all decided then." I looked at mum who looked away, chewing on her lip. Sariel met my eyes levelly but his face was closed into his usual expression of boredom. I wondered what was going on behind that carefully applied façade.

Does Asmodeus always get his own way? I asked.

Yes. Always.

There was no answer to that, nothing more to be said, and so I excused myself and took a shower. I was careful to ignore the fact that the dirty water was tinged with old blood and I could see bruises across my stomach. They followed more or less exactly the line of where my cut had been. It was healed completely — no scar, not even a faint pink line, just a few bruises and the dull ache of my memory.

I admired it in the bathroom mirror — the flat clean planes of my stomach unmarred by that horrible ragged cut that David had made into my skin. I swallowed when I thought of him and closed my eyes against the thought of what Azrael had probably done to him. And the others. All those kids, dead? Eaten? I began to shake and sat down on the edge of the bath, taking deep breaths to stop myself from pitching over.

Are you ok? Sariel's voice was soft and cautious.

No, I told him honestly. *I just want to wake up.*

He sighed. *I'm sorry, Emily.*

I got dried and dressed and then headed downstairs. Mum and Seth had both gone to work, leaving me a note detailing what time they finished, what time they'd be home, how much food was in the fridge, how many times during the day I should pee. Well, ok, maybe not the last one but it all felt false and ridiculous and I was annoyed with them anyway.

CHAPTER TWENTY-TWO

Sariel was sitting at the kitchen table nursing a mug of coffee. He rose and poured one for me.

"I can get my own coffee, Sariel," I snapped. "I'm not made of bloody porcelain all of a sudden!" I scowled and sat down heavily at the table. "Sorry." I mumbled.

"You should call Annie and Dylan," he said. "They've been going crazy."

I grinned. Yep. That sounded like the gruesome twosome. I lifted the phone and called Annie's house. Her mum answered but told me that Annie was out so I called Dylan. His brother, Steve, answered. "He's out with Annie, Emily. Aren't you guys meeting up?" I scowled an excuse into the phone before throwing it back into its cradle. Obviously they weren't that concerned.

Sariel watched me over the rim of his mug as I searched down the back of the sofa for a scrunchie and then tied my hair back in a loose ponytail. I sat back down at the table trying to act calm when my insides were churning with annoyance and fatigue and anxiety. I turned a false smile on Sariel. "So, great protector. What are we going to do today?"

"I'm going to answer your questions today, Emily," Sariel said, staring into his cup of coffee. "Whatever you ask, I'll answer."

"Anything?"

"Anything."

I nodded and sipped my coffee. It was good – strong and hot. My brain immediately began to fill with question after question. So much I wanted to know. I shook my head to clear it a little. I needed to think about it.

I looked up at him. "I'm not under house arrest or anything am I?"

He frowned. "I'm not a gaoler, Emily."

"Ok, Can you take me somewhere? I need to think before I start asking questions."

He nodded and we gathered ourselves together and got into his car

— a Renault Clio, which was rather more sensible for our road than his usual ostentatious suv.

"Where to?" he asked cheerfully as we pulled away from the curb.

In the end there was only one place to go.

We pulled up outside All Saints church and I got out and began the walk towards the front door. If I'd expected Sariel to be upset or surprised about my choice of destination then I'd been wrong. He'd made no comment at all, just nodded as if he'd expected it and driven us there.

I stopped at the door and turned to him. "You won't burst into flames if we go in here or anything?" I asked wryly.

Sariel grinned. "Let's find out, shall we?" He moved past me and inside. I followed and felt the calm envelop me as soon as I stepped into the foyer. I closed my eyes and took a deep breath before following him into the main church.

As before, the place was quiet and virtually deserted. I walked over to the candles and lit one again before walking to the very front pew and sitting down. Sariel had retreated down the other side aisle and into the shadows behind the columns. He hadn't burst into flames or been struck by divine lightning but he obviously wasn't as comfortable being in here as he liked to make out.

I lost myself for a while going through everything that had happened since the day we'd come home from school to find mum in tears and Rosie in the kitchen. There was so much and it was such a short time ago. I wasn't certain where to begin with the questions, or where to end.

I was so engrossed that I almost didn't hear someone sliding into the pew behind me. Almost. It could've been anyone — one of the elderly ladies from before, briefcase guy, a mafia don with an attack of guilt - but I had a sudden flash of intuition.

"Are you going to try to save my soul today, Father?" I asked softly.

He stilled in surprise and then chuckled softly, leaning forward and pillowing his arms on my pew. "Should I ask how you knew it was me?"

I shrugged. "You smell holy," I told him.

He raised an eyebrow but said nothing.

"I'm sorry if I did it wrong," I said, thinking he had come to complain about the candles.

He turned his head and studied me.

"I'm not here to complain about how you strike a match…" he began.

"I meant the…" my hands fluttered in front of me…"whatever you call the stuff you say as you light it."

Father Cassidy smiled. "Somehow I didn't have you pegged as the kind of person who cared for the conventions of religion."

I rolled my eyes, "Oh, really. And what kind of person did you have me pegged as? A heathen?"

He grinned and gestured to the far aisle where Sariel had come to stand in the light. He was watching us carefully. "Boyfriend?"

I shook my head. "No, just a friend."

The priest nodded thoughtfully. "Can I ask you something?"

I thought about that. This seemed to be a day for questions. "Go ahead."

"Ok. Well, people usually come here when they're in trouble. When they come across a problem or a situation that they feel they can't manage to overcome or understand on their own."

I turned to face him and held up my hand. "I think I know where you're going with this, Father. Let me answer your question."

He frowned. "You don't know what it is yet."

I smiled. "I think I do. Sariel is not my abusive boyfriend, he's probably one of the reasons I'm still sane. My mother is not cruel or vindictive or handy with her fists, she's a kind, caring woman who loves me very much. My brother is an…well, he's a decent bloke and, even though we fight a lot, I love him to bits. I came in here 'cause it's quiet and I like the calm of the place – it helps me to think. I don't need to be saved or read to from the good book. And I don't need someone telling me that God loves me and will keep all the evil ones from me if I believe in him and keep all his rules and regulations, come to church seventeen times per week and purge my soul by confessing that I held hands with Adam Farlow one night." I took a breath and looked at the priest. He didn't look upset, angry, confused or anything else I'd expected, instead he looked intrigued.

"Do you believe in God, Emily." he asked carefully.

I looked towards Sariel who had moved down the aisle and was now only a few pews away.

I shrugged. "What does it matter?"

The priest made a face and stood up as Sariel slipped in beside me. "Good morning, Father," he said smiling his 'could-charm-ice-from-Eskimos' smile. Father Cassidy smiled right back at him and they shook hands. I winced, waiting for Sariel's hand to start smoking. It didn't of course.

"Fascinating name you have, son," Father Cassidy told him.

"Yes, Sir."

"'Sariel' was a fallen angel you know?" The priest told us, still smiling.

"Wow. Told you I was an angel, babe." Sariel was smiling too but I could sense his sudden discomfort. It was as though I could feel his heart hammering against his rib-cage and I shivered as a thrum of gathering power pulsed from him. I looked up and his eyes had darkened to a deep blue.

His smile was slipping and so I took his arm, smiling brightly at the priest.

"Lovely to see you as always, Father. Take care."

I pushed Sariel down the aisle and out into the foyer, pulling the main door open as he stumbled a little. We made our way to the car and pulled out and onto the main road again.

"I guess I know the first question I want to ask," I said as Sariel maneuvered the car down Main Street.

"Shit." He mumbled.

CHAPTER TWENTY-THREE

We settled at the kitchen table for almost a minute, during which time I fidgeted and started a lot of sentences without finishing them. Sitting opposite each other with a table between us didn't feel right. I sighed and pulled Sariel into the living room, depositing him on the sofa while I sat on mum's ancient and patched easy chair.

Okay, that was better. I felt more relaxed at least. Sariel hadn't said a word, had just watched my increasing nervousness with a bemused expression. Now he looked grim, he knew what was coming.

"So," I began, "Any question?"

"Yes. Was that question one?" Sariel grinned. I rolled my eyes, "Sorry, thought I'd lighten the atmosphere a bit."

"Yes, very noble of you. Right then; Are you named after a fallen angel?" I watched him carefully as I asked. He twitched ever so slightly. "You said that you'd answer any question I wanted to ask." I reminded him, earning a glare. I smiled.

"Okay, then. No, I am not named after a fallen angel." He lifted his brows in challenge.

I took a breath and felt my heart pound a little faster. "Are you the fallen angel called Sariel?" I asked and forced myself to look into his eyes as I waited for his answer.

He breathed in slowly and breathed out again, weighing up his options maybe. His eyes dropped from mine. "Yes," he said softly. "I am the Fallen called Sariel." He closed his eyes.

I frowned. He looked ashamed. I slid off the chair and onto the floor, dropping my head and craning my neck to look up at his downturned face. He opened his eyes and they were the palest I'd ever seen them. He blinked at little at seeing me so near.

"Want to talk about it?" I asked.

"Do I have to?" He asked. I shook my head. "Then, no, I don't want to talk about it."

I sat back on my heels and thought about my next question. What did I really want to know? Was I going to end up looking like Azrael? Who were the people that Sariel was supposed to be protecting me from? What was it like to fall from heaven? Was he a demon now? I chewed on a nail.

"Can I ask another question?"

Sariel looked up again and seemed to give himself a mental shake. "Of course."

"Hmmmm. Ok. When Seth and I turn eighteen, will we wake up that morning and look like Azrael?" *Please say no, please say no, please say no,* I whispered to myself.

"No, as the product of a ... relationship between a human and a demon Lord you may or may not gain certain abilities. These will manifest sometime during your eighteen year. Scaly skin and cloven hooves are not in your future." He paused. "Unless of course your ability is shape shifting in which case you can appear as Azrael's twin should you so wish." He smiled as I made a going-to-vomit face.

Trying to keep the relief off my face was impossible. Sariel smiled back. "Seth cheered," he said, "You at least kept your dignity."

I giggled at that and then frowned. "You mean Seth already knows all this?"

Sariel shifted a little. "Well, we had a lot of time to talk in the hospital after your, um, accident, if you still want to call it that."

"Until you can prove otherwise then it was an accident." I snapped.

"As you wish. Any other questions?"

"Well, what did Seth ask?" I folded my arms across my chest and scowled at him.

"His first question was what kind of enemies does Asmodeus have," said Sariel, his lips twitching in a half smile. "Why are you so pissed that he spoke to me already."

"I'm not pissed, well, ok, maybe a little but neither of you told me any of this." I was whining but I couldn't help it.

Sariel sighed and shook his head. "So do you want me to tell you?"

"Tell me what?"

He raised his eyebrows. "Who Asmodeus' enemies are." He clicked his fingers in front of my face. "Stay with me brainiac."

Brainiac? "Quit watching Hannah Montana on your days off, Sariel." He chuckled and I felt my face flame. "So, tell me already. Some of us are aging here."

He tutted at my little strop, grinning. "Asmodeus has more enemies than any human or demon could count. Other demons wanting to take over his empire, humans who want to take over his empire, humans who stumble over the truth, the archangels…"

"Wow, wow, wow,wow, back up there cowboy. Humans who 'stumble over the truth.' Bet they don't last long." I shamed myself by doing a typical teenage move – closing my eyes, turning partly away and tossing my head. The whole already-had-this-conversation-with-Seth thing was still stinging.

"Actually the brotherhood is well organized, well funded and extremely knowledgeable of demonic methods. They're slippery little suckers." He grinned.

"You're impressed by them?" I was surprised.

"Well, yes, I suppose so. Although I'd like to find out who's behind them."

"You can't just dig into their minds and come up with the answers?"

He shook his head and rubbed his chin. "No, that's just it, recruitment is done by lower level employees, each individual only ever sees the one person for the entire time they are active within the organization. No-one really knows enough and getting to those higher up the ranks has so far been impossible." He shook his head, smiling.

"Okay. Um…what job do you do for Asmodeus?" I'm not sure who was more surprised by the question – me or Sariel.

He knit his brows together and then sighed deeply. "Well, you really know how to get to the heart of the thing, I'll give you that," he said with a sad smile. "What do I do for Asmodeus? Well, you could say that I fix things for him."

"What kind of things?" I asked, intrigued by his reaction to a seemingly simple question. "I mean, are you like a handy man? Or a plumber?"

He smiled at that and then grew serious again. "Maybe a fixer is the wrong way to describe it. Hmmm. Maybe I should say that I locate problems and, should the need arise, I arrange for the problem to be taken care of." He looked at me carefully, willing me to figure it out.

I swallowed. "Do you kill the, er, problems?"

Sariel sighed and made a face. "I have done, yes, but usually I pass that rather distasteful job on to someone else. I much prefer to use the science of fear to the use of force."

I nodded slowly. "So my knight in shining armour, my great protector, uses his gift from God to sniff out threats to the great empire of the demon Lord Asmodeus and, if necessary, arranges a murder?"

A nerve twitched in his jaw and Sariel's eyes darkened with anger. I forced myself not to shrink away from him, although the temptation to turn tail and run was very strong. Finally he nodded. "That sounds about right, yeah."

"And how long have you been performing this glorious duty?" I asked stiffly.

"For longer than I ever thought it would be possible to perform such a task and not lose my sanity," he said softly, his voice barely above a whisper.

"You have a choice, Sariel." I told him, thinking that I sounded like a huffy six year old.

He laughed. "What choice is there, Emily Carson? What choice do you believe I have?" I sighed and looked away from him but his swift hand caught my jaw and turned my eyes back to his. He searched my face. "Please, let me hear this great wisdom that you have to impart, oh great child of the dark one." He sneered and my temper rose.

"You could say no," I suggested snapping the words out and pulling away from his vice-like grip.

Sariel's head fell back and he laughed loudly. "Oh, well, why didn't I think of that?!" He jumped to his feet and began pacing. "Such a simple word, isn't it? No. You think that using such a simple word in the face of a demon lord means anything to him? Especially coming from one so low as I am."

"You're an angel, that's not low!" I shouted at him. "You stood in the presence of God, Sariel. That's NOT low."

Sariel stopped pacing. He moved sinuously over until he was standing right in front of me, his breath on my face when he spoke. "And where was He when they found me and ripped off my wings? Where was He when they took me down and tortured me? Where was He when I begged for death? When I begged for release from torment?"

"Why did you fall?" I asked, my voice shaking. I was scared of him now, truly afraid of the anger in his eyes and the venom in his voice.

Sariel blinked, seemed to realize where he was and took a step back. I swallowed my fear and followed him. "Why did you fall?" I asked again.

His face fell and twisted into a grimace of agony. "Don't make me..." he began.

I made myself move, made myself speak. "Why did you fall?" I hissed, pushing my face into his.

He looked at me for a long time. "Let this go," he whispered but I shook my head and he sighed. "I stood with my brothers on Mount Hermon and I saw His creation. I watched them live and die. They had free will and they used it without knowing its power, without understanding what a gift it was. Some of us went among the humans, talked with them, showed them how to do things that would help them to survive. I saw the women and I...wanted them." His eyes closed. "I took a human wife and I showed her the secrets of heaven, Emily, and for that sin I was cast from heaven, down among the humans. I may have been an angel but I wasn't prepared for living on the earth. The demons found me. They tracked me for days, weeks, months and then they caught me. They caught me and punished me."

"By ripping off your wings?" I asked in horrified fascination.

He nodded, keeping his eyes closed. "A fallen is insignificant to them – an enemy discarded to be used as they wish. I was weakened by my fall, disbelieving maybe. Fighting back was beyond me just then." He opened his eyes and I bit my lip against the pain in them. "I am immortal in the truest sense of the word, Emily. I cannot die. But I can feel pain and they had such fun designing new tortures for me to endure and recover from. I endured and I healed, endured and healed over and over and over until I prayed to Him for release from this world, from my torment. I repented my sin, I begged for his forgiveness and do you know what happened?"

I blinked away tears and put up a hand to stop him. I knew that I didn't want to hear this. In fact, if I could have taken my question back right then, I would have. It hurt to hear this. I wanted to tell him that I was sorry, sorry for everything he'd been through, sorry for my mightier-than-thou attitude. He grabbed my palm and glared at me fiercely.

"Nothing happened, Emily. He was no longer listening." Sariel threw my hand away from him and sat down, burying his face in his hands.

My face crumpled and I cried for him then, hot tears slid down my cheeks and dripped off my chin. I sat down beside him and wrapped my arms around his stiff shoulders.

CHAPTER TWENTY-FOUR

I made tea for us both and we sat there in the living room without speaking for what felt like forever. I couldn't think of anything to say. 'Sorry', seemed to me to be woefully inadequate. For once my brain was a blank, perhaps I was in shock a little. I mean, a year ago there were no such things in my cozy little existence as demons, or angels, never mind fallen angels. And right here in front of me was a fallen angel who'd had his heavenly wings ripped off by demons who then proceeded to torture him. And now he worked for a demon lord as a kind of psychic-investment-protection-hit man type dude. It was all bewildering.

When I couldn't stand it any longer I began to clean again. Hoovering under Sariel's feet while he sipped tea and watching me zoom around behind our trusty Henry hoover. I polished too – squirting Pledge around with great abandon and trying not to look too pleased when Sariel sneezed and moved himself to the kitchen.

The bathroom was next and I scrubbed the tiles until they gleamed, polished the shower door until it sparkled and got down on my hands and knees to clean the floor with a billion bathroom wipes. I was starting on the dust bunnies hanging under the door when I looked up to find Sariel watching me. He was leaning against the banister with his arms folded and he blinked slowly once he caught my eye.

"Are we going to talk about this or are you going to continue to dodge the issue?" he asked.

I blustered and fussed and made excuses for a while but finally we sat down on the top stairs of the little landing.

"So..." he began.

"So," I said, staring at my shoe laces, my hands, the cobwebs on the landing window.

"Emily," Sariel warned.

"Well, I don't know now." I whined.

"What don't you know?"

"I don't know if I want to know anything else now," I wailed. "I mean, the stuff I thought I wanted to know just seems really…childish."

"Compared to what?" Sariel frowned at me

"Well, compared to everything you've been through."

He sighed and there was an edge to his voice when he spoke again. "It was all a very long time ago, Emily. I don't want or need your pity; I want to get on with now. Ask your questions, because once we get all this out of the way there's still a lot to do."

"Like what?"

"Is that one of your questions?" He lifted an eyebrow and smiled pleasantly.

I rolled my eyes. "Here we go again. No, that is NOT one of my questions."

Sariel folded his arms. "Then I refuse to answer that particular question until you ask the questions that have been on your mind." He tossed his hair like a diva in a strop and looked away.

I grinned and slapped him on the arm. "Now, who's being childish?"

He narrowed his eyes at me. "Is THAT one of your questions?"

I giggled. "No." I took a deep breath and settled myself. "Ok. Um…We covered the scales and hooves thing, the enemies thing…I won't have to eat babies will I?' He shook his head. "Or drink blood?" Another shake of the head, though not so emphatic this time. "Oh, so now I know that weres are real, what about the other stuff? Are vampires real?"

He made a face. "Well, vampires are just a type of demon really."

I shuddered and rubbed my hands over my face. "God is real, demons are real, werewolves are real, vampires are real. Bloody hell. Um, have you ever met Lucifer?"

"Only when he was an angel. Not since."

Laughter bubbled out of me and Sariel frowned. "Sorry," I told him, "but what a line that is…'yeah, me and Lucifer, we go way back, man. Since he

116

was an angel' that's brilliant." I laughed some more and Sariel watched me as though I was mentally unbalanced.

"So, does Asmodeus pay you?" I asked once the giggle-fest had passed.

"Well, he keeps me under his protection and provides me with food to eat, clothes to wear, a place to sleep..."

"But no money?"

Sariel shook his head. "If I am to go somewhere a car is provided, or a plane. All other expenses are charged to him."

"So you have his credit card? Cool. We could do some damage with that!" I said clapping my hands with glee. "I'm joking." I said when I saw his face. "Jeez, you fallen angel-slash demon types have no sense of humour."

"We prefer to laugh when something's actually funny," Sariel said drily and I stuck out my tongue at him.

I blew out my breath and thought about it. What more did I want to know? Until I turned eighteen, no-one knew what little extra special something daddy dearest had donated to my genetic make up so that was a dead end. 'Oh, I know!' I sang happily. "What if I don't have any special gifts?"

Sariel's brows drew together. "I don't know." he said.

I tilted my head and studied him. "You're lying." I told him.

He sighed and bit his bottom lip.

"You promised you'd answer..." I began.

"Yes. Yes, I know," he snapped. "Fine, any of Asmodeus'...children who have failed to gain significant gifts before they turned nineteen were..." He paused and chewed the inside of his lip.

"Were what?!" I bit out.

"Well, their protection was removed and they were left to fend for themselves." He finished and slumped back against the stairs.

I digested that information. "How many of them survived?" I asked in a small voice.

"None."

I nodded and then brightened. "But I can communicate with you mind to mind, right? That's a good thing, right?" I was grinning like an idiot but Sariel's expression didn't encourage me much.

"I told you before, Emily. That gift is not demonic."

"Well, you can HEAL, Sariel. I wouldn't imagine that's a terribly demonic gift!" I spat at him.

"No, it's not. That is a heavenly gift." he said gently.

I shook my head. We were getting into choppy waters again. I needed to change the subject. "Ok, well, anyway. What about my dreams – the garden, the book place – you made a big song and dance about that. What's the deal there?"

"Song and dance? I did not make a…" Sariel began angrily. He stopped himself and took a few calming breaths. "Ok. Remember I told you that it was important not to tell anyone about those dreams?" I nodded and made a get-on-with-it motion with my hands. He scowled. "Well, that's because the places you go in your dreams are not YOUR places."

My eyes widened. "Pardon?" I asked in my most sarcastic tone. "They are MY dreams so how can they not be MY places?" I made a pffft sound and smiled patronizingly at him. "Don't be ridiculous."

Sariel leaned forward. "They are not YOUR places, Emily. They are MY places. The book place? That's my knowledge, everything I have learned in my life. The garden? That is my place too, the place where I was once happy and at peace. Or perhaps you're going to tell me now that you once visited the Garden of Eden and then recreated it in your dreams? Eh?"

I gaped at him. "The G…G…Garden of Eden?" I whispered.

CHAPTER TWENTY-FIVE

I shook my head "I can't believe the Garden of Eden is in England," I whispered.

"What?!" Sariel barked a laugh. "What are you talking about?"

I frowned at him. "I was there, in the garden. You must've taken me there 'cause I sure as hell don't know where it is and it can't be too far away 'cause it didn't take too long to get there."

Sariel studied me for a while. He was obviously waiting for something...a penny to drop maybe? I concentrated hard, closing my eyes. What was I missing? I thought about the car coming towards me, the shock of the icy floor, the beauty of the flowers, the caress of the breeze, the stars twinkling in the dark purple sky.

I opened my eyes and my mouth dropped open.

I was in the garden.

Just like that.

The scent of lilies was in my nostrils and I could hear bees fussing around the tulips somewhere close by. It was mid-day here with the sun high in the sky – I could feel its heat on my skin.

"Wha...? How?" I turned around in a slow circle. Sariel was behind me, standing at the door to the book room.

He lifted an eyebrow. "Still think the Garden of Eden is in England?"

I shut my mouth with a snap. "I don't understand," I mumbled to myself. I chewed my bottom lip, thinking furiously. Sariel had said something about the book room; that it was his knowledge. His knowledge added up to a lot of card points at Waterstone's. I frowned at him. "Are you going to enlighten me?"

Sariel smiled, a completely genuine, unguarded smile that lit up his eyes and took my breath away. "Nah, I'm having fun now," he drawled.

I put my hands on my hips. "I don't know what this is and I'm getting just a bit freaked out now, okay. So will you tell me what's going on here?

Please?"

He sighed. "Well, since you said please." He reached out a hand and, after a very brief hesitation, I took it. He opened the door to the book room and led me inside.

There was a fire burning in the hearth this time. It cast comforting, cozy shadows around the cavernous room where the ice had all but disappeared. There were two chairs now, both as frayed and worn as the original had been but all the more comfortable for it, and we sat down in them. I stretched my feet out towards the heat of the fire, leaned back into my chair and sighed in contentment.

The fire cracked and spat as it burned, orange flames mingling with yellow and the odd flicker of blue. It was beautiful and mesmerizing and I thought that I could have watched it for hours. I forced myself to turn away from it and back to the matter at hand.

Sariel smiled at me. "You seem to have the ability to stray into my mind at will, Emily. I would love to know how you do that."

"I can't do that! I've never done that!" I exclaimed. "It takes a lot of concentration for me to be able to even talk to you that way."

He leaned his chin on his hand and looked at me closely. "And yet here you are," he said softly.

I frowned. "What are you talking abou..." my voice trailed away and my eyes widened.

"Eureka!" Laughed Sariel, sitting back and getting comfortable again.

I looked around the room. "This is inside your head?" I asked.

"Yep."

"And the garden is inside your head?"

"Yep."

"But we're ... here. I mean, I can feel the heat of the fire," I reached out my hand and felt the warmth from the flames seep into it. "I can feel the fabric on this chair." I tugged at the chair, feeling the places where the cloth was worn. "If we go outside I can smell the flowers, I can feel the grass, I can hear the birds and the crickets and the bees. I can look up and pick out Mars and Orion's Belt. How is this possible?" I was fascinated.

"Maybe I'm lying," he said with a sly smile.

I studied him. "No, you're not." I said with certainty. "I would know."

He laughed and stood up. "Shall we walk?"

I followed him back outside and we followed the path across the bridge and through the trees on the other side. I kept touching the flowers, smelling them, feeling the rough bark on the trees, the waxy leaves, and the velvet petals on the pansies.

"I had a lot of time to remember," Sariel told me, "And a lot of pain to escape from. I escaped deep into a daydream of Eden as I remembered it. Such perfection in every detail, such beauty." He shook his head. "I took each memory I had, everything I learned about the heavens and the earth and I examined each of them for some clue, some reason, some way to get back. My knowledge, my memories are all in there." He gestured back towards the book room. "To be honest, it's been a while since I was back there, although I still walk in the garden from time to time." He smiled and reached out to caress the perfection of a peony.

"So this is all from you?" I breathed. I was in awe, astonished.

"And now do you understand why I asked you not to tell anyone about it?" He asked.

I nodded. "Yes, this is private. This is yours." I turned my face to his, suddenly sad. "I won't come again. I'm sorry."

Chapter Twenty-Six

And just like that we were back on the stairs with the riser digging into my back and the scent of lemon bathroom wipes filling the air.

Sariel sighed. "I didn't say you couldn't go there, Emily. You found it when you needed to and you find it again pretty much every night."

I gaped. "I do?"

He nodded. "I find a new daisy chain every day and believe me when I tell you that I don't make them!" We grinned at each other and then I studied my hands.

"What are you thinking about?" Sariel asked.

"If no-one else knows about your ...places and I didn't know about you when I first went there, then how did I find them?" I tapped my chin with a finger and thought about that one. Sariel was silent and I looked up at him. He looked serious and worried. "What is it now?" I asked.

He brightened. "Nothing we need to worry about now. Any more questions?"

I was going to shake my head when one occurred to me. Sariel looked at my expression and leaned back into the wall. "This doesn't look good," he mumbled.

I bit my lip. "Okay one of the last times I was in your garden, I mean , the Garden of Eden, I followed the sound of a voice and this weird thing happened. It was like I was looking through someone else's eyes. I saw a man who was chained up and he was really scared and I hit him. Except it wasn't me who hit him." I shook my head. "I know this sounds weird but I can't think of any other way to describe it." I looked up at Sariel. His eyes were closed and he had turned his face away a little. Sariel? Was that you who was hitting that man?" I heard my voice catch and he turned slowly back towards me, opening his eyes.

He nodded and I felt as though I'd been drenched in ice cold water. "Why?" I stammered. "You're an angel. Why did you hurt that man?"

Sariel sighed and rubbed his hands on the knees of his jeans. "I was sent to interrogate six men. We had information that they were being financed by one of the other demon lords and were coming after you and Seth. It was my job to find out the details and perhaps follow the trail back to the demon lord responsible."

"And you couldn't just read his mind?" I was bewildered at the idea that Sariel was capable of real violence, although part of my brain was reminding me that he was my body guard. What did I expect? Should he have a pocket full of feathers to tickle information out of bad guys?

Sariel shook his head. "They were prepared for that. They had all been chosen because of their ability to resist any kind of compulsion or mind control."

"And did you get the information?" I asked.

He shook his head again. "No. They didn't tell us anything but two of them had photographs of you and Seth in their possession when we found them."

"And where are they now?" I asked, not really sure if I wanted to know the answer.

"Alive." I frowned, wanting to get to the bottom of it NOW. And then I realized that maybe my brain had had enough to deal with for one day. I sighed and rubbed my eyes. Information overload. "Any more questions?" Sariel asked gingerly.

I shook my head. "No, I think I'm all up to date. For now." I added.

Sariel nodded, relieved, and checked his watch. "Right then. Let's go and pick up Seth and Arkron."

I blinked. "For what?"

He reached down a hand and hauled me to my feet. "Training."

"What?!"

CHAPTER TWENTY-SEVEN

Our 'training' began that afternoon at the back of our school, out of sight of the road and away from the houses at the top of Rainey Street. It was, Sariel explained, a crash course in self defence. We had three weeks left until school began and he wanted us to have a grounding in the basics by then. Seth's burly new best friend, Arkron, would help although I was pretty sure that if he ran at me I'd run screaming in the opposite direction.

I'm not sure what I was expecting. I suppose when someone says self-defence you might think about those demonstrations that the police sometimes put on down in the shopping centre or maybe something like karate with the white pajama thingies that they wear. Well, to Sariel the art of self-defense involved killing us first. We sprinted between cones, we did star jumps and stretches, jogged on the spot and then sprinted again. I was just thinking that death was imminent when he announced that "Okay the warm up's over, let's do some training."

Seth and I both gaped at him in horror. 'Start training'?! Arkron almost fell over laughing and earned a glare from both of us.

It was fun, aiming punches, learning to control the power of the punch, curling my hand around so that I didn't end up with a broken thumb (who knew you could break your thumb by punching someone?), learning to dodge and sway out of range, bobbing and weaving like Mohammed Ali. Sariel said we were naturals with real power to our punches – although to be honest, it was easy to put power behind a punch aimed at Sariel after he'd made us do almost forty star jumps. By the time the sun was setting we were soaked in sweat and exhausted but it felt good.

It became routine. Sariel and I hung out every morning and then he made himself scarce while I met Annie for lunch, or Dylan and Annie came around – although the three of getting together was happening less and less often since they were now officially loved-up and I felt like I was just getting in the way when we were all together. – once Seth finished work (around 3 or so) Sariel and I picked Arkron and him up and we headed somewhere to train. It was usually the school, occasionally the forest, once in our back garden (although jogging around the perimeter of our postage stamp garden was hardly a challenge) and once at the primary school playing fields, which was a disaster since the caretaker's house overlooks the school and he spotted us and came running.

We had graduated from punches to kicks and I was the queen of angling a kick exactly where it would do the most damage – I had Seth writhing in agony more times than I could count which was hugely fulfilling and had Sariel wincing in sympathy for him. The warm up continued to be a pain in the neck – and in every other muscle we possessed – but I was starting to really notice a difference in my body (more toned, less puppy fat) and my abilities (I was most definitely stronger). It was strange to be so suddenly *aware* – that's the only way I can describe it. I was *aware* of my body, of my movements, the muscles I was using for even simple tasks like making my bed or carrying the trash to the bin. And beneath that was the scary awareness of the damage that could be done just by aiming a kick in the right place or a punch to the right bone.

Chapter Twenty-Eight

Our birthday is on August 30th – mostly it's annoying to have a date so close to the start of the school year but it means that we can be a bit flexible on the whole 'when-shall-we-party' thing. Usually we have a get together with our friends (movies, dinner out, dvds and a sleep-over, something like that) during the week before and then a birthday tea at home with mum, grandma and gramps. Gramps always said we were like the Queen – having an 'official' birthday and an extra celebration too.

We already knew that this year would be different (Annie and Dylan would be together-together for a start and did I really want to celebrate my birthday with Amber? Hell, no!) but the announcement that Asmodeus would be throwing a party for us in London was completely unexpected.

"Why would he do that?" Seth asked Sariel and Arkron who were sitting at our kitchen table drinking coffee and eating doughnuts. Well, Sariel was drinking the coffee, Arkron was putting the doughnuts away so fast he was practically inhaling them.

"So you can meet the family," suggested Arkron through a mouth full of chocolate frosting.

Sariel grinned at him. "Yeah and the others."

"What others?" Seth and I asked in unison.

"You will be introduced to the crème de la crème of demon society, folks. Asmodeus will wan to show you off." Arkron grinned showing his chocolaty teeth. I grimaced and poured him another coffee.

"Yeah, and I'm willing to bet you won't be allowed to wear those," said Sariel pointing to my jeans and trainers.

"Good luck with that," mumbled Seth. "Mum reckons if she ever gets married we'll have to use a jack hammer to get her out of them."

I wisely ignored him, except for maybe standing on his foot. "Well, what will I be expected to wear?" I whined.

Sariel took his time, licking every last crystal of lemon sugar from his fingers before answering. "A dress, obviously."

I moaned. "A dress?! But I don't like dresses! I look like the village idiot when I wear a dress."

"There's a plant hire place in Stowmarket," suggested Seth helpfully. "We could hire the jack hammer by the day. Shouldn't take more than three days to get them off her."

I thumped him in the ribs and turned back to Sariel. "Well, what will you all be wearing?"

"Suits and ties. According to Rosie it'll be a classy event." Arkron told me and Sariel nodded smiling widely.

"So, I have to wear a dress to my own birthday party and you guys get to wear stuff that you pretty much wear everyday anyway? No fair!" I stamped my feet like a three year old, making them all stare.

"Would it make you happy if I wore a dress too?" asked Sariel, sugar sweet.

I glared at him, thinking furiously. "I will not wear a dress unless you …get your hair cut!' I said triumphantly, folding my arms and sticking my tongue out at him.

"Hard to believe she'll be seventeen this day next week, isn't it?" Seth stage whispered to Arkron who snorted.

Sariel was looking at me wildly. "What do you mean? You can't negotiate this, Emily. You HAVE to wear a dress."

"Then you HAVE to get your hair cut!"

He ran his fingers through his shoulder length hair, frowning at me. I glared back. The atmosphere in the room had suddenly changed. Arkron set his mug down slowly and pushed his chair back from the table, watching us both.

"Hey, guys, let's calm down here," Seth said wading in with his big size tens. "Nobody needs to do anything they don't want to do. Isn't that right?" Arkron made a non-committal noise in his throat and Seth rolled his eyes.

"She MUST wear a dress," Sariel hissed.

"Then he MUST get his hair cut. And not just a couple of millimeters, I mean cut short!" I refolded my arms and stood up a little straighter.

Thankfully the phone rang and it was Amber wanting to organize a night out for our birthday. I made frantic neck-cutting motions as Seth explained that we would be leaving for London on Tuesday so we only had Monday night. He turned away from me, nodding and saying "uh, huh, uh, huh," a lot. I followed him, getting in his face. He closed his eyes and said "That'll be great, sweetheart."

I turned away, disgusted, making vomiting noises which creased Arkron up but made Sariel frown even harder. 'Childish,' he mouthed at me. I mimicked coming at him with scissors and he tutted like an old maid. Sometimes winding people up was just too easy.

This discussion isn't over, Sariel told me

Get a hair cut or I don't wear a dress.

You would defy Asmodeus?

I've been defying my mother's wishes for me to be pink and frilly for almost seventeen years and she scares me a lot more than he does.

He rolled his eyes and turned his attention back to the coffee.

Seth put the phone down and came back to the table grinning from ear to ear. "They're going to open the club for us – private party and all that. We can invite as many people as we want. Amber's going to arrange catering. Isn't she great?"

"Fab," I drawled, biting into a doughnut.

CHAPTER TWENTY-NINE

The Party was predictably yawnsome. Well, at least for me it was. Everyone else seemed to be having fun. Maybe you have to dance to enjoy clubs, or drink a lot of alcohol and then vomit in the toilets for half an hour (I saw you Sandra Parker!). Or maybe you have to be in a couple and constantly touching or kissing or giggling with your heads close together. (Jealous? Moi?)

Between them Amber and Seth invited most of the senior school – I invited Annie and Dylan, although talking to them gave me a headache (or maybe it was just watching them gaze into each others eyes every twenty seconds). Annie and I talked about going to the pool again sometime, or maybe out to see a movie but neither of us sounded totally certain that it would happen, or that we really wanted to. I told her about the party in London and she told me about her mum's latest hobby – candle making – and the conversation stalled. Dylan sat beside Annie and fidgeted, glancing my way every now and again but saying absolutely nothing. It was frustrating and depressing and I couldn't seem to find the right words to bridge the huge gap that seemed to be opening between us.

After ten minutes of excruciating silence, Dylan and Annie got up to dance and didn't come back. Annie looked back at me once or twice and Dylan even waved me up onto the floor but I shook my head and concentrated on watching the back of Adam's head. The 'it' crowd were sitting at a large round table on a slightly raised platform to the left of the dance floor. Amber had her arm slung casually around Seth's shoulders and Sarah was sitting on Adam's lap. I pretended that she wasn't there and willed Adam to look around. He didn't and I got eye strain.

By eleven I'd had enough of sitting by myself watching couples grope each other on the dance floor or make out in the shadows. I made my excuses and left.

Sariel fell into step beside me as I walked down past the factory and turned onto Market Street. I stuck my hands in my pockets and marched on with my head down.

"Good party?" he asked cheerfully.

"Nope."

"Saw you talking to the were,"

That made me smile. Adam had said Hi and told me I looked really nice as we all went in. His eyes had been looking into mine when he said it and his smile had been...

"...at that prat."

I stopped walking. "What did you say?"

Sariel sighed. "I knew you weren't listening. I said that it's a pity that you only have eyes for him. There were loads of guys there looking at you, four of them asked you to dance and you turned them down 'cause you were so busy looking at that prat."

"He is NOT a prat," I squeaked before marching off again.

"Look, all I'm saying is that you spent a miserable night when you could've been having fun."

"How could I have had fun when I was sitting on my own all night?" I swore at him and began walking faster.

"You weren't on your own all night. Annie and Dylan were at your table for ages and that other girl from your school with the long skirt and the blonde hair..."

"Claire."

"...Yeah, she was chatting to you as well. And then when the others were dancing you kept glaring at them."

"Dylan had his tongue so far down Annie's throat I'm surprised she could still breathe." I snapped. "And Amber's a cow. Watching Seth make a fool of himself around her makes me feel sick."

We turned into Dean's Avenue. I was practically running now, so angry that I could've spit bullets.

"He really likes her, Emily. Shouldn't you just be happy for him? If he's happy then you should be too."

"He'll get hurt, Sariel. Amber'll use him until Ritchie comes back on the scene and then she'll dump Seth. You know as well as I do that she's out of his league."

"I disagree," Sariel grumbled as we turned onto our street. "Seth's a good looking boy and he's tall, athletic, funny and definitely not a prat."

"What? Now you want to date him too?" I hissed, laughing and flinging myself inside.

Behind me Sariel whispered a goodnight as I slammed the door closed in his face and marched upstairs.

CHAPTER THIRTY

I sat in the garden pulling up daisies and weeping silently. Above me the stars sparkled in the perfect night sky and all around me was alive with night animals and soothing scents of lavender and orchid.

"I promise this is the last time I come here to cry," I said aloud. "You can come out Sariel, I know you're there."

He emerged from the trees to my left, barefoot and wearing his jeans and an old Iron Maiden t-shirt. He sat down beside me.

"I'm sorry," I mumbled.

"For what?" he asked casually.

"For being so mean earlier. You're right. I know I should be happy for Seth and for Annie and Dylan. I'm just…"

"Jealous?"

I bit back an angry retort. "Maybe."

He sighed. "I went too far, Em. All I really wanted to say was that you sitting waiting for Adam Farlow is a waste." He pushed a stray tendril of hair away from the side of my face, tucking it behind my ear. "You're so very young, and so very pretty. There are guys lining up to ask you out but they know you're going to turn them down. And there's only so many times they'll be willing to get knocked back before they give up."

I sighed and nudged him with my shoulder. He nudged me back grinning. "So we're good again?" I asked.

He nodded. "We're good. Now get some sleep."

I frowned at him. "I thought I was asleep."

CHAPTER THIRTY-ONE

Tuesday was a day of firsts.

We drove to a small airfield near Wymondham and boarded a private plane which took us to Stanstead where we met a long black limousine and joined the traffic heading into the capital.

I'd never been in a private plane before (very luxurious but the loos are still cramped) or a limousine (incredible, luxurious and slightly embarrassing, we could see all the people gawping in as we passed!) but both experiences were overshadowed by my first views of London.

We crossed the Thames over Tower Bridge, passing the Tower of London and then Sariel (who was riding in the front with the driver) asked if we'd like to take in some sights. Seth and I bounced from one window to another as we passed by the rebuilt Globe theatre, the Tate Modern and the London Eye. We crossed back over the Thames via Westminster Bridge and then Buckingham Palace was in front of us.

"Oh, stop! Stop!" I shouted and Sariel laughed.

"Plenty of time, Em," he consoled. "You'll be here for 5 days."

We pulled up outside the Ritz Hotel and my mother's eyes practically popped out of their sockets.

"Oh. My. God." I managed to squeak as Sariel stepped out and opened our door, extending his hand to help first my mother and then me out. Seth followed and we tried our best to look nonchalant, as though we stayed at places like the Ritz all the time.

The hotel lobby was a study in reds and creams with a spectacular arrangement of flowers on a table in the centre and people gliding around. As we stood waiting for Arkron to check us in I looked up and gasped. I could see all the way to the glass domed ceiling, past the iron railings of each floor. I nudged Seth who took a look, grinned at me and then tried discreetly to nudge mum.

"Over there is the grand staircase," Sariel whispered into my ear. "And through those doors is the famous Ritz restaurant."

"Wow," I breathed, drinking it all in. I think it was possibly the first time in my life that I felt underdressed in my jeans and trainers.

A young woman in a Ritz uniform came over to greet us. We all shook hands and she explained that we would be in the Green Park suites which had been configured as per Mr. Asmodeus' instructions, to provide accommodation for all of us plus an extra room for our security staff. She called to another uniformed employee who took us to our room.

Well, when I say a 'room', I mean a whole bunch of them.

The suites were huge with big beds, separate living areas, more bathrooms than we would ever need and an extra room through an adjoining door. The furniture looked antique and I was almost afraid to sit down on the chaise in our suite. My mum oohd and aahd over the curtains which had more swags and tails than I'd ever seen before. It was incredible and slightly scary for people who were used to an old second hand sofa and IKEA separates.

The bathroom in the suite that mum and I were going to share was the same size as the entire lower floor of our house and had so much marble and mirrors in it that I felt totally exposed and freaked out every time I went into it. How would I ever pee in there?! I wondered if maybe Sariel and Arkron would have a smaller bathroom.

Their room turned out to be slightly smaller with two twin beds and a much more conservative (but still humungous) bathroom. I used it immediately, much to everyone's amusement, just in case I couldn't face using the other one.

There were views from all the rooms out over Green Park and I loved it immediately. It reminded me a lot of the walks near the forest in Dean's Lynn – open meadows and shady trees with sun dappling the ground and glittering on the wrought iron lights dotted here and there. Unfortunately it seemed that we wouldn't be getting out for a walk in it anytime soon as Rosie appeared to dampen my spirits. And she was smiling which made it even worse.

The reason for her happiness was simple – over the next few days she was to take mum and me to a beautician and then shopping for clothes. The bitch.

I know that going to a beautician is a big treat for most people, something that they look forward to. I mean, some people spend days in places called spas and say that it's great. I do my own nails, thank you. I also do my own hair and if I wanted someone to pamper me I could think of a better way to do it than have someone rip the hairs from my legs using wax strips. Who thought of this stuff? It must've been a man.

I had my eyebrows waxed, my legs waxed, my bikini line waxed (why would you do that to yourself?!) and then I had a 'relaxing' back massage followed by a facial. Mum came out of her room glowing with health and beauty. I came out walking like John Wayne with a face the colour of a tomato.

And then my torturer dropped another bombshell. "See you tomorrow for your tanning session, Emily," she called cheerfully. I appealed to mum for mercy but she just laughed and told me how much better I looked with slim eyebrows. Traitor.

We had lunch in a brasserie somewhere off the Mall and then we went walkabout, taking photos of each other like proper tourists. Sariel and Arkron stood off to the side, amused, with their arms folded and their eyes watchful. At Trafalgar Square, we begged and pleaded until they allowed a passer-by to take a photo of all of us together, arms linked and smiles wide as pigeons fluttered about and the sights, sounds and smells of London surrounded us.

We had dinner in one of the conference rooms at the hotel. It was incredibly beautiful – a table of polished walnut big enough to seat ten comfortably. Asmodeus was there with three men I didn't know. Mum was introduced to them before dinner and Seth and I briefly shook hands with them but I got the impression that they were business associates and that Asmodeus didn't want them getting too much 'family' info.

Sariel, Arkron and Rosie were at the far end of the table from Seth, mum and I, next to the businessmen. Asmodeus sat at the head of our end of the table with mum on his right and Seth on his left. The conversation was lively and centred around the food (which was beyond incredible) and our thoughts on London. The fact that a pigeon had taken a particular shine to Arkron and left him with a little memory on his shoulder, which housekeeping were currently removing, was brought up several times. Arkron took it all in good heart; whenever he could drag his eyes from Rosie that is. Ok, yes, the cow knew how to dress – she was wearing a floor length navy skirt of what looked like wool with a matching cardigan and a slim belt. The material clung to her and made a sound like the breeze through the trees when she walked. I idly wondered about the build up of static electricity around her as she ate her dinner – would her hair begin to stand on end? Sariel made a choking noise and I leaned forward slightly to look down the table. He took a drink of his water, his face slightly red with the effort of not laughing.

Are you eavesdropping? I asked.

You were projecting very strongly, I couldn't help it.

I thought about that as I chewed on a perfectly cooked hassleback potato.

Does that happen often?

What?

That I project into your head without intending to? I thought about the morning after the summoning when he'd been asleep in my chair and I'd imagined kissing him.

What do you think woke me up?

I jumped and felt my face flush. *Stop that!*

I'm not listening in, you're projecting!

Then you'll have to teach me how to stop.

"Are you ok, Emily?" asked my mum. "You look very hot."

I smiled shakily. "Just eating too much, mum." I gestured at my plate. "It's all so lovely."

Asmodeus chuckled. "Leave some room for dessert, Emily. It's your favourite."

My head snapped up. *How would he know?!*

Smile and nod like a lady. Sariel warned.

I smiled at Asmodeus and nodded. "Yummy." I said stiffly.

CHAPTER THIRTY-TWO

Back in the suite I begged mum to let me use the phone and finally she agreed that I could make a three minute call to Annie (you don't have a day like full of firsts and not share it with your BFF, besides, I really wanted to make peace with her).

Annie answered on the second ring.

"Great! I was hoping you'd call. Where are you staying? What's London like? Did you get a meal on the plane? Are there skyscrapers?" She was in one of her slightly dippy but mega excited moods which I love.

"We're staying at the Ritz."

"Be serious!"

"Cross my heart. London is huge with a capital H and we saw the London Eye and our suite is the same size as our whole entire house."

"No way! You're in a suite?!"

"Yes way! And we flew down on a private plane so there was no meal but we had a coke and then we got a limo to the hotel and oh my God, I just feel like the poorest person on the planet in here. It's mad with antiques and the bathroom has all these mirrors in it so I'm really embarrassed to pee and stuff. Oh, and Rosie took me to a beautician."

"You? Went to a beautician?" Annie giggled.

"Yeah, yeah, laugh it up. I got my legs waxed which was completely insane. I swear the pain was mega intense. How do Amber and Sarah do that so often? Oh, and they waxed other bits that we won't talk about too."

Annie giggled again and I found myself laughing with her.

"I wish you were here, Annie," I told her somberly.

There was a moment's silence.

"Annie?" She sniffed and I realized with horror that she was crying. "Are you okay?"

She sniffed again. "I'm just so glad to be talking to you, Em. This whole thing with Dylan has messed everything up. We were all so close and now we never seem to talk. I wanted to sort things out at the party but I just couldn't think what to say, how to even start the conversation. Is it too weird?"

"You and Dylan?" I asked.

"Yeah. I mean. Should we just go back to being friends?"

"What?!"

"Nothing's worth breaking up a friendship, Emily, and you're my best friend, you and Dylan. I don't want to lose that." She sniffed again and I felt absolutely miserable with guilt. I wanted so much for things to go back the way they were, I even opened my mouth to tell her. And then I bit my tongue. What was I thinking?! I was the worst friend in the universe – the most selfish person ever to exist. I could maybe have blamed it on the demon blood in my veins but I would only have been lying to myself.

"Annie, you and Dylan are great together," I told her. "It's taken me a while to get used to it and yeah, I'm maybe a bit jealous too. Oh, not about Dylan," I added hastily as she squeaked at the other end of the line. "I mean, I love him but not like *that*! I just, well, I felt real awkward and I didn't know how to fix it. I mean, this is all new for us, right?"

"Yeah," she said and I could hear the relief in her voice. "We're all finding it weird and awkward."

"Look, let's get together when we get back home. We could meet at the rec grounds on Sunday afternoon and discuss tactics for surviving our first week at school. You game?"

"Definitely! Um…"

I knew what she wanted to ask. "Yes, Annie, of course Dylan's invited too. Both of you are my friends and I want it to stay that way. We can get all this awkwardness out of the way over a game of football and an ice-cream float at the diner."

Annie laughed. "Sounds like a plan. Thanks Emily. I'm really glad you called."

I smiled into the phone. "Me too. Gotta go and get some shut eye before the torture begins again in the morning."

Annie giggled. "Ok. Have a good time on Friday night. Call me on Saturday – I want to hear all about it."

I promised I would and hung up with a smile on my face.

CHAPTER THIRTY-THREE

We all slept well and I managed to shower at the speed of light the next morning, averting my eyes from my newly hairless legs and worrying what Rosie would consider it essential for me to have plucked or tweaked or waxed next.

Breakfast was a quiet affair – we ate in our rooms. Mum and I lounging in our huge fluffy robes and munching on toast, fruit, cereal and yoghurt. I burped loudly and mum giggled. "I won't need to eat again until tonight," I grumbled rubbing my belly. "Shouldn't have eaten so much."

Mum grinned. "Nonsense, I'm sure we'll do some more sight-seeing today. All the walking will soon burn it off. Wonder how Seth's getting on with Asmodeus?"

I grinned. "Yeah, first night sleeping in the same suite as a demon lord. Bet that was a bundle of laughs. Wonder if they stayed up late watching reruns of 'Desperate Housewives'?"

Mum laughed as our door got a knock and she answered it. Sariel was waiting there, shaking out the sleeves of a starched white shirt. Standing beside him was a small girl with sort, spiky plum coloured hair and a doll-like face. Sariel looked serious and unhappy. Doll-face was smiling and looked us over with cold dark eyes. I stood up, pulling the robe a little more tightly closed and waited for the news.

"Morning, Joanna, Emily," Sariel said, closing the door behind them. "This is Alexa. She's going to be watching your backs today."

"Why?" I asked and mum shot me a look.

Sariel sighed and opened his mouth to explain. Alexa stepped forward, the same pleasant-but-fake smile on her pretty face. "Our master has requested that Sariel leave his associates to their flight today so I am to escort you to your appointments."

My mother smiled at her. "Thank you, Alexa. What time do we need to be ready?"

Alexa checked a dainty gold watch. "Oh, I think you probably have just over an hour before the car arrives."

Mum nodded. "In that case, I'll go and lay out some clothes and grab a shower." She grabbed my arm as she passed and hissed "Be nice" into my ear.

I watched her leave and then turned to Alexa and Sariel. "Where's Rosie?" I asked.

"Oh, she'll be along presently," said Alexa. "May I?' she indicated the sofa and I nodded, turning my attention to Sariel.

"Will you be away long?" I asked.

He glanced at Alexa and then shook his head. "I don't think so, maybe a few hours but the timing of their flight clashes with your appointments so …" he trailed off, fighting with a dark red tie. I frowned and waved him over.

"So you might be able to meet up with us later?" I asked, knotting the tie expertly and standing back to admire my handiwork.

"Thanks," he checked his appearance in a mirror. "I'll be here when you get back." He looked to where Alexa was sitting and then back at me. "She's a good protector, Emily. You'll be safe."

I nodded, biting my lip.

I don't trust her, I told him.

He took a deep breath in, exhaled. *She may not be Annie or Dylan, Emily, but she's good at her job.*

I nodded and pasted on a bright grin. "I spoke to Annie last night and we're meeting on Sunday. Turns out we're all feeling weird about stuff."

Sariel smiled and play-punched me on the arm. "Good for you. So you're feeling a bit better about it all?"

I nodded. "Yeah. Maybe I'm maturing into a lady."

Sariel snorted with laughter and I was about to retort when our door opened and Seth came in, stopping when he caught sight of Alexa who bounced up from the sofa, eyes narrowing.

"Alexa!' Sariel moved so fast he was a blur. One minute he was beside me and the next he was in front of Seth, arms extended. "This is Seth, Alexa.

He's Emily's twin."

Alexa relaxed immediately and her suddenly feral features slipped into an innocent smile again. She shook hands with Seth who shivered ever so slightly, and then she sat down again, crossing her dainty legs and clasping her knee.

Seth made a face at me and we hugged.

"So, did you have fun last night?" I asked.

He grinned. "Yeah, it was okay. Arkron and I played poker with peanuts for ages and then I went to bed. The dude was winning every hand! Asmodeus was out late with his business partners but we had breakfast together this morning and I'm going out with him later to get clothes for this shindig on Friday night."

I nodded. "Yeah, we're going out to get clothes today too." I rolled my eyes. "Just what I need – shopping for clothes with my mother and Rosie, queen of the low cut top and short, short skirt."

"Nothing wrong with low cut tops and short, short skirts," mumbled Sariel, leaning against what was probably an antique writing desk.

"You haven't seen Emily's legs," said Seth making an oh-dear-me-what-a-pity face. "Gramps says he's seen better sticking out of a nest." They chuckled and I curled my top lip at them.

"She'll be wearing a demure dress not a short, short skirt," said mum coming back into the room.

"Ah, yes," said Sariel. "That'll be interesting. Good luck with that."

He and Seth high-fived each other, grinning like idiots.

"Well, isn't it lucky that you'll have some free time today, Sar," I said with a too-bright smile.

He frowned at me. "I know I'm going to regret this but, why?"

"It'll give you time to go and get that haircut." I licked my forefinger and drew a pretend 1 in the air.

"Now, wait a minute, Emily," Sariel whined as I headed for the bedroom. "I never agreed to that."

"No haircut," I told him pointing at his head. "No dress," I pointed at myself and slipped inside the door with a victorious smile.

CHAPTER THIRTY-FOUR

Rosie picked us up bang on time and took us for more torture. It was excruciating. I had to strip, put on paper knickers and then stand in a cubicle with my eyes closed behind weird goggles and my arms outstretched while a blonde girl with a bored expression sprayed me with fake tan. I have NEVER been so embarrassed in my life.

I looked in the mirror when she was finished and squawked in panic – I was orange! I was frantic but after a thorough inspection, Rosie assured me that it was perfectly normal for the colour to be a little 'extreme' to begin with – by Friday it would be perfect. Her parting comment that I 'looked better even if I did resemble the stunt double for an oompa-loompa' left me fuming and trying furiously to think of ways to get out of attending the party.

And then, about two hours later, we were trying on dresses and I was thinking that turning seventeen was a lot more hassle than turning sixteen had been. I refused to look in a mirror, hating the fact that no matter what colour I wore I was still going to look like a carrot wrapped in fabric.

My mum chose a beautiful but plain coral wrap-over dress in a beautiful, light, silky fabric. It was only the fourth dress that she tried on but as soon as she pulled it over her head she sighed with contentment and was adamant that 'this is the one'. I had to admit that she looked amazing in it – fresh and young and…happy? I thought about that as the assistant brought an assortment of gowns for me to try on.

After turning down the young woman's offer of 'help to dress' I sat alone in the spacious changing room and panicked for a few minutes before pulling the first dress on and heading out for mum, Rosie and Alexa's scrutiny. It got the thumbs down, as did a frothy yellow number, and a cream satin, and a pale pink brocade. I stopped looking at the colours and the fabrics, pulling dresses on and off on automatic pilot. I wondered if Sariel had got his hair cut and vowed that I'd check on him, via the garden, later. If I survived the trial by couture.

I stepped out into the private viewing room in what may or may not have been the thirtieth dress that I'd tried on. Mum's hand went to her mouth and she stood up slowly. Alexa, drinking tea from a rose-patterned china cup, looked around, scanned me and nodded. "Nice." She said.

Rosie paced around me, checking the fit, the view from the back, the view from the side, the view from the front. No-one was more surprised than I was when she gave me a genuine smile and said "It's perfect."

I pulled the dress off and slipped back into my jeans, relaxing immediately at the feel of them. Pulling my trainers on was even better. I felt complete again, more like myself than some brunette Barbie doll.

And the day wasn't over.

After a quick lunch, the car took us to try on shoes and my boredom threshold was reached fairly quickly. Matching shoe-colour to fabric samples of our dresses really didn't interest me so I laid my head back on the plush sofa of the 'day room' (It's a shoe shop for crying out loud!) and concentrated on finding my way to the garden.

One minute I could smell expensive perfume and shoe leather, the next I was immersed in sunshine and orange blossom. I opened my eyes and grinned. I was back and the garden was in full bloom – colours were exploding everywhere; blood red roses, pure white gardenias, dark purple tulips, every shade of green on the trees and shrubs, every shade of blue across the sky. I lay down on the grass for a while, stretching out and pretending to make snow angels without the snow.

"Shouldn't you be trying on dresses?" Sariel asked.

I sat up and he was sitting beside me, fiddling with a blade of grass.

I looked him up and down. "Shouldn't you be getting a haircut?"

He laughed. "Maybe later. I've been sent on another errand. I have to go back to the house."

I frowned. "What do you mean? What for?"

Sariel turned to me. "It's business, Emily. I have to go back. You're okay with Alexa, aren't you?"

"Well, no-one's killed me yet, if that's what you mean so yeah, I suppose so but…"

"But what?" he was frowning now.

I didn't have an answer for him because I didn't know why I didn't like him being away. There was no reason for me to feel so…not right.

I shook my head. "It's nothing. I'm just not having a good time and I need someone to bitch to about it."

He laughed. "You need someone to take it out on you mean."

"Yeah that too." I sighed. "Suppose I'm going to have to go back to annoying the hell outta Seth then."

"You definitely should. He's been getting it easy these past few months."

I grinned and twisted around. My mum was calling me from somewhere far away. "Get back there, I think they've found your size." Sariel told me. He grasped my arms and gave me a push that sent me flying backwards and into my body again.

Cassaforte di soggiorno, quella cara.

Whatever. Quit trying to mess with my brain by speaking in languages I don't understand. I grumped as mum gave me a poke and told me to 'take a walk in them, dear.'

I stumbled and weaved across the thick carpet in a pair of stilettos with heels so high I was practically stilt walking in them. I looked at Rosie who was biting a nail and looking at me as though I was a new breed of rodent that she had just discovered.

Alexa was pursing her lips. "I think those are too high for her," she offered helpfully. Rosie gave her a withering look that made me grin.

"You may be correct, Alexa," she said and turned to my mother. "Perhaps we should go with the midi heel for her rather than the tower. What do you think, Joanna?"

My mother looked at me tottering and nodded. "I think that would be less dangerous for all of us," she said as I finally lost my balance and fell in a heap.

What a day.

Chapter Thirty-Five

$\mathbf{S}$ ariel was gone for the rest of the day which mainly consisted of more clothes shopping (yawn), Rosie fussing over our lack of make-up (double yawn), a trip to a theatre in the West End (amazing) and a midnight feast (Seth and I met up in my room and pigged out on mars bars and family sized packs of Doritos).

It felt like old times – the two of us whispering to each other with our mouths full and freezing when we heard a noise in case mum caught us sneaking food from the fridge. We sat on the floor, side by side, with our backs against the bed and Seth was in the mood to chat, so we did. We talked about Annie and Dylan, and I admitted that I felt left out now; we talked about Amber and him and I tried to explain that I was afraid for him but I'd try to be happy if she was his choice; we talked about turning seventeen and what the last two years of school was going to be like. We talked and ate and he called me an oompa-loompa and I called him a tragedy on legs, we thumped each other with pillows, giggled a lot and talked some more.

At some point, I fell asleep and woke up early the next morning tucked into bed with my robe still on and discarded crisp wrappers littering the floor. It made me smile 'though and I felt like I'd connected with Seth again. It was a good feeling.

Alexa was in the living room when I brought out my plastic bag of wrappers and she watched me with her flat eyes as I crossed the room and dumped my trash in the beautifully decorated waste paper bin under the writing desk.

"Sariel has been...detained." She said with her eerie smile and oh-so-bright voice.

My heart fell a thousand feet. "What do you mean 'detained'? Is he ok? When will he be back?" I asked in a rush, which made her frown a little before she recovered her composure.

"His business took a little longer than our master expected. He should be back from Italy in time for the party," she sounded rehearsed, like she was making a little learned-by-heart speech.

"Italy?" I yelped. "Why is he in Italy? He 'should' be back for the party or he *will* be back? Did he get a haircut? 'Cause, number one, if he's not going to the party then I'm not going and ,number two, if he hasn't got his hair cut then I'm not wearing a damn dress!" I didn't mean to yell, I really didn't but once I realised that I might be going to the party without him something snapped. Something that I'd been holding inside since Seth and I found out about Asmodeus and this whole hornet's nest had first been stirred up.

Arkron must've hit the floor of his room as soon as my voice began to rise because by the time my little speech was over he was in our suite, shirtless and wearing a pair of the most bizarre 'little devil' boxer shorts I'd ever seen. He was carrying a gun too, which should've scared the living daylights out of me. Instead I told him to "point that thing at someone else" and walked past him without another glance.

Mum came out of her room like a shot too – her hair in disarray and the strap of her nightdress sliding down her shoulder. I know she said something but all the sounds were muffled, all the oxygen seemed to have been sucked out of the world, leaving me in a little bubble of misery and shutting everyone else out.

By the time Seth arrived, I was heading for the bathroom leaving the room in a state of agitation and shock. At that moment, I didn't care. Whatever thread of sanity I'd been hanging onto seemed to be slipping away as I locked the bathroom door behind me and slid down onto the floor, put my head in my hands and began to sob.

CHAPTER THIRTY-SIX

I took a bath because it seemed like something that people did to relax and calm themselves. My tan had faded from Loompaland orange to Californian bronze. It made me look odd – the whites of my eyes looked whiter, my teeth practically looked radioactive. In the bath I stretched my long, smooth legs out of the water, marvelled at the dark purple nail polish on my toenails and perfectly shaped fingernails and wondered if Adam would like the new me. I was suddenly a study in well-groomed teenage perfection and it felt completely odd.

After my bath I wrapped myself in a huge fluffy towel and made my way quietly back to my room past the silent, worried faces of mum and Seth. I lay down on the bed and wondered how to claw my way back after my little outburst. Why did it matter if Sariel was there or not? What was wrong with me?

Rosie announced herself with a quiet knock on my door and then she slipped into my room, much to my annoyance.

"Not really in the mood for visitors, Rosie." I told her, covering my eyes with my forearm.

Ignoring me as usual she sat down on a chair by the window. "Sariel will be home for the party," she said tonelessly.

I sighed. "I suppose I should apologise to Alexa."

"Why? She's an idiot anyway, she gets shouted at all the time and it means nothing to her – she performs like a good little marionette but she doesn't do much in the way of thinking." Rosie was looking out the window as she spoke, careful not to look in my direction.

"Well, everyone else then."

Rosie leaned forward, leaning her elbows on her knees. "Look, Emily. You've had a major upset in the past few months. You've been under a lot of pressure ever since. To be honest, I'm surprised you've lasted this long without cracking up. Sariel's kind of been your rock, your ally. It's no wonder that you've come to ... rely on him, is it?"

I considered that. "I guess not."

"Of course, there may be more to it than that," she continued, her gaze fully on me now. "I mean, Sariel's male and you're a very pretty girl. If he..."

My anger flared and I concentrated very hard on breathing slowly. How dare she. "No, Rosie. Sariel's been a gentleman. He's never made any moves on me. He wouldn't." I wondered if knocking her onto her back and scratching her eyes out would be considered appropriate right now or if it would get me into more trouble.

She smiled. "Of course he wouldn't, Emily, but the question had to be asked. You understand that, don't you?"

I managed to nod and after facing me down for a few more seconds, she left.

Breathe, Emily. Calm down. Your heart's pounding so fast.

His voice in my head made the tears come again. *Sariel.*

Are you hurt?

No, no it's ok. I just had a little ... episode.

What happened?

I sighed. What was I supposed to say? *I don't know how to explain. I'm kind of embarrassed now.*

Show me.

I sat up. *How?*

Just remember it as clearly as you can. I'll be able to see, remember?

No. You'll think I'm a lunatic.

He laughed. *I already think that. Let me see.*

I felt my face flame as I remembered, and I remembered more than I thought – Alexa's little frown, Arkron's boxers, mum's face, an ocean of tears, my long, slim, tanned legs rising from the bath all soapy and wet, Rosie...I clamped my mind down on her.

What are you hiding? He asked

I don't want you to see.

Please, Emily.

I remembered what Rosie had said. I felt the heat of my anger again, this time it was matched by the heat of my embarrassment.

Sariel was quiet for a long time. *Its okay, Emily. I'll be home tomorrow. Let the anger go – it never does any good.*

You sound like Oprah.

She's a smart woman. You okay?

Yes. I just want this over with. I don't know if I can be around all this for much longer.

Emily…about what Rosie said…

It's okay, Sariel. I'm almost seventeen remember. I'm a big girl now. I can deal.

Er…yeah. Ok. I'd better go. Please try not to start any more fights 'till I can get there to protect everyone.

Ha ha. Very witty.

Lo manco anche, Emily.

You have to stop that. What language is it?

Italian.

It's beautiful, like music. What did you just say?

He didn't answer and I went about getting dressed and making my apologies.

CHAPTER THIRTY-SEVEN

We went to do more sight seeing in the end, with Arkron, Rosie and Alexa all very much in evidence. We took a trip on the London eye – organised by Asmodeus, so there were strawberries and champagne for us while we marvelled at the views. And, yes, they were spectacular. Seth and I nibbled on strawberries and tried to beat each other in spotting landmarks – mum wouldn't allow us any champagne, unfortunately, but that didn't spoil the mood, which had lightened considerably once I said sorry to a bemused Alexa and a troubled looking Arkron. A hug for mum and Seth had helped too – Seth had held me tight and whispered a promise of another midnight feast and a 'proper' talk.

The day passed in a blur of motion – Madame Tussauds, St. Pauls' Cathedral, London dungeon, the Tower of London. We managed to fit lunch in somewhere, photos outside Buckingham Palace and a walk in Green Park before we made it back to the hotel. My feet were killing me but it had been a fun day. I just still felt that someone was missing and it was starting to bug me.

Rosie came by with our dresses and shoes for the party, along with some extras that she'd ordered for dinner.

"Tonight?" I asked.

She nodded. "We're to be the guests of Mario and Isabella D'Anucci on board their yacht."

I gulped and Rosie grinned and patted my arm, "Don't worry, Emily. You'll be fine. They're good people." I raised an eyebrow and she rolled her eyes. "Yes, they're human." She laid an outfit on the bed for me, hung my party dress in the dressing room and left muttering to herself.

So we dressed – mum in a beige tulip dress with beading across the shoulders and back, me in a duck-egg trouser suit with a cream, mandarin-collared shirt underneath. Mum refused to let me wear trainers and so I was reduced to wearing the court shoes that Rosie had left for me. I glared at myself in the mirror as I brushed my hair until it shone and then pulled it up in a ponytail.

Seth and Asmodeus came in – both looking dapper in pleated trousers and open necked shirts. Asmodeus twirled mum around, telling her that she looked beautiful while Seth and I made faces at each other behind their backs.

The car picked us up around seven and took us to the yacht, which was moored at St. Katharine's and was like a small city on the water. I gaped at it as we climbed the gleaming steps onto the deck. A man in a waiter's uniform took our coats and provided us with drinks – champagne for mum and Asmodeus, cherry coke for Seth and me, water for Rosie and Alexa. Arkron was nowhere in sight but I was sure he was somewhere close – he never wandered too far from Seth.

Isabella and Mario were in their late fifties with olive skin, bright eyes and beautiful accents. Mario had salt and pepper hair that was receding slightly in front but he was a genial host and had a loud, booming laugh that made me giggle. Isabella was about an inch taller than her husband and a real chatterer although I guessed that she was also a shrewd woman – she watched us all carefully for maybe the first five minutes before she began to speak and it was easy to see that she had us all sussed. She was carefully polite to Asmodeus, more relaxed with my mother and friendly but conservative with Seth and me. I liked her.

We had dinner on deck, served by discreet waiters who seemed to appear and disappear at will. The food was glorious – simply cooked but beautifully presented and I had to will myself not to wolf it all down but to eat slowly, like a lady.

After dinner, the adults had drinks and Seth and I were introduced to the games room – pool tables, table tennis, a wii, xbox 360 and a playstation 3. We played a game on everything and were just finished trying to kill each other on Call of Duty when I realised that Isabella had come into the room. Nudging Seth, I stood up and smiled at her. "I'm sorry, I didn't hear you come in," I said and she smiled. Seth began to put our games away.

"Don't worry, quello piccolo, I like to see you enjoy."

I cocked my head. "What does that mean?" I asked.

Her eyebrows rose. "Quello Piccolo? Oh, forgive me. It's nothing but an endearment. It means 'little one.'"

I nodded. "So, you're Italian?"

Her smile widened. "Yes, we are. You have an ear for languages?"

I shook my head. "I heard someone speak it and thought it was beautiful."

"Ah," she looked a little disappointed.

"Can you teach me to say something?" I asked, sitting back down on one of the chairs.

Isabella considered that for a moment. "I don't see why not. What do you want to say?"

"Oh, anything. What about the simple stuff? Like 'hello'?" I felt Seth sit down near me.

"Ok, to say hello you say 'ciao.'"

I screwed my face up. "Isn't that goodbye?"

She laughed. "No, 'goodbye' is 'arrivederci.'"

"Oh," I whispered the words to myself and then said them aloud, trying to put the same accents on the sounds as she had.

Isabella clapped her hands and gestured to Seth who said something like "Cho" and "Arribaderki".

We all giggled. "More?" she asked and Seth and I nodded.

"Hmmm," she stroked her chin. "What to teach you? What would seventeen year olds like to say in Italian? Hmmm. Do you have boyfriend? Girlfriend?" Seth nodded and I shook my head. "Well to your girlfriend you could say 'sembrate stasera bello.'"

Seth tripped over the words and then said them again with a thoughtful smile on his face. "What does it mean?" he asked.

Isabella smiled. "It means 'you look beautiful tonight,'" she said and

Seth flushed.

"And for you, quello piccolo, hmmm. Perhaps you have a boy you like, no?" I thought about Adam and smiled. "Ah, so you could perhaps say to this boy 'lo gradico mólto.'"

I parroted her and she clapped her hands again. "This means 'I like you a lot.'"

I grinned at her. "And if I wanted to say…thank you?"

"Ah, very simple. You say 'grazie'. Is easy this one?"

We nodded, repeating 'grazie, grazie, grazie' until she was happy with her pronunciation.

One of the waiters knocked the door softly. "The car has arrived for your guests, padrona."

Isabella smiled and nodded. "It seems that it is time for you to go back." We all stood up and Seth and I thanked her. "It was my pleasure. So long since I have taught my language. You practice, yes?"

We joined the others back on deck, retrieving our jackets and thanking them profusely before we walked back down to the car. I was last off the boat and, on impulse, I kissed Isabella on the cheek. "Can I ask you something?" I said softly.

She nodded, studying me with her clear blue eyes.

"I'm sorry for the pronunciation but what does 'Lo manco anche' mean?"

She smiled. "It is good, your pronunciation. It means, um… 'I lack also'," At my confused expression, her eyes glittered with enjoyment. "It could be used to tell someone that you miss them too."

Apart from the mellow, subdued light from inside the boat, the night was dark and I was glad because I'm sure my face flushed a billion different colours of red as I stuttered a thank you.

Isabella took my hand. "Perhaps you do have a young man," She said with a knowing smile. "Although you are not entirely aware of it."

I managed a smile and hurried to catch up with the rest of our party as they slid into the waiting cars. My heart was pounding so hard that I was certain everyone could hear it. I felt jittery – as if I'd had too much caffeine – and warm – like I had a little internal heater currently blasting volcanic heat through my blood stream. I smiled a lot on the way home, joining in the conversation as much as possible but holding a little piece of secret happiness close to my heart as well. Sariel had told me that he missed me and for a few precious minutes as we rode from St. Katharine's back to the Ritz, nothing else mattered.

CHAPTER THIRTY-EIGHT

My euphoria didn't last of course.

As with all matters of the heart, doubt set in. Yes, Sariel had said those words but as far as he was concerned I was a child, less than a child; he was ageless, immortal and I was seventeen; part demon where he was an angel; my genes came from hell, his direct from God; I was only his job, my welfare was linked to his well being. Nothing more.

I looked at myself in the bathroom mirror and frowned. He was tall, dark, gorgeous, strong, gorgeous, he'd met God, oh, and did I mention that he was gorgeous? I was tall for my age, weedy with average brown hair and average sized boobs. Unless he was especially partial to skinny nerds then there was no way that he...

I spun away from the mirror and folded my arms angrily, determined to get such stupid thoughts out of my head. It was ridiculous. I needed chocolate.

And Seth provided.

We ate our way through Snickers, Double Deckers, Ripples, Giant Buttons and a bag of salted peanuts. Seth had even found some cherry coke – although we both concluded that it wasn't the *real* cherry coke, it was more like coke with cherry if you know what I mean. Trust me, they're NOT the same.

As we munched we talked about Asmodeus (still scary), mum's past (Wow. Go mum!), what it was like living at the Ritz for a few days (amazing how fast you get used to sitting on antiques), Arkron (over muscled but surprisingly ok for a demon), Alexa (freak), Rosie - super-sexy (according to Seth) but super-bitchy, on a par with Sarah (my tuppence-worth))

Then it was Sariel's turn to be rated.

"He's a good guy," Seth mused before studying the label on his can of 'coke with cherry'.

"Yeah," I muttered. "Good guy."

"So…you like him?" asked Seth, still intent on his label.

"Like I said – he's a good guy."

"Yeah. I mean you really like him?" Seth sneaked a glance at me and looked away.

I sighed and turned to face him. "Spit it out, Seth."

"Mum's just worried, Em."

"Mum's worried? And she couldn't talk to me herself?" I slumped back against the bed and folded my arms.

"Oh, don't get like that. She didn't want you to freak out or think she was getting all…interfeery."

"Is that even a word?"

"You say 'gazillion' and 'chillax'. They're not words." I rolled my eyes and opened my mouth to argue. "Oh, no you don't!" Seth sat up. "I know your game, Emily. Start a fight about nothing so I'll forget what we were discussing. I'm not letting this go."

My mouth had fallen open. "I do not…" I began.

"Yes you do. So, Sariel?" I shrugged and looked into the peanut bag in case any super-salty crumbs were left. "Emily!" Seth snatched the bag from me. "Do you like him?"

"Like I said…"

"NO, Emily. Do you like him, like him?"

I sighed. "Maybe," I admitted in a whisper.

"You know what he is, right?" I nodded. "You know he's older than you by centuries, right?" Another nod. "And you know that…"

"Oh for goodness sake, Seth!" I blurted, pushing away from the bed. "I know all this, ok. I've spent all night telling myself not to be so stupid, that he couldn't possibly feel anything for me. I'm only seventeen, I'm his job, I'm a skinny little nerd with a weird trans-Atlantic accent and tiny boobs…"

"Ewww. Do we have to discuss your boobs?"

"Not helping!"

"Sorry but, well, ewww." I sighed and went to the mini-bar. "Er...what are you doing?"

"Relax, Seth, I'm not about to start knocking back the Jack Daniels, I'm just looking for more chocolate."

"More chocolate? We just ate the chocolate equivalent of two small countries, Em!" Seth pointed to the pile of wrappers on the bed.

"I know, I know. Damn!" I closed the mini-bar door again. "There's no chocolate in there anyway." I sat down heavily on the end of the bed.

Seth came around and sat down beside me, putting his arm around my shoulders. I leaned against him. "What if he did?" He asked softly.

I shook my head. "Not going there, Seth. Tra-la-la-la-la." I put my fingers in my ears.

Seth grinned. "Okay, okay, jeez, stop killing that cat." He ducked as I fired a pillow at his head. "Hey!" We settled down again. "So, party tomorrow night, huh?" I nodded. "All dressed up and no-one we know. No pressure on us then?" We grinned at each other. "Can you sleep?" I shook my head, feeling way too wired on sugar to even attempt it. "Wanna fight? I mean like Arkron and Sariel showed us?"

I jumped up, shook out my hands and legs and moved into a defensive stance. "You're going down, sucka!" I hissed.

Laughing, Seth jumped up, shook peanuts and salt from his pyjama bottoms and put up his fists. "Bring it on sista!"

By the time Arkron rushed in I had Seth in a headlock and was trying to stop him twisting long enough to punch him in the face. Arkron leaned against the wall, watching us.

"A little help here, Ron?" Seth asked.

"You let a girl get you in a headlock, you deserve to work your way out of it yourself," Arkron told him with a grin.

"The only reason...ooof...that she managed it was that I...ow, Emily... couldn't stop laughing at her attempts to kick higher than my kneecaps." He finally managed to twist far enough around to push me back onto the floor and began tickling me. Our laughter probably woke half the hotel.

Arkron yawned. "If you two aren't going to do any more damage to each other than tickling then I'm going back to bed."

Seth turned to say something to him and I took my chance, slipping out from under him and jumping onto his head with a roar. Rolling his eyes, Arkron left us to it.

CHAPTER THIRTY-NINE

Friday dawned and I crawled out of bed around seven, determined to get a walk in Green Park again. I took a quick shower, changed into grey sweats and an old t and headed for the door. Alexa was standing outside, her back to the door and he arms clasped neatly behind her back.

"Good morning, Miss Emily," she said without turning around. "Rosie said to let you know that the hairdresser will be here at eight so I'm afraid you won't have time to sneak off wherever it was that you were sneaking off to."

I wandered over to stand next to her, folding my arms and leaning against the wall. Alexa kept her eyes fixed straight ahead. "What, you aren't looking at me now?" I asked.

She sneaked a glance and grinned. "The master has instructed me to practice being discreet in case I am required for tonight."

I frowned at that. "So if you have to come with us tonight then you're not allowed to look at us?"

"There will be many important people at the gathering and I am not worthy of meeting their eyes." She tilted her head to the side as she thought for a moment. "Nor am I worthy of speaking to them. I should practice silent obedience." She mimed zipping her mouth closed and throwing away the key.

I watched her for a moment as she became first still and then absolutely motionless. It was as though she had turned into a pillar of cement as I watched. Fascinated I moved in front of her. Alexa's eyes did not blink, her chest did not rise and fall as she breathed, there were no involuntary twitches or slight swaying. I moved right up into her face. "Alexa," I whispered. "Are you still in there?" Silence. I shook my head, grinning. Demons were weird with a capital "W".

I turned around to scan the corridor, intending to make an escape to the park while Alexa was practising her silent routine. Unfortunately Rosie was standing watching me, her arms full of boxes.

"And you are going where, exactly?" She asked.

I thought about lying but decided very quickly that there was no point. "I was trying to sneak out for a walk." I admitted.

Rosie looked pointedly at Alexa.

"Yeah, well, she's practising the whole creepy silent and still thing so I figured it was as good a time as any."

Rosie sighed and gestured to the door, which I reluctantly opened, and we went inside.

Mum was awake and lying on the sofa reading a romance novel and looking relaxed and beautiful. "Where were you two at? I've just ordered some coffee. There was a note on the table to say we needed to be ready for a hairdresser at eight. Surely that's a little early. The party isn't until tonight. We have plenty of time."

Rosie was setting her cargo on the writing desk. "I have plenty of time to make myself look good. You two will need every second of the hours between now and whatever time the car comes in order for you to be fit for presentation to the gathering."

Gathering? That was the second time I'd heard that word. It made me feel uneasy. "I thought it was a birthday party for Seth and me," I murmured.

Rosie's lips curved in a sly smile. "But of course it is, Emily. When a number of our Lords come together for any occasion, we call it a gathering. It's simply a mark of respect." Her lashes fluttered in an attempt to look innocent. I wasn't fooled.

As mum and I watched, Rosie unpacked some of the boxes – there were the shoes that we had ordered, new make-up in a variety of colours, all manner of clips and bobbles for our hair, underwear for both of us, nail kits, little sealed dishes of cotton wool and a small box of dough nuts. I looked up at her. "I was hungry and they looked good," she admitted, grabbing a chocolate glazed beauty and biting into it. "Mmmm."

The coffee arrived around the same time as the hairdresser. Sorry, I mean the hairdressing team. I gaped as our bathroom was rapidly transformed into a salon, complete with young girls to wash our hair, two women to apply some kind of conditioning treatment and an array of magazines for us to read as we waited.

It was a bizarre morning. The conditioning treatment took an hour after which our hair was washed again and dried by yet another two women who said nothing as they dried and kept their eyes averted from ours at all times. They had obviously been well schooled in demon manners and I longed to whisper to them that I was human and they could chat if they wanted to. Rosie's glare as I opened my mouth kept me silent 'though. It seemed that the rules of etiquette went both ways.

The hairdresser left and was replaced by beauticians who gave us facials (again) and a truly embarrassing all-over body scrub followed by manicures and pedicures. My nails were painted in a light shade of mauve, which seemed to have the properties of mother-of-pearl. I moved my newly perfect nails from side to side as they dried, watching the shimmer of colours flash through them like mini-rainbows.

We had lunch in our room and I called Seth who was had been out playing Squash with Arkron for most of the morning. They were going to have a swim in the pool later and then the hairdresser was coming to them along with the tailor to make final adjustments to their suits. He almost fell off his chair laughing when he heard that we'd been getting beautified since eight. He simmered down when I asked if there was any sign of Sariel. He checked with Arkron and reported that he wasn't expected until around five in the evening. The car would be coming for us around seven and it was expected that we would probably be allowed to join some of the younger members of our family at a private club after the party.

"What club?" I asked pouting now that I knew Seth was having a fun day and Sariel wasn't around yet. I wasn't sure which would win out when he finally arrived – the urge to hug him or the urge to punch him. I had both.

"Well, apparently our uncle owns a private club somewhere in Soho and we're allowed to go after we've spent a couple of hours at the fancy shindig."

"Does mum know?" I asked, looking for an excuse not to go. The idea of spending time with adolescent demons did not appeal.

"Think so," Seth said, allowed he didn't sound sure. "Gotta go, Em, lunch has arrived and I'm starving!" He hung up and I chased some lettuce around my plate for a while before switching on the TV and watching the lunchtime news.

"Seth ok?" Mum asked.

I nodded. "He's playing squash and swimming today," I grumbled. "And he says that we're going to some club tonight after the party. Did you know about that?"

It turned out she didn't and, after several phone calls back and forth between Rosie and Asmodeus, my mother finally lost patience and asked to see him. I watched her march off in front of Rosie towards Asmodeus' suite with a huge grin on my face. My mother in a bad mood was not to be trifled with. She'd kick Asmodeus' ass if he were out of line on the subject of what her children were permitted to do.

I kicked back in the suite and watched the Disney Channel for half an hour until they came back. Mum was smiling, but not I-showed-him smiling, it was more like a confused what-the-hell-just-happened smile and when she asked to lie down for a while, complaining that she had a major headache, I knew what had happened – Asmodeus had messed with my mother's head.

I paced, I fidgeted, I picked things up and set them down, I rearranged the furniture, I needled Rosie endlessly about what they'd talked about ('I can't say, I wasn't in the room'), called Seth endlessly (he was still out apparently) and then finally, exhausted, I lay down on the sofa and feel asleep.

Chapter Forty

When I woke, about an hour later, my old friend the beautician had arrived back with two helpers and they were checking out Rosie's new make-up purchases, all of them nodding and pointing and smelling and testing.

Mum was sitting in a white, tilting chair that they must've brought with them. She gave me a cheery wave and a huge smile, nodding towards the gaggle of beauticians in their starched white uniforms and bleach blonde hair.

I watched curiously as they went to work on my mum's face using different fluids from little expensive looking bottles first and then carefully applying make up, under advisement from Rosie. There seemed to be a hundred little pots open on the table, cotton wool balls were used at a crazy rate, scary looking eyebrow tongs were deployed and then acres of mascara. Lipstick was applied, blotted, applied, blotted, and sealed. For someone who had no idea about make-up the whole process was enthralling and slightly disturbing. All this work for one night? I considered my mum to be beautiful without all the stuff that they were ladling onto her face but even I had to admit that, when they were done, she looked incredible; like a super-model with high cheekbones, dazzling eyes and flawless skin. Mum was thrilled too, constantly checking herself out in the mirror.

Then it was my turn. I already had a feeling that having people tweak and prod and flap at me wasn't my thing and the hour I spent having make up applied cemented that feeling into a fact. It was awful – uncomfortable, boring and embarrassing as someone filled in all my imperfections with a ton of heavy concealer and clever tricks with blusher.

Rosie commented that the colours they had chosen worked well with my tan and the shade of my dress, complimenting my nails and highlighting my youth. My heart sunk as I remembered the dress and I wondered if Sariel had kept his side of the bargain. I wasn't in the mood to play nice if he hadn't. "Has Sariel arrived yet?" I asked. Rosie frowned and shook her head.

"It's not five yet, his flight has probably touched down by now but he won't have made it back to the hotel."

I nodded as if it didn't really matter and went back to being miserable under the hands of the beauticians. "Is Seth back?"

Rosie nodded and checked her watch. "They should be having a snack soon. We will too and then the barber will be arriving. Oh, I must ring the dresser." She scurried off.

"What's a 'dresser'," I asked no one in particular.

There was silence and all the beauticians froze looking at each other. "Um...I think it's someone who helps you to dress, Miss," whispered one and was immediately shushed by the others. Everyone looked strained and nervous so I decided not to push it and kept my mouth shut for a change. Someone to help us dress? So now we couldn't pull on a dress and a pair of shoes? What was wrong with the world?!

The beauticians finally finished, proudly holding up mirrors so that I could look at myself. I stared. And stared. And then stared some more.

The young woman looking out of the mirrors was a stranger – she looked incredibly pretty with her tanned skin and smoky eyes. I turned this way and that looking for a blemish but there were none. It was disconcerting, as though I was wearing a perfect mask over my usual face. I managed to stutter a thanks and the beauticians left with satisfied smiles on their faces.

A snack arrived and we ate tiny sandwiches, nibbled on biscuits and drank tea from the usual fine china. Going back to Pound stretcher mugs would be weird after all this!

Seth popped his head in the door to let us see his hair and his eyes nearly popped out of his head when he caught sight of mum and me. "Holy crap, Emily! You look gorgeous!" he yelped.

I punched him on the arm. "You mean that I don't usually look gorgeous?"

He grinned but didn't stop staring, which was annoying. His hair was lightly shorn, artfully tousled and smelled of expensive styling products. It suited him and I told him so adding an, "Amber'll love it," quip that made him smile widely.

Rosie shooed him out after about ten minutes, telling him that our hairdresser was on the way with the dresser. I groaned and flopped onto the couch again. "Can't I just stay here and you lot can party?" I whined. "I'm pooped."

"Sariel's back," whispered Seth as he headed for the door and my stomach did a little flip flop of excitement and relief. I controlled my face with an effort – I was determined not to let them all see that it mattered.

"Good," I said, "Make sure he gets that haircut."

Seth ducked out as Rosie went for him again and I relaxed a little. If Sariel were back then maybe it wouldn't be so bad.

Sariel?

Just back. How's it going?

Bloody awful. We've been stuck in all day having people paint our faces and stuff. I'm bored.

He chuckled and I smiled to myself. *Hope you've managed to stay out of trouble*, he cautioned.

I've been so totally well behaved and not-me that it's a wonder my mother still recognises me. I told him.

Really?

I made a face. *Well, kindda. I'm trying really hard not to ask too many questions and stuff but there's so much going on. For instance; what's a 'gathering' and does Asmodeus have the ability to mess with mum's mind?*

A 'gathering' is simply a meeting of demon lords and their houses, or families. Why do you ask about Asmodeus?

'Cause mum went to see him, all riled up 'cause we were being allowed to go to a club later and he hadn't told her about it. She comes back all kind of confused and dreamy and everything's forgotten. Oh, and she's got a headache and has to lie down.

Sariel sighed. *It is well within Asmodeus' abilities to influence her. As can I, remember?*

I thought about that. *Could Asmodeus influence me?*

I don't know. Even 'though I can't it doesn't mean he wouldn't be stronger. Be careful around him and we'll hope that you never have to find out. Has Rosie been…talking to you again?

No, she's been watchful but tight lipped about you. Seth and I ….I stopped.

What?

Oh, nothing. Twin stuff. I decided it might be a good idea to change the subject. *You got the hair cut yet? I'm not getting into a dress until you have.*

Not yet. So you're not dressed yet?

Is this where you get all weird and ask me what I'm wearing?

Would you tell me if I did?

I hesitated, grinning and feeling all girly and giggly. *Why Sariel. I do believe you're flirting with me.*

Before he could answer Rosie shook my arm. "You humans need so much sleep! C'mon, Emily the dresser and stylist are here. Let's go."

It took over two hours for mum and I to be dressed, styled and prepped to a level that satisfied Rosie. And yes, the dresser did actually help us to dress. Although I drew the line at having help with my underwear! That was just too icky.

My dress was a revelation. I didn't remember it at all. It was raw silk in a dark purple that shimmered through shades of red and blue depending on where the light hit it. The left side was slit almost to the thigh and, although the front was quite a high boat-neck, the back dipped alarmingly into soft, Grecian-like folds that revealed a huge amount of my tanned skin – all the way from my shoulders to the small of my back. I was glad that it had a built-in bra structure because there was no way to wear one and disguise it. It felt all at once decadent, comfortable, alarmingly revealing and incredibly beautiful.

The shoes were higher than I was used to but not so high that I was tottering. They fit perfectly – their thin straps wrapping around my ankles several times and my perfectly painted toe nails peeping out the top.

There was a wrap to go with the dress – a simple swathe of matching silk that slipped around my shoulders and felt like feathers brushing my skin. I left it off while my make-up was re-touched and gloss was brushed onto my lips. Then the stylist got to work with an array of tongs and strighteners, clips and clasps, pulling my hair up high at the back and dropping little tendrils of it down at the sides to frame my face.

Rosie checked us out and nodded. We were ready to go.

CHAPTER FORTY-ONE

The elevator seemed to miss floors – diving to the reception area before I was quite ready for it. I willed it to go slower because I was starting to feel more than a little nervous, my stomach full of butterflies all fluttering around and threatening to throw the sandwiches and tea back up.

We left the elevator and headed out to the car – a limousine tonight. I looked for Seth but Alexa informed me that the men had 'gone on to renew old acquaintances without the distraction of the women'. I wanted to ask if Sariel was with them but I was learning to keep my mouth shut.

Mum showed her nerves by chattering non-stop the whole way to the party venue. It turned out to be a private house set in its own grounds with a long sweeping driveway in front. It was easy to imagine this place with carriages outside and servants lining the entry. The house itself was large and beautiful with high ceilings, muted lighting and an amazing collection of paintings that had me goggle-eyed.

It also had a huge number of people milling around in evening dress but I was trying very hard to ignore them all and concentrate on walking – one foot in front of the other. My heart was pounding, my hands were shaking and I was close to vomiting with sheer terror. Meeting new people was not my thing, meeting new demons was an exercise in absolute horror. I kept walking, following Rosie and mum with Alexa behind me, my eyes slipping over faces until I found the one I was looking for.

Seth was standing in a loose huddle of older men. He was wearing a conservative navy suit and tie with a light blue shirt. He looked scrubbed, sophisticated, debonair, and handsome. Not my twin. Until he looked up and saw us, then he relaxed, his face melted into a huge smile and he excused himself with a whisper and came to greet us, hugging mum and then me.

"He's getting Dad a drink, Em. We have to be careful how we act and talk here. This is serious shit." And then he was complimenting Rosie on her almost-there red dress and nodding towards Alexa, that smile still on his face but fixed now that I was studying him. There was stress around his eyes and in the way he held himself. I struggled to process everything. Someone was getting a drink for Asmodeus and Seth was scared which meant that I should be afraid too.

I turned slightly towards the bar and met Sariel's eyes.

He was carrying a tray with several flutes of champagne on it and they were all in danger of slipping off as he drank me in. That's the only way I can describe it – his eyes travelled from the top of my head to the tips of my perfectly pedicured toes and he gulped visibly. Something warm stole its way into my stomach and settled there like a hot, heavy rock. I felt shy and excited both at once.

I gestured towards his hair and gave him the thumbs up. His hair was now short – cropped tight in at the back and shaggy over his fringe making him look younger and making his incredible eyes even more noticeable. With the hand not holding the tray he pointed towards me and mouthed 'wow'. We grinned at each other and then he walked forward, blanking his face as he passed the drinks around.

He stood behind Asmodeus' left shoulder while the men chatted, stealing glances my way every now and again. I could almost feel the weight of his eyes on me as I followed Rosie and Seth to the small bar area and ordered a diet coke with ice. Seth ordered the same and we chose a seat until Asmodeus was ready for us.

"You will be introduced by Asmodeus first and then you will mingle with the guests, escorted by your bodyguard," Rosie whispered to us. "And you will only speak when spoken to." She stared at me hard. "Anything you say or do here will be noted and if you were to say something…incorrect to one of the gathered Lords, it would reflect badly on your father. Do you understand?"

I looked out over the crowd, caught the naked looks of curiosity and nodded. I had absolutely no wish to meet these people, things, beings, whatever they were. And I had even less of an urge to piss any of them off, Asmodeus included. Tonight I would be on my best behaviour because I was honestly scared.

I wanted to talk to Sariel; I wanted some kind of reassurance, some guidance. Tonight, in this place, wearing these clothes and amongst these strangers, I was aware of my age, my lack of true knowledge and, more than ever before, my mortality.

A man stopped at our table. He was tall and thin, his cheekbones prominent, skin stretched tight over bone. There were dark circles under his large eyes and his black suit hung on his wasted body. His eyes were the only thing about him that looked alive – they blazed insanity and eagerness. I looked up at him slowly, feeling dread slip icy fingers across my bare shoulders.

"Daughter of the darkness," he hissed and licked his lips.

Rosie stiffened beside me.

I decided to play it safe and nodded to him. He laughed – a sound like the rasping of sandpaper and I cringed. "A pretty trinket you are. I imagine you will taste like roses and sunshine. Perhaps I'll put in a bid when the time comes."

Asmodeus appeared at his shoulder, a smile on his lips. "Nybbas, my old friend. I see you have met my daughter before I have had the chance to introduce her to anyone else."

The man in front of us paled even further and turned to Asmodeus, wringing his hands and quivering. "I did not mean to push myself forward, dark one but she smells so good." He inhaled, closing his eyes and shuddering. "I was unable to resist."

Asmodeus leaned in close to the man and whispered into his ear. Nybbas' eyes widened and then fell to his feet as he nodded and then backed away from us.

Asmodeus held out his hand. "Come, Emily. It seems the rabble will not wait for us to settle. We will start the introductions. Not you, Joanna," he said as my mother rose to her feet. "Seth has already been introduced to a few. He will stay with you for now. You and I shall talk to our guests together later."

I took his hand, keeping my face blank as revulsion washed through me. I let him fold my arm over his as he led me away from the table and towards the first small group. "Did Rosie speak to you?" he asked softly, the smile never leaving his face. I nodded. "Good." He patted my arm and then we were there and all faces in the group turned towards us.

"Ladies and Gentlemen, may I introduce my daughter, Emily."

I nodded to them, making sure I had a smile for each of them, meeting their eyes for the briefest of moments. A woman moved forward. She was small and plump with rosy cheeks and exquisite green eyes. "So lovely to meet you, Emily. We've been waiting for a long time to catch up with you. My name is Lilith. Tell me, how are you finding the Ritz?"

"It's beautiful. Very comfortable, thank you." I replied, enunciating my words carefully.

Lilith smiled. "This is Cacus," she nodded to the man on her left who bowed stiffly, "And Nickar," another bow, "Mammon, Sitri and Anzu." More nods, more bows. "We are all Lords. The others here are of our houses. Do you know what that means?"

She raised an eyebrow.

"Your families and your ...staff?" I ventured.

Lilith nodded. "Those belonging to our houses are under our protection. A slight on one is a slight on all." Her eyes glittered and she and I looked at each other for a few seconds. She turned to Asmodeus. You forgot to tell us that she was a beauty, Asmodai. Is that why you've been hiding her for all these years?"

Asmodeus chuckled. "Emily and Seth were only recently found, Lilith. As you are, no doubt, aware."

Lilith smiled. "And you are seventeen today, yes?" I nodded. "What a perfect age to be experiencing your first gathering. I hear you've been targeted." She tried to look anxious for me but failed miserably. "I hope you have provided her with protection." Her gaze returned to Asmodeus who nodded.

"I have." He said simply. "In fact, you may be able to help me with a quandary, my friends," he raised his hands beseechingly to the others.

"What kind?" asked one of the men, Nickar, I thought his name was. He was a striking man with skin the colour of dark chocolate and flat eyes. His voice was nasally with a southern accent that sounded fake.

Asmodeus smiled and slung an arm companionably around my shoulders. I had to struggle not to throw it off and run screaming from the room. The smell of him filled my nostrils – burnt flesh, mint and acid mixed with honeycomb. "I was just trying to decide which of her bodyguards should accompany her tonight." He gestured and Alexa moved out of the shadows, followed by Sariel. Both of them stood silently, their eyes lowered, their hands clasped behind their backs.

I kept my gaze level as my heart plummeted to the bottom of my stomach.

Lilith walked forward and around the two of them, her hand caressing Sariel's shoulder as she passed. "You've cut your hair, y'assina eloi." Sariel didn't move as she circled them again.

"Apparently, Emily refused to come tonight unless he did," said Asmodeus, laughter heavy in his voice.

Lilith turned back to me, her eyes wide and her eyebrows lifting high onto her forehead. She clapped her hands and her laughter rang out around her. Several further groups turned to look. She dipped her head in my direction, giggling again. "Truly?" I wanted to contradict them – I'd said I wouldn't wear the dress, not that I wouldn't come – but it didn't seem like the right time or place so I nodded. She turned back to Sariel. "It seems you have found your Delilah," she told him, making a number of those listening in laugh and talk among themselves.

Lilith turned to Asmodeus whose face was calm and clear. "Send the fallen one, Asmodai. If he will cut his hair for her then he would surely die for her." "And what's your opinion, Emily?" asked the other woman in the group. I turned to her and smiled into her narrow rat-like features.

"It will be as my Father wishes," I said sweetly, willing my voice to stay steady. There were aahs and murmurs all around us and I returned my attention to Asmodeus.

He smiled and nodded to Alexa who backed away, but not before I saw a look of relief cross her face. My heart lifted and Sariel's eyes flicked briefly in my direction but his face was impassive. If he was happy still to be there, I couldn't tell.

CHAPTER FORTY-TWO

We spent a few more minutes in the company of Lilith and the rest of the coffin-crew, as I named them, (remembering their names was going to be close to impossible anyway.) and then, after some whispered instructions from Asmodeus, Sariel took hold of my elbow and led me away.

We spent perhaps another hour mingling with the crowd in the downstairs of the house. Sariel introduced me politely to many of them, priming me about them beforehand, and then stepped back for me to chat for several agonising minutes before we moved on again. My feet were starting to ache from the unaccustomed height of the heels and my face was starting to stiffen from trying to hold a smile in place for so long.

"Almost there, you're doing well," Sariel whispered as we moved from the hall to the drawing room via the conservatory and the living room.

"My feet are killing me," I hissed through my smile.

"Don't tell any of this lot – they like to witness pain," Sariel smiled at the first of the group as my brain digested that little of piece of information and I wondered if throttling your bodyguard would be enjoyable for them to watch too.

We circulated, smiled, made small talk, and passed Seth with Arkron, my mother with Asmodeus, Lilith cradling a goblet of what I hoped was dark red wine and Rosie purring into the ear of a small blond man with a nervous pout and half of his right ear missing.

A woman dressed in black and white came to the door of the drawing room and announced that dinner was served in the ballroom. The guests began to move towards it and I made to follow but Sariel caught my arm and held me back. I frowned at him.

"You will go in with Asmodeus, Emily. This is your birthday party after all," he said and I studied him for traces of intentional sarcasm. His face was inscrutable so I concentrated on pushing into his head a little. "Not here," he whispered harshly. "There are too many sensitives here tonight and you're a strong broadcaster. They could sense your power."

I nodded as Seth arrived with mum on his arm followed by Asmodeus, deep in conversation with Rosie and Arkron. Sariel stepped back as Asmodeus took my mother's arm and indicated that Seth should take mine. I turned back to Sariel. "Aren't you coming?"

He shook his head. "We are not permitted to dine with the pure bloods," he said softly, his eyes not meeting mine. I know I paled, I could feel it happen. Whether it was from anger at such a slight against him or fear about going into the midst of them without him, I'm not sure. Seth and I trailed after Asmodeus and mum but my eyes didn't leave Sariel until the last second so I caught his worried grimace as the doors to the ballroom closed behind us.

CHAPTER FORTY-THREE

The ballroom was huge with long elegant windows down three sides and a ceiling painted to look like a summer sky with little cherubs leaning down from clouds or playing harps whilst winging their way across the vast expanse of blue. The walls were also blue although the shades darkened the nearer they got to the floor.

There were eleven chandeliers down the middle of the place and directly under them was a long table. Our 'guests' were standing behind their chairs all down the table, their faces turned towards the entrance expectantly as we entered. A hush fell as Asmodeus directed us to our seats and then he took his own at the head of the table.

The guests waited until he sat down and then there was a cacophony of noise and movement as everyone followed suit. The chatter was loud and the mood seemed to slowly shift from contained to happy, excited and then exuberant as the courses were served and the wine flowed.

We dined on soups and breads, fruit and salads; then steak, chicken, pheasant, pork, a mass of vegetables and side dishes that took my breath away; next there were sweets of more cream and fruit and ice and cake and biscuit and pastry than I could name. I ate sparingly, nibbling small amounts and trying not to stare at the huge platefuls that the others were eating. This was gluttony taken to extremes and I felt uncomfortable watching it happen.

Seth was beside me and for once he seemed to have very little appetite. His eyes were fixed on the floor every time I looked at him. Finally I nudged him and glared. He nodded towards the floor and I studied it as discreetly as I could.

I had taken the floor to be stained in a dark wood varnish with whorls and curls of colour here and there. On closer examination, it appeared to be a view down into an abyss with tormented faces screaming up at us, their hands raised in supplication. I looked around, aghast. In one place near Seth's left foot a face seemed to press right up against the floor, the features squashed. It put me in mind of games that Seth and I used to play as small children – squashing our faces against the glass in shop windows to make each other laugh. This, however, was nothing to laugh about. Coupled with the high gloss of the floor, it seemed that we were looking down on the entrance to Hell itself through a floor of glass that would forever keep the tormented souls below.

I put my fork down and lifted my napkin, pressing it to my mouth to control the nausea that threatened to return my half-digested profiteroles to my plate. I looked up at Seth. His face was very white and grim but he was attempting to smile as the woman in the seat opposite asked him how he found London.

And so it went on. Cherubs above us, tortured souls beneath and demons all around. Anxious laughter threatened to bubble up and I forced it back down, very aware of Asmodeus' scrutiny.

The party got rowdier as a tall, slim blonde wearing a pink sequined dress that left very little to the imagination was helped onto the table at the end farthest from ours. To loud cheers and claps she walked her way carefully up towards us, her long legs and nimble feet missing the plates and glasses. She stopped in front of Seth as the whooping, cheering and clapping rose to a crescendo and then she leaned down, bending from the waist, reached out and pulled him to his feet with his tie. Seth's eyes were wide and he looked around in embarrassed confusion. My mother's mouth was agape, and she looked to Asmodeus for reassurance. Asmodeus was watching Seth closely, studying his son's reaction. I filed that info away for future reference and turned back to my brother who was now being thoroughly snogged by the crazy blonde.

Job done she grinned at my brother and slowly wiped her lipstick from his lips with her thumb, her eyes locked on his. She walked back down the table as some of the lords and their friends threw money at her and then helped her down and back onto her chair.

Seth turned his wide, slightly glazed-over eyes to me. "What the hell was that?" he squeaked.

Glancing at Asmodeus I told Seth, "I think that was some kind of weird initiation type thing." Asmodeus smiled and clapped his hands for quiet. It descended immediately and everyone looked towards him.

"Shall we have cake?" he asked and the room erupted into more shouts and catcalls.

The main door opened again and four men wheeled in a trolley draped in a red material. On top sat a four-tier cake of chocolate and strawberries decorated with discs of icing. I looked closer as the cake was pushed to stand at Asmodeus' left hand. The discs were decorated with elegant swirls – a '1' and a '7'. It was beautiful. Mum gave me a shaky smile as the lights in the room went down. I heard Asmodeus say something under his breath and then the candles on the top of the cake gave a tiny hiss and splutter as they all lit at once.

One of the waiters pulled my chair out to allow me to stand. Another did the same for Seth. We stood awkwardly as Asmodeus beckoned us to come up beside him. Standing there at the head of the table, looking across all those faces shining in the flickering light from our birthday candles I felt a kind of fearful claustrophobia. We were surrounded, my mother, Seth and I. And even if, at that moment, I could have made myself move to run out of the room, where would I go? We could never hide from these beings again – I felt the truth of it right down into the marrow of my bones.

They began to sing 'Happy Birthday', some in perfect pitch, some so far out of tune it was more of a banshee wail. Then we blew out the candles to applause and laughter. For a few moments there was blessed darkness, peace from their scrutiny and Seth took my hand and squeezed – either to reassure himself or me.

The lights came on and we blinked in the sudden brightness as Asmodeus cut the first slice of cake with a long thin silver knife and fed it to my smiling mother. The image of her standing there, so beautiful in her fine dress and perfect make-up, her eyes showing terror, her mouth smiling and strawberry juice sliding down her chin was frozen in time for me for just a moment. I closed my eyes to push away a feeling of premonition that sent icicles through my blood, and when I opened them, the world had moved on and it was time to sit down again.

I managed a few spoonfuls of the rich chocolate cake. It was liberally laced with kirsch and made my eyes water and my throat burn. Seth managed a whole slice, grinning like a village idiot as a man came up and slapped him on the back, murmuring about the kiss of a succubus. I filed that one away for future study when I got home.

The thought was no sooner in my head than Asmodeus was checking his Rolex. "The car will soon be here for you both," he told us with a huge grin. "I have persuaded your mother to allow you to go to a club for a few hours." He smiled at my strained face. "Don't worry, Emily. None of us old fogies will be going. It'll just be the young bucks. Anzu!" A man further down the table stood up. I recognised him as one of Lilith's coffin crew. "Your sons are waiting to look after my children, yes?" Anzu nodded and his eyes brushed across my face before he looked back at Asmodeus. "Anzu owns the club," Asmodeus was telling us in a conspiratorial whisper. It's a … private place so you will be safe and among friends. Enjoy yourselves but remember who you are." He looked at me for a second, his eyes hard. I nodded and Seth and I pushed back from the table, smiling at waving as our party guest shouted their goodbyes.

At the far end of the table, I caught sight of the walking skeleton, Nybbas, who had approached out table when we had first arrived. His smile was odd, almost misshapen and it wasn't until he widened it and I caught sight of his teeth that I understood why. Nybbas had fangs and he bared them at me menacingly, his lips pulling back from his gums, before melting back into the crowd. I shuddered and hurried from that room as quickly as I could.

CHAPTER FORTY-FOUR

Outside in the hall Rosie was waiting for us. "Sariel and Arkron are in the car already. You know where you're going, who you're meeting?"

"No!" I said sharply. "'Anzu's sons' is the only clue we've had. And no doubt they'll just be one long giggle-fest. You okay?" I asked Seth. He nodded and smiled but there was a brittle quality to it.

"What happened?" Rosie asked him, her gaze taking in his white face. She straightened up his tie at the door.

"I got kissed by some tall blonde while all these old people clapped and cheered," he said. "Do you mind? You're cutting off my circulation."

"Sorry," Rosie said cheerfully, loosening the tiny knot that she'd made in his tie. "So they had a bit of fun with you, eh?" She grinned and turned to me. "What about you?"

"They obviously took one look and decided I wouldn't appreciate getting snogged by any of them," I told her, reaching for the car door.

Arkron was already in the back seat. "You got snogged?" he asked, his obsidian eyes wide.

I threw myself in beside him, frowning. "No, Seth did." Arkron reached around me to high-five my brother who grinned ridiculously. Rosie slid into the front seat and Sariel gunned the engine." Who is that weird dude, Nybbas?" I asked. "And what's with the fangs?"

Sariel glanced at me in the rear-view mirror and then turned his attention back to the road. "He seems to have taken quite a shine to you, Em."

"Yeah, lucky me. Who *is* he 'though?"

"Vampire." Rosie told me, expertly reapplying her lipstick.

I closed my eyes, leaned my head back and sighed. "Great. Just great. I may never sleep again after tonight. Damn demons singing happy birthday out of tune and vampires with their fangs out. And then there was the cake full of bloody alcohol."

Sariel grinned. "How do you know there was alcohol in it?"

"Mum loves those things you get at Christmas – y'know? The chocolates with the stuff inside them."

"Liqueurs," Seth said helpfully.

"That's it, yeah. Anyway, Seth and I found a box one year, we must've been, what? Eight? Nine?"

"Eight, I think,"

"So we ate about half the box and spent most of Christmas morning hung over." I grinned at Seth and he laughed.

"Remember that time we stayed with Gramps and Grandma? They went to bed and we raided their sherry and port? Filled the bottles back up again with berry juice." Seth chimed in. I nodded, giggling.

"So," Sariel said with a slow smile. "You two aren't as sweet and innocent as you look."

"Oh, shut up and drive," I told him, folding my arms.

Rhianna's 'Shut up and Drive' came blasting from the car's speakers and Arkron grinned. I looked up in surprise. "How'd you do that?"

"Another of my many gifts," Sariel told me.

"Wow," Seth said nodding. "Useful dude to bring to a party."

"Just down here and then take the next right," Rosie was saying. "You'll know it when you see it.

CHAPTER FORTY-FIVE

Club 'Hades' was at the far end of a row of bars and strip-clubs. ('Classy area,' Seth whispered as we drove up.) The outside was plain apart from the sign that had the name in neon red and nothing else.

There was a doorman on duty with two beefy bouncers who were holding back a crowd of would-be clubbers that stretched all the way from the club entrance to the end of the block.

Sariel stopped the car at the entrance and Arkron climbed out to open our door. I frowned. "I'll wait for you." I told Sariel.

"Um…I'm not allowed to go in," he said carefully.

"Pardon?"

"Rosie and Arkron are permitted but Anzu's eldest son and I have… history. I'm not allowed to go in there."

I folded my arms. The fear I'd felt in the ballroom was fast being replaced by a slow burning anger at the whole situation. "Then you can take me back to the hotel. I'm not going in there without my bodyguard and, as far as I'm aware, that's you."

Arkron was staring from the door and Seth waited, one foot on the pavement outside. I head Rosie sigh.

"Emily, you have Rosie and Arkron with you. You don't need me. Besides, you know the rules…you can't make things look bad for Asmodeus." Sariel was aiming for a neutral tone but I heard the hesitation in his voice.

"Rosie," I snapped. She poked her head into the back of the car. "Get my father on the phone." I spat the words out, my eyes blazing and my heart thudding. Sariel's eyes widened and Rosie gasped.

"Emily…" Sariel warned.

"No, Sariel, not this time. I've done what I was told all night. I've been sweet and subservient to those…those…things even while they cheered and applauded my brother getting some female's tongue stuck down his throat and my mother getting fed alcohol laced cake by a demon Lord. It's not in my nature and I'm damn well putting my foot down. Either we all go in or I go home. Right now."

Rosie stepped away from the car and I waited, my eyes locked on Sariel's. He chewed his lip.

"Asmodeus says that if you Sariel can go in." She paused. "If you can convince Anzu's sons to let him."

I nodded and climbed out after Seth. Rosie tucked her phone back into her clutch bag and we waited for Sariel to park the car and walk back. Arkron was staring at me in amazement. "What?" I asked.

"You have guts, Emily. I'll give you that." He said. "I just hope you get to keep them."

"Why wouldn't I?" I asked.

"Ever seen a woman get gutted?" he asked, his dark eyes suddenly very serious.

"No," I whispered, feeling cold all over.

"Well, I have," he said. "It's not pretty." Glancing around at the crowd, he followed Rosie inside. Sariel took my elbow and propelled me after him.

"Did you hear that?" I whispered. Sariel nodded. "Think he's yanking my chain?" He shook his head. "Crap."

Inside the club, past the main foyer we got into a lift and went down, and down, and down, and down. When it felt as 'though we might just be in the bowels of the earth, we came to a stop, the doors slid open and our senses were assaulted by loud pumping music, strobe lights, gyrating bodies and the smell of alcohol, sweat smoke and heat.

The club was an average size with a long bar running down the left side. There were booths and tables on our right; and in front of us, on a raised dais in the middle of the dance floor was the dj station. Farthest away from where we were standing were several more enclosed booths with privacy glass which frosted over when someone went inside and closed the door.

Rosie led us to the bar and spoke to one of the barmen. He glanced at us and then nodded, pulling a cell phone from his pocket and making a call.

He directed Rosie to one of the private booths and we made our way through the crowd.

It was slow going and we were jostled and bumped from all sides as the dancers twisted and rotated around us. I kept my eyes down and followed Seth with the comforting presence of Sariel close behind me.

At the booth, Rosie knocked and we waited. There was a shout from inside and we trooped in. I half hid behind Seth as I looked around. In the dictionary, under the word 'decadence' there should be a photo of this room, I thought. It was incredible – a mirrored ceiling, red and black walls of a silky material, thick carpet of a deep ruby red, small tables holding half drunk glasses of who knows what. And dominating it all was a round bed in the middle. Currently reclining on the bed was a young man and a startled looking girl of about 19. She blinked rapidly as she looked at us, her pupils huge and the whites of her eyes startling in the mellow lighting. She was wrapped in a swathe of black satin with her shoulders and legs bare. Her toenails were painted blood red.

I turned my attention to the man. He looked perhaps in his early twenties with delicate features and pale skin. He was wearing a black, Hugh-Heffner-type robe and his pale, thin legs protruded from the hem like little white sticks. He smiled "Welcome, welcome, welcome." He turned to the girl. "Leave." She stood up and slipped past us and out the door. It made a shhhhh noise as it closed and the glass frosted over again.

"So," he said, leaning back on his elbows. "You're Asmodeus' most recent gets, eh?" He waited and then lifted an eyebrow. "Well? Cat got your tongues? Introductions please."

Clearing his throat, Seth stepped forward and held out his hand. "I'm Seth."

The man shook my brother's outstretched hand. "Well met, Seth. I'm Dennis, son of Anzu."

Well, I mean, come on! I couldn't help it; I dissolved into fits of laughter causing everyone in the room to turn in my direction. 'Dennis' looked mightily surprised and that just made it even funnier.

"I so sorry," I wheezed to Sariel. "I'm just having a 'Bill' moment. 'Dennis the Demon'. That's just brilliant!"

Stifling a smile, Sariel turned to Dennis. "I apologise for Miss Emily, Sir. She's had a very exciting night and she was very nervous to meet you. It seems her nerves have gotten the better of her."

Dennis pushed himself up off the bed and came to stand in front of me. The top of his head reached my chin and he had to look up at me. I pinched my arm behind my back to stop myself from laughing again and forced a calmness to my face that I certainly didn't feel. Dennis looked me over from top to bottom, the sweep of his gaze was like the rasp of a cat's tongue. I felt it as though he had physically touched me and I couldn't repress the shiver that slipped down my spine.

Dennis stepped closer, until his face was only inches from my neck, and then he inhaled deeply. His gray eyes closed and he trembled a little. He stepped back and looked me over again, scratching his chin with his palm. "Well, well, well. Emily, wasn't it?" I nodded. "Don't you just smell good enough to eat?" he chuckled and his tongue snaked out to wet his lips.

There was a knock at the door and his face changed. "What?" he snarled, rage darkening his features.

The door opened and the dj came in. "Daeshan says you have VIPs. He suggested we might play some music they would like." He looked excited, eager, and human.

Dennis smiled. "Well, Emily? What would you like to hear?"

I raised an eyebrow. Good sense was telling me to keep my mouth shut but another part of my brain was telling me to push it a little. Let the claws out. Live a little. Yeah, whispered Good Sense, and have your guts ripped out before morning.

"What about "Rockin' Robin" by Michael Jackson. That's my favourite. I gushed.

The dj's mouth dropped open, Dennis stared at me for a moment and then he began to laugh. "Oh, you are priceless, Emily. I like you." He turned to the dj. "Let's have a club mix until 12 and then slow things down a little." He turned back to me. "Now, let's see if we can't get you and, what was your name? Oh, yeah, Seth. Let's get you and Seth something to drink, shall we?"

We headed for the door only to find our way blocked by a man mountain with green reptile eyes and a broad chest. Sariel was behind me again and I felt him stiffen as the man in front of us looked past me. "What's the wingless wonder doing here?" He asked, his voice like a rumble of thunder.

"Who?" Dennis saw Sariel for the first time. "Who let you in? Guards!"

I moved in front of Sariel and smiled at Dennis, looking up at him from under my lashes. "I'm sorry, Dennis. I asked him to come. He's my body guard y'see and I'm so new to all this, it makes me kindda nervous."

Dennis looked up at me and sucked his teeth as he thought about it.

"And you are?" The man from the door had come into the room and moved to stand beside me. I felt Sariel tense to move forward and waved a hand at him. I turned slowly to face the muscle.

"I'm Emily, daughter of the dark apparently. Who are you?"

The snake eyes glittered. "I am Daeshan, son of Anzu, steward of the ninth gate," he glanced at Sariel, "and I have not finished with this one yet." He moved forward and I put a hand on his chest. He looked down, frowning. "You would stop me?"

"I am not finished with you, Daeshan. My bodyguard is of my father's house and therefore under his care. A slight on my father's house is a slight on my father and I'm sure you don't want that kind of trouble tonight."

He chuckled, a deep, low sound that vibrated under my hand. "No, Emily, daughter of the dark. I have no wish to have the wrath of the house of Asmodeus come down on me tonight." He jerked his head at Sariel. "It seems we must continue our...discussion some other time, fallen one. The she-cat fights your corner. Ilomai y'camalas." With a final nod towards his brother and a glance my way, Daeshan turned around and melted into the crowd outside.

189

Dennis clapped his hands. "Drinks!" he shouted and headed for the bar, a swathe of the dancing crowd opening up to let him pass. We followed quickly. "What did he say to you?" I asked Sariel above the heavy thud of the music.

"It's not important."

"I want to know." Sariel shook his head and I sighed loudly.

Behind me Rosie whispered, "Daeshan told Sariel to watch his back."

I shrugged. "So he was just being all stupid and macho? Typical."

Rosie shook her head. "Didn't you know? It was Daeshan and his house that found Sariel and ... removed his wings."

I stopped walking and Sariel turned to see why. He saw my face and glared at Rosie. "She didn't need to know."

Rosie pushed past us. "Yes, she did."

CHAPTER FORTY-SIX

It quickly became apparent that Dennis was trying to get me drunk. He pushed drink after drink into my hand and I 'accidentally' left them behind on tables, in the toilets, on the bar. I took a few sips of one and almost choked. "There's a reason they call it 'firewater,'" Sariel told me; handing me his glass of water (Dennis refused to serve him anything else.).

Arkron was standing off to the side, his eyes riveted on the spot where Seth was dancing with Rosie. "Why doesn't he relax?" I asked. "It's not as if Rosie bites."

Sariel gave me a funny look and then smiled. "I don't think it's Rosie he's concerned with. See that girl beside Seth? The one with the strawberry blonde curls?"

I looked. "The one who keeps trying to grab his ass?"

Sariel laughed. "Yes, she's one of Anzu's Tetrax demons. They can be very sweet until they get into a rage and then they're lethal."

I paled and signalled to Arkron. "Make him sit down," I mouthed. Arkron shrugged and re-folded his arms.

Dennis bounced up beside me again. "I simply must have the next dance, Emily," he slimed. "I won't take no for an answer this time."

I smiled at him. "Of course, Dennis. Anything you say."

Grinning happily, he went to order another drink and I sighed. "How are we going to get out of here?"

"Well, you're just going to have to pretend to get drunk and then I can take you home." Sariel told me. I glared at him.

"You couldn't have told me this an hour ago? How long would it take me to get drunk? How should I act?"

Sariel laughed. "Ah, sweet, innocent, Emily." I elbowed him, hard. 'Ow! Okay, okay, maybe another half hour, he probably thinks that you talking to me is a side affect of all the alcohol he's been giving you, and y'see the girl with the dark hair?"

"The one dancing on the podium thingy?"

"Yes, start copying her after a bit."

I looked at him, eyes wide. "I am NOT dancing on one of those things."

"You just have to act like you're letting go a bit, like the alcohol has loosened you up, made you a bit kindda giggly. Once Dennis believes that then you can start saying that you're going to vomit and I can take you home."

I nodded. "Ok, I can do that." I straightened my shoulders and watched the brunette laugh as she slipped from the podium and was caught by one of the men watching her. By the way," I turned back to Sariel. "Why does Dennis keep sniffing me? Is he a vampire?"

Sariel made a face. "Dennis? No! What makes you think that?"

"'Cause that Nybbus dude was sniffing me as well. It's weird don't you think?"

Sariel frowned. "Come here," he said pulling me over until I was wedged against his side.

"Okay, this is weird," I told him. *And very, very nice*, my little inner voice whispered as Sariel leaned in and inhaled, his breath tickling my cheek.

"Ah," he said, pulling away so suddenly that I almost fell over.

"Ah?"

"Yeah, um. I'm not sure how to put this..."

"What? I used deodorant and everything..." I began to panic sniffing at my hair and my dress.

"No, no, no, Stop that!" Sariel pulled my arms down as I attempted to smell my own armpits.

"Well, what then?"

"Hmmm. See, when a half demon starts to...change, to gain their powers, they start to smell like...well..."

"Oh, God! Is it like sulphur? Rotten eggs? Mildew?" I wailed.

"No, Emily," Sariel smiled. "They start to smell really...good. It's, well, it's...do you know what an aphrodisiac is?"

I gave him a look. "Sariel I'm seventeen, not seven."

"Yeah, ok," his eyes travelled the length of my body and back to my eyes. "I see that."

A shiver trailed over my skin and this time it was nothing to do with fear. I gulped and tried to get my brain back onto the problem at hand. "So you're telling me I smell so good right now that it makes guys like Dennis... like me? Ewww."

"Not just guys like Dennis," he whispered as Dennis came over and pulled me into the crowd. I glanced back but Sariel's face was lost in shadows and the music changed from fast heavy beats to mellow and slow. Dennis grinned and pulled me close, pressing his lips to my neck and taking a deep breath. I rolled my eyes. It was going to be a long half hour.

Dennis may have looked weedy and eccentric with his silk robe and his stick insect legs but he was also very strong and seemed to have about eight hands, all of them attempting to touch me at once. I giggled, struggled, slapped his hands away playfully, and danced on the podium in the end just to get away from him. All the while he watched me with hungry eyes, his little pink tongue wetting his lips now and again. The music changed again, became hypnotic and I felt certain that if I had actually been drinking all that alcohol, I would have been in a total trance by now.

Complaining about my feet, I managed to convince a very sweaty Dennis to take me back to the bar. Sariel was still sitting on his stool with Seth to his right, chatting animatedly to Rosie. Arkron was standing with his back to the wall scanning the crowd. As we left the dance floor, me weaving a little and shaking my head as though I was trying to clear it, Dennis smacked my behind with a high-pitched little giggle and I decided that enough was enough. Slamming into Sariel's chair, I wrapped my arms around him.

"Sariel," I crooned loudly, "You haven't been paying me any attention."

Surprised, Sariel opened his mouth to respond and I jumped on him, covering his lips with my own. He tasted like sunshine and honey, sweetness over a hint of spice and I felt a little ripple of happiness echo through me.

Sariel had grabbed my arms to push me back and now he pulled me closer instead, his eyes closing as he deepened the kiss. One of his hands slid into my hair, pulling a clasp out and letting some of the silken strands glide down over my shoulders. The other slid onto my back, trailing across my skin in a gentle caress. Then he froze, breaking the kiss and staring at me, his eyes dark. I swallowed and said loudly. "I think I'm going to be sick."

Rosie grabbed me and propelled me through the crowd and into the bathroom, throwing out the gaggle of beauty queens that were standing in front of the mirrors brushing their hair and plumping up their boobs.

I hovered over one of the sinks, waiting for my breathing to get back under control. Rosie waited.

"I want to go home now," I told her and she nodded and flipped out her phone.

"Sariel, I think you should bring the car round. The little princess is pissed." she said and snapped it shut again.

CHAPTER FORTY-SEVEN

The ride home was quiet. I tried to catch Sariel's eye but he kept both of them firmly on the road so I was left to wander if he was cross with me for kissing him in front of everyone and then I wondered how cross he would get if he knew that I wanted to do it again. I clamped my brain down on that thought in case it would stray from my mind to his.

Rosie complained a few times about having to leave early and I caught her trailing a finger down Seth's thigh, their eyes locking. Maybe Seth smelled good too. Ewww.

My night just kept getting better.

As we exited the lift at our floor, a hotel employee was waiting to tell me that 'Mr. Asmodeus has requested your presence in the drawing room'. I frowned and made some comment about needing to lie down but the man persisted. "He said as soon as you came in, Miss." I nodded and glumly followed him, sensing everyone's eyes on me as we headed across the hall and into the suite that Asmodeus was sharing with Seth.

Three goons met us in the small foyer and instructed the man that his job was done. He left with a startled glance in my direction as goon number 1 opened the doors to his right and ushered me in.

Asmodeus was standing in the dark, silhouetted against the window. I walked to the middle of the room and waited.

He turned around. "Would you prefer some light, Emily? Or is your head sore?" There was laughter in his voice.

I swallowed. "I'm fine in the dark."

He chuckled. "Some people are afraid of the dark, or maybe afraid of what might be waiting for them in the dark. Shadows can hide anything, can't they? And then your mind plays tricks, hears noises where there are none, imagines movement under your bed or in your wardrobe. And once that fear takes hold, Emily, it becomes truth. There's something under your bed because you believe that it's there. The monster waiting to eat your heart, the bogey man with the eyes like starlight, the little green men who've come to take you away." He stopped talking and waited. I wondered if he was waiting for some kind of reaction but I wasn't in the mood to give him any. We were both silent and the room became eerie in the lull of conversation.

"I know you don't like me," he finally said softly, his voice a whisper in the stillness of the room. He walked from the window and into the deep shadows to his left. I squinted, trying to keep sight of him but he seemed to melt away. "I know that you skin crawls when I touch you, that your mind rebels at the idea of your mother once finding her way into my bed." His voice seemed to come from everywhere, still soft but resonant. "That's where she is now, by the way, in my bed." He waited again. I bit my lip, feeling my shoulders tense with the effort of ignoring him and he laughed. "Not rising to the bait? Pity, I would've enjoyed sparring with you, I hear you enjoy a good debate."

I could feel goose bumps crawling up my arms and my back, a feeling that he was moving around me as he spoke. My lips quivered and I pressed them shut. There was no way I was going to show him how much he scared me. I could still do that and be civil, right?

"So, shall we talk about what happened tonight?" he hissed into my right ear and I jumped, biting off a gasp. I snapped my head around but he had dissolved into the inky blackness again. "Anzu is an old friend, his sons are well known in our community and it seems that Dennis (I stifled a grin) has taken a shine to you. Anzu's house is wealthy and powerful, Emily. The fact that one of his sons deems you fit to be a bed partner is a great honour." Again, he waited and again I bit my tongue. Arguing with that assessment was, I thought, not a good plan. "Now I know that you and Sariel have become close." The word was whispered into my left ear and I shuddered and closed my eyes. "The fact remains that Sariel is a nothing, a fallen. Your so-called God of Love cast him out. He was dismissed, forgotten and left for us to find. Did he tell you what we do when we find them? The fallen?" Asmodeus came to stand in front of me, his eyes glittering and his mouth smiling tightly. "They provide us with such sport, Emily. We chase them down, stalking them for days, weeks, months and then, when we catch them, we take their wings. Then we see if we can break their spirit. That can provide entertainment for years. Angels heal quickly, did you know that? And archangels? Well, they are incredible. Sariel still had angel dust on his wings when we caught him." He looked excited by the memory and he sucked in a shuddering breath. I allowed myself a grimace of disgust and stepped back.

Asmodeus moved right up close to me, his hot breath on my cheek. "We broke every bone in his body, Emily. You should've heard him scream. Every hurt we found for him healed. Every fresh break knit together. Daeshan spent so long in the depths with him that he is no longer entirely comfortable above ground. It was...interesting. And for all of that we couldn't quite break him, couldn't quite take his soul. He kept some of that spark, that piece of angel, kept it locked away very tightly and, in the end, I decided to champion him. All the better to have him close so that I can watch him. I can know when he breaks and I can claim him." He moved away and I swallowed the tears that threatened to spill down my cheeks. I fisted my hands; for the first time in my life I wanted to hurt someone. I wanted to hurt this man the way he had hurt Sariel. I felt the heat of my anger turn into cold rage, felt the ice flood my blood and the arctic chill of it calmed me. I opened my fists and breathed slowly again.

He was gone back into the shadows but I was so hyper-aware that when he tried to push carefully into my mind, I felt it. His touch inside my head was delicate but I could taste the wrongness of him at the back of my throat. His very presence on the edges of my consciousness was foul and I felt contaminated even though he couldn't find a way to force his will on me.

"I knew your mind would be strong, Emily. I could taste your power from the first night you walked into my house. I don't even think you know what you're capable of but oh, what a fine addition to my house you'll make. And when your next birthday comes and your full strength comes into being, well, the houses will line up to make a bid for you."

I frowned. "What do you mean?"

"Aha! A response! Finally. I thought that perhaps your little dalliance with Sariel had left you mute. You are not a pure blood, Emily, so you are… down the food chain a little, is how I think you would put it. Your power, however, your … gifts, make you exciting to us. New blood doesn't come along very often and when it does it makes for an interesting change, a little bit of excitement in our otherwise humdrum existence. We crave it, Emily." He moved back in front of me again and took my chin in his hand. "We crave the taste of something new, the feel of that fresh raw energy and to be the first to feel it, to taste it? Well, that is a gift beyond price." He dragged his thumb over my lips and I almost choked on the tainted taste of him.

I was confused, my mind so full of the horror of him that I couldn't think straight. "You're going to marry me off?" I asked aghast.

He laughed loud and long. "No, no. You're mine, Emily. You belong to my house. We will, however, sell off that which you have yet to gift to a man." He raised an eyebrow and walked away again.

I felt a tear slide down my face. "Monster," I whispered.

"Perhaps." He was behind me again.

"I won't let you, I'll tell…"

"Who? Who will you tell? Will you run to mummy? The priest in that little church you've been visiting." I looked up. "Oh, yes, I know about that. I see everything you do, everywhere you go, and everyone you're with. You can't run anywhere, Emily. There's nowhere to go. You can't get help because there's no one to help you. You try pedalling this story to anyone and you know what they'll do? They'll lock you up. Poor, sad, crazy Emily. Lost her mind. Went bananas." He laughed.

Another tear joined the first as I felt the truth of his words. No escape, nowhere to go, no one to tell. Trapped.

"Oh, and one more thing, Emily." Asmodeus stepped up behind me and wrapped his arms around mine. I struggled for a moment but it was like being wrapped in steel. His voice was a feverish whisper against my ear. "If at any time you forget that you belong to me I will take your mother and I will

paint the lowest corridors of hell with her blood. You know the place I mean."
His tongue rasped across my ear, leaving a wet trail. I gagged and he let go of
me, chortling.

"Sariel will continue to guard you until I tire of watching him fight
his nature. You bring him such delicious pain." His laughter drifted away and
I waited until he was silhouetted in the window again. His back was turned
to me and I knew that I had been dismissed so I turned and left the room,
walking zombie-like back across the hall.

CHAPTER FORTY-EIGHT

Our suite was quiet and deserted, the lights low. I slipped my shoes off and walked barefoot to the window, throwing the curtains open and pushing the window wide so that the noise and smells of the park and streets below hurried in. I gulped in the air, revelling in the taste of the traffic, the scent of the wet pavements and the sweet, fresh fragrance of the trees. I wanted to shower, to scrub the putrid smell of that monster from my skin but I knew it wouldn't do any good – his essence would stain my soul forever.

The connecting door opened and closed. I didn't turn around, kept my face in the bracing air.

"Your thoughts…so sad…so angry…so despairing." Sariel was behind me. "Did he hurt you?" He asked softly, turning me around. I dipped my head so he couldn't see my expression but he tipped my chin back up and I opened my eyes. "Emily…" his face fell.

"I'm trapped, Sariel. He'll sell me off to the highest bidder next year. One night only, folks! Roll up! Roll up!" I giggled hysterically. I clapped my hand over my mouth and lurched away from him. "I shouldn't even be telling you or he'll…" I froze. "He never cared about her, did he? Never felt anything but the need to father some offspring to help him line his pockets."

Sariel shook his head and pulled me down onto the sofa. "They bore so easily, Emily. Eternity is a long time to spend eating and drinking and trying to cause chaos. You are an escape from it, you and Seth - unknown quantities in a life of such monotony."

"He said that she's in his bed again." I wanted to rinse my mouth out. "Is she?"

Sariel sighed. "Your mother is …easily persuaded. For Asmodeus it's easy to whisper into her mind and make her turn to him." He pulled me into a hug and then leaned his forehead into mine. "We're going home in the morning, Emily. You'll feel better when you get back among your own things."

I didn't have the energy to argue. I suddenly felt so tired, completely exhausted, but I wanted to make one thing right first. "I'm sorry for earlier," I told him, keeping my eyes closed. "Will he ... punish you?" My voice shook.

"Forget about that," Sariel said softly. "Sleep now." My head slid onto his shoulder and he pulled me onto his knee. "Siete sembrato stasera bello, Emily." He whispered his lips grazing my cheek. "That means 'you looked beautiful tonight'".

I smiled. "Grazie, Sariel." I whispered around a yawn. "That means thank you," I told him as my eyes closed and his surprised chuckles followed me into my dreams.

Chapter Forty-Nine

Here's an interesting fact; no matter how much chaos the rest of your life is in, you still have to go to school. It's bizarre. Dad's a demon? Nasty, but don't forget your 3000 word essay on the Chinese revolution. Met a vampire? Ewww, but make sure your uniform has no creases – don't want to be scruffy on your first day back. Afraid of what's going to happen to you when you turn eighteen and your dad sells you off to one of his fiendish friends? Pity. But don't forget your lunch money.

So there we were again, crowded on to a stuffy, smelly school bus at ten minutes past eight on Monday morning, schoolbags in hands, lunch money in pockets and uniforms freshly laundered. All around us there were chattering kids in various states of euphoria and depression, wriggling uncomfortably in over-starched shirts or standing up to roll up the waist of an over-long skirt to mid-thigh instead of mid-ankle.

Seth and I stood in the middle of this organised anarchy, both of us hanging onto the overhead bars, swaying and bumping around corners and over uneven roads. I wondered if this felt as surreal to him as it did to me. Maybe the past week had been a dream – too much cheese one night before bedtime, or an overdose of cola bottles maybe. That could cause it, right?

Annie got on at the last stop before Market Street and waved up the bus at me. Today, especially for the first day back, she had dyed her hair maroon which matched the stripes on our ties. I grinned. We'd spent Sunday afternoon together – Annie, Dylan and me – and it had been wonderful. Like it used to be before they joined the ranks of the permanently-joined-at-the-hip.

Once Annie had finished being stunned by my tan, hair, nails etc.etc. and Dylan had stopped looking at me oddly ("You sound like you but you don't look much like you.") we had spent a pleasant hour kicking a football around at the recreation grounds on the East side of town. Until the ten year olds from Crawley Street had come over and challenged us to a game with the football itself as the prize. Fifteen exhausting minutes later, we'd slumped into a booth at the diner and gone Dutch on an extra large ice-cream float with cola.

"How can ten year olds be hard to beat at football?" asked Dylan with an expression of complete confusion on his face. "I mean, we're taller than them, we're older and so we've played more football, we're meaner…"

"Speak for yourself," Annie interrupted, yanking the straw from me before I slurped all the cola.

"…And we're stronger. How did we lose my football?"

I giggled. "We'll stump up for a new one, won't we, Annie?"

Annie nudged him and laid her head on his shoulder. "Yeah, quit worrying about it, sweetie."

Dylan leaned down and pressed a kiss to her cheek. He sighed in contentment and set his chin on top of her head. I waited for the awkwardness to start, for the vomit-o-meter to fill up past maximum but this time when I looked at them I saw how good they were together and I felt good for them. It felt right.

This morning it still felt right and Annie's smiling face at the front of the bus gave me an inner glow that lasted until fifteen minutes into the new school year.

Predictably, it was Sarah who ruined my good vibe.

We were in our form room sorting out our schedules with our form teacher, Mr. O'Halloran. I had chosen five subjects for As level – Maths (predictably), English, History, Physics and Chemistry – so sorting out a timetable was a nightmare. Mr. O'Halloran was, however, a Saint and perhaps also a wizard equal to if not better than Dumbledore himself so we managed to get everything fitted in and still have free periods for study and two sessions of gym (oh, whoopee).

Anyway, happy to be finished I had moved my baggage to the back of the classroom and was checking out the list of books I had to pick up when a shadow fell across my desk. "Hi, Emily. I think you're going to be in my English class."

I looked up, confused by the voice and found Sarah smiling down at me. I looked behind me to see who she was talking to but there was no one there. I looked back at her. "Are you talking to me?" I asked in a voice that (embarrassingly) squeaked.

Sarah threw back her glorious mane of hair and gave a throaty giggle that immediately had most of the males in the room panting. "Oh, Emily, you are just so funny," she drawled. "Mind if I sit here?" She pointed at the empty seat beside me. Stunned into silence I could only nod mutely. I glanced around the class to see if this was weirding everyone else out as much as me. Seth had his face stuck in his schedule list, an expression of total bewilderment on his face, as Amber pouted beside him, trying to attract his attention. Annie and Dylan were standing next in line at Mr. O'Halloran's desk, comical twin expressions of astonishment on their faces as they caught sight of Sarah making herself comfortable beside me.

I'm sure my face had taken on a rigid 'someone-help-me' look and I tried to find some reason to high-tail it outta there but Sarah had started talking.

"So, this dump is, like, such a drag after London, right? I was born there, did you know that? We moved here 'cause mum got, like, fed up with the whole big city experience and wanted us to grow up somewhere quieter." She snorted. "Well, they certainly found somewhere quiet, right?" I managed a nod and tried to damp down the fact that I was freaking out. "Anyway, we had such a great time at your party. We should totally do that again. I mean, like, soon. We should check our schedules and see when to get Amber's dad to let us have the club again. Give me your number and we'll hook up sometime this week." She dug her small, pink, sparkly cell phone out of her bag and looked at me expectantly.

"Um, I don't have a phone," I croaked. Cringe.

Sarah blinked rapidly for a few seconds. "Oh, ok. We'll just call round sometime." A shadow crossed her pretty face and she checked the slim gold watch on her wrist. "Where is that boy? He got sent for extra homework diaries ages ago."

As if on cue, the classroom door opened and Adam came in, carrying a large number of hard-backed school diaries. He set them down on Mr. O'Halloran's desk with a thud and the teacher nodded his thanks.

Sarah waved enthusiastically to catch his attention and, when he did look in our direction, his amazed reaction to the two of us sitting together was hastily covered up with a lop-sided grin that made my stomach do flip flops. He pulled a chair out from the table in front of us and sat down as Sarah took up another one-sided conversation.

"So, it must be great to meet your dad, right? Especially when he's, like, really rich. And it was so nice of him to put on such a big party for you. I mean if he does that for your sixteenth then your eighteenth is going to be amazing." I wanted to disagree with that little observation but she was still chattering. How did any of her friends get a word in edgeways with this girl? "So, Amber said that Seth told her that you stayed in the Ritz? My mum's stayed there quite a few times when she meets dad for business dinners and stuff. Was it, like, really amazing? Did you see any celebs? I'd love to meet Victoria Beckham 'cause she's, like, amazing." Anyone like to guess what Sarah's word of the day was? "Adam could chat to David about football and Vick and I could talk fashion. We could double-date!" She giggled again and some more people turned to look our way. Pretty much most of the class were watching now, all catching flies with their chins hitting the floor.

Dylan and Annie were still talking to Mr. O'Halloran but Dylan kept glancing my way, worry making him frown. Finally he whispered something to Annie and then, taking a deep breath made his way through the rest of the gawking class until he was standing at the end of Adam's table. He coughed into his hand and Sarah looked up, a frown crinkling her smooth forehead – no Botox yet then.

"What is it, nerd-boy. We're talking here." She growled.

Dylan swallowed nervously – his Adam's apple bobbing like a little yellow bath duck. "Er, well, Emily, Annie was wondering if you could bring your schedule down so we can have a look? Hers won't work out so Mr.

O'Halloran's wondering if he made a mistake on yours."

"Get lost feeb," Sarah said and turned back to me. "Honestly, the people who just should never have been born." She flicked her hair dramatically.

Dylan chewed on the inside of his cheek and looked at his shoes. I sighed and stood up, pulling my bag with me. "I'm coming, Dylan," I said loudly and Sarah blinked furiously again, as if she couldn't quite believe her eyes.

"Where are you going?" She asked in astonishment.

"To talk to my friends." I told her slipping around the end of the table and hooking my arm into Dylan's. "Thank you," I whispered and he smiled a super-happy Dylan smile.

"But I wasn't finished talking to you," squeaked Sarah behind me.

"Yeah? Well, I was finished talking to you," I told her with out looking back.

Wow, being a total cow actually felt pretty good.

At least it felt pretty good for the 3.2 seconds it took for Dylan and me to walk across the classroom. Kids were whispering at my back as I stood in front of Mr. O'Halloran's desk and pretended to search my bag for my class schedule. I glanced at Annie and she raised her eyebrows questioningly. I shrugged. I was feeling guilty as hell. Just because Sarah was usually a bitch didn't give me the right to be one too. She'd actually been nice for almost five whole minutes – surely a record – and I'd just sat there being confused and anxious.

And then it hit me – how did she know about London and Asmodeus? Oh, of course. Seth and Amber. Seth had told Amber who had told Sarah and the whole world and his lunchbox probably knew by now. Great.

CHAPTER FIFTY

I spent break with Dylan and Annie, studiously ignoring Seth who was doing his best to appear confused by my cold-shouldering him. He had other problems too - Amber was following him around like a lost puppy, taking his hand as they walked in the corridors, running her fingers up and down his arm when he was talking to his other friends. It made me feel a bit sad for her to be honest, like she was trying too hard to keep his attention. The tables, it seemed had turned. Last year, Seth had been the lost puppy and now he was the one in control. I'd obviously got it all wrong in my original assessment of their potential relationship – I needed to watch more Oprah.

At lunch I decided to get some time to myself (and also give Dylan and Annie some time to cosy up – no way was I going to sit beside them while they made out. Yeuk!) so I headed out of the main school and into the quad to eat my lunch at one of the picnic benches.

I'd just finished wiping the crumbs from my ham, chicken and potato salad sandwich (don't knock it 'till you've tried it!) when Adam sat down beside me on the bench. Thankfully I wasn't still eating so I didn't immediately choke in astonishment. I also managed not to blush furiously, hyperventilate or start talking about the weather.

We sat together silently for a few minutes and I was able to study his utter gorgeousness from the corner of my eye. Adam Farlow was sitting beside me. OMG. Outwardly his body language screamed 'relaxed and hunky male' but his eyes darted all around, constantly scanning the playground and the other benches. I began to get seriously paranoid. If he didn't want to be seen with me then why was he sitting with me?

Or maybe he was looking for dangerous would-be kidnappers. Maybe weres had the ability to sniff out threats like that – you know, like Spiderman's tingly spidey-sense. I began to look around too. Not really certain what I was looking for but figuring that any kind of threat would reveal itself. Besides, Adam would protect me!

Adam coughed into his hand and I was so wound up looking for a super scary demon-ninja hit squad among all the school uniforms that I almost jumped three feet into the air. We looked at each other.

"Er, about earlier," Adam said.

"Huh?" It was all I could manage to say as my heart rate slowly returned to normal.

"Y'know. The whole thing with Sarah."

"Oh, yeah."

"You were in the Suffolk Digest, on the Society Pages."

"Huh?" Oh, me and my amazing conversational abilities. How will Adam ever be able to resist my wit and charm?

"There were photos of the party in London."

"Huh?" Oh, my God. Please let me be able to add more to this conversation! Adam is actually talking to me – in broad daylight, without being chained to a cafeteria table - and all I can manage is 'huh'. Aarrrgh!

"You looked amazing." He grinned. "I don't think I've ever seen you wear a dress." My blush was probably hot enough to equal some nuclear reactions. "And Seth in a suit? Man, those were sick threads."

"Yeah, sick threads. That they were." Great, now I sounded like Yoda.

"So the guy you were with – cousin? Family friend? Boyfriend?" Adam was scanning the playground again.

"Um, it's kindda complicated." How was I supposed to describe Sariel?

I'm your bodyguard.

Quit listening in! I can't tell him that anyway, can I?

Adam nodded, distracted. "So anyway, Sarah saw the photos and the write-up."

"There was a write-up? About us?"

Adam nodded. "Yeah, all about your Dad and his businesses." He waited.

The penny dropped. "Ah, so Sarah sees that my Dad is loaded and suddenly I'm good enough to talk to? Nice." I shook my head. Typical, and I had even felt guilty for being bitchy to that cow!

"I just thought that you should know – you looked pretty freaked out about it." Adam's attention was back on me again and his eyes were just incredible - deep blue, the colour of oceans, a girl could get lost in those eyes and not care.

I may vomit if you don't stop.

That's it! You need to teach me how to mask my thoughts. Or at least not project them so strongly.

Why?

Because I don't want you listening in all the time. It's embarrassing.

Sariel chuckled. *I find it entertaining.*

Shut up.

I concentrated on smiling at Adam. "Yeah, I was a bit spooked. I mean, Sarah's never been my number one fan or anything. Thanks for the heads up."

He nodded and stood up, pulling his bag onto his back. Oh, no! Don't leave! My brain is just starting to produce actual words!

He turned to walk away and then swung back and leaned a knee on the bench seat, moving forward until his head was millimetres from mine. "Um, Emily. I was wondering if you would…" he paused and chewed on his bottom lip. He grinned a little self-consciously and shook his head, pulling away.

"What? Spit it out, Adam."

He leaned back over again and I could smell imperial leather soap laced with some light aftershave. It was delicious and I may have momentarily just closed my eyes and inhaled. Looked gorgeous, smelled gorgeous, had eyes the colour of the ocean and a voice like caramel. What's not to like?

He's an ass.

Butt out.

"I was wondering if you'd like to meet me sometime?"

"Huh?" I didn't blame my brain for shorting out just a little. Had Adam just asked me out?

"I mean, are you busy tomorrow night? Say around nine?" I shook my head. Attempting to speak would just produce another grunting sound anyway. Adam's smile was dazzling. "Great! Meet me in the orchard behind Myles' factory, ok?" I nodded again. Adam leaned a little closer. "Come alone," he whispered against my ear, his breath tickling me pleasantly and making me shiver. I nodded again and he was gone, leaving me in a state of exquisite confusion.

Bloody human teenage hormones.

Go away, Sariel.

CHAPTER FIFTY-ONE

I think it's pretty safe to say that I floated through Tuesday on a magic carpet of heavenly anticipation.

Adam had asked me to meet him.

Secretly.

It was all just so ridiculously romantic – we were, in my mind at least, Suffolk's answer to Romeo and Juliet and naturally (this being my fantasy world) this would be the first of many secret dates that would blossom into a real 'relationship'. We would eventually go public of course, declare our undying love for one another, get married and live happily ever after.

Lord help me but I was turning into a Disney Princess!

Sariel's voice broke into my thoughts many times during that day. If I was aware of the concern in his tone as he made light-hearted comments on mundane stuff then I tuned it out. I was buoyant with happiness for the first time in ages and no one was going to ruin it for me.

It wasn't a total surprise when I saw him waiting for me at the school gate, casually ignoring all the admiring looks and the whispered, giggly comments. I think that deep down I'd been waiting for this, knew why he was there, but again I ignored it and proceeded to give him a step-by-step account of my day on the off-chance that he might just have missed one stimulating second.

And yes, I possibly noted the signs of his agitation as he drove me home – his white knuckles on the steering wheel, his lips pressed tightly together into a thin hard line and his silver-blue eyes glaring, Clint-Eastwood-like, beneath his frowning brows.

We were maybe four streets from home when he jerked the steering wheel to the left and stopped the car. My lengthy description of the changes to the Bunsen burner set up in the chemistry lab trailed away as he turned his stony face in my direction.

"I'm going with you," he said in a 'don't-argue-with-me' tone that immediately got my back up.

"I beg your pardon?" I asked in my very best attempt at and ever-so-English accent.

"Cut the crap, Emily. You are not sneaking off to meet this guy on your own."

I folded my arms and glared at him. "Says who?"

Sariel jabbed a thumb at his chest. "I say. Or would you prefer we tell your mum and dad and let them decide?" He raised an eyebrow.

"I'm not having you tag along on a date, especially when I've waited so long for it. This is Adam Farlow, Sariel! Adam! It's bad enough that you'll be listening in but…"

"Sorry? Rewind just a tad there, Emily. A date?" Sariel laughed theatrically. "You seriously think that Adam Farlow is taking you to a rotting apple orchard for a date?" He laughed again.

If scowling was an Olympic sport then I'd be a sure thing for the gold medal – I could scowl like the witchiest witch who ever lived – a dementedly angry witch at that. I scowled at Sariel and wished that my demon blood had at the very least given me laser beams in my eyes to fry up all the annoying male idiots who seemed to cross my path on a daily basis. I was a male idiot magnet. "Just because *you* think that a skinny little nerd from a council estate can't date a rich, good looking, tall, blond rugby playing rowing captain doesn't mean that Adam can't look beyond all that and see *me*." I blinked away a sudden attack of hot tears.

Sariel sighed and looked away for a moment. His right hand was constantly making and unmaking a fist and I wondered if he wanted to punch me as much as I wanted to laser-fry him just then.

"So, why all the secrecy?" He asked finally. "What about Sarah? Did you think about her, Emily?" his eyes searched mine and I had to look away. No, I hadn't thought of Sarah – she'd been a background spectre but I'd ignored her presence in the great Adam/Emily equation. "I know that you've liked this guy for a long time and the fact that he's asked you to meet him must feel like a dream come true but…." Sariel rubbed his eyes. "All I'm saying is that it doesn't feel right to me. If he doesn't think enough of you to date you openly then he's not worth it. You'll end up getting hurt because he'll stay with Sarah and you must know that."

I grimaced and looked at my feet, flinching when Sariel's hand gently touched my cheek and turned my face back to his. "Don't do this, Emily," he whispered. "Don't get hurt."

I heard what he was saying, I understood it all but the truth was that I didn't *want* to hear it *or* believe it. In fact, I was downright angry with Sariel for pointing out all the things that I was afraid of. This was Adam Farlow for goodness sake! This might be my only opportunity and he was trying to put me off. I sighed in annoyance and then drew in a deep breath. "If you promise to stay well back then you can come along but I am going to meet Adam tonight, whether you like it or not."

Sariel held my hot, angry eyes for a few more seconds and then dropped his hand from my face.

"Like I was ever going to let you go alone," he muttered.

I gave him an Olympic-gold scowl again and my anger flashed to the surface. "That's right," I snarled at him." I forgot that you have to watch out for me. Wouldn't want to upset Asmodeus now would we?"

With a low growl, Sariel shifted the car into gear and swung us back into the early evening traffic. I folded my arms across my chest and spent the rest of our short journey quietly simmering with anger and more than a few niggling doubts.

CHAPTER FIFTY-TWO

Ask anyone the first thing they noticed when they first drove through or past Dean's Lynn and at least 90 percent of them will say the forest. On the satellite photos that we saw in geography class during our first year in town, Allenton forest is a fat crescent of lush green cradling the whole west side of the town and a portion of the north too - it runs along behind the church and all the way over to the site of the old factory.

The factory used to belong to the Myles family who once owned a large portion of Dean's Lynn land. They farmed a huge orchard on the edge of the forest from the early eighteenth century and built the factory to produce their famous cider ('Myles cider, Best by Miles') which was apparently a Suffolk institution. The last of the Myles family, Arthur, died in 1963 and the factory closed shortly afterwards. The land, however, was never reclaimed and the factory and orchard were left to the ravages of Mother Nature and Old Man Time.

Like all kids in town, Seth and I went through a phase of exploring the forest – first following some of the County Council walks and trails and then branching out (pardon the pun!) on our own into the less accessible areas. The orchard was, as far as I remembered, a place of dense trees, tangled weeds, moss on the ground and on the tree trunks, strips of gold sunlight slipping through the branches and, above all, silence. It was *not* the most romantic place to meet for a date. However, I wasn't thinking about that.

It was easy enough to get out of the house. Mum was watching Family Fortunes and Seth was in our room doing homework so when I told mum that I was thinking of going for a walk she looked up, frowned briefly and then told me not to be too late, nodding in Sariel's direction when he got up and pulled on a coat too.

We walked silently down to the bottom of our street and then turned right towards the rec grounds. I waited for Sariel to complain, to try to talk me out of it again, but he stayed quiet, striding comfortably beside me as though we took a walk to the orchard for me to meet the most popular gut in school behind his girlfriend's back every night. I pushed that thought away and got back into my 'married with children' fantasy again, grinning dreamily to myself as we walked down Market Street and across to Orchard Bray which led to the factory. I turned to Sariel. "You can leave me here. I know this area really well so I'll be okay."

Sariel pursed his lips, looked at me for a second and then, shaking his head, walked across the road and on up Parker Avenue towards the far side of town. I watched him go for a moment; suddenly the idea of walking the rest of the way on my own wasn't so appealing. Wimp! Giving up at the first hurdle. I ought to be ashamed of myself. I straightened my back and then walked to the top of Orchard Bray, crawling through the hole in the fence and onto the grounds of Myles' factory.

The main building was a huge, rusting shell on my right, criss-crossed by crumbling support beams and vague shapes of machinery. What had once been the west wall still had a smattering of windows with glass in their frames and they reflected the last rays of early September sun setting through the trees on my left. It was kind of beautiful in a weird and spooky way.

I walked on past the outbuildings, which still had a faint but nauseating smell of dead yeast, sugar and rotting apples, and towards the eight feet high red brick wall. In the middle of the wall was an arch with the Myles coat of arms carved into the keystone. There had once had an iron gate but it had long ago fallen into the vegetation beyond and was now indistinguishable from the ground. I had arrived at the entrance to the orchard.

I walked through the arch, with the butterflies in my stomach doing back-flips and my supper of toast and jam threatening to make a reappearance, down the remnants of a path, past rows of overgrown apple trees and down towards the firebreak. Adam was waiting, his back to me as he kicked a stone around among the debris on the ground, and I had a moment to calm myself, be amazed at my good fortune and admire his broad shoulders and tousled blond hair. He was actually here. I was actually here. This was actually it.

CHAPTER FIFTY-THREE

"Hi, Adam," I said softly, congratulating myself on how confident and relaxed I sounded. He looked up and I waved then dropped my hand. Good start, wave at him like a three year old. Yep. So mature.

Adam's shoulders dropped a little but he turned around with a smile on his face. "Hey, Emily. Thanks for coming," he said. "No trouble finding the place then?"

He sounded weird and instinctively I backed off a little. "Er, no. Seth and I used to come up here a lot when we were younger," I told him, watching as his eyes darted from one side of the clearing to another.

"Yeah, me too," he gave a little chuckle and looked down at his feet.

Maybe he was embarrassed. Uncertain what to do with me now that he had me there (I could make several suggestions). Or perhaps he was having second thoughts.

"So, you want to take a walk?" I asked quickly.

"Er," he looked around again.

I waited.

"So, um, how've you been?" he asked.

I frowned. Was this how a date with the hottest guy in school was supposed to go? "I've been fine." I replied. "You?"

He shrugged. "Yeah, good. I've been good."

"Great." Wow. We were really doing great in the conversation stakes. Adam shuffled his feet once more and stuck his hands in his jacket pockets. I wanted to be patient, really I did. I wanted to be enjoying the moment – being alone with Adam and all that jazz – but I was getting impatient and, yes, I was a bit annoyed with him for being so weird. We'd survived being eaten by a demon together for goodness sake! And he'd seemed so much friendlier at school.

"So, London was good then?" He asked.

I looked at him for a moment and he couldn't seem to meet my eyes.

Hmm.

Okay so patience is not my strong point at the best of times. I am willing to endure a certain amount of waiting when I consider it necessary or perhaps prudent but this? This was just annoying.

"Adam, why did you ask me to meet you here?" I asked, taking a step towards him. My voice carried and I paused, tilting my head to the side and listening. The orchard was certainly a quiet and tranquil place but it had gone beyond being peaceful and was now eerily soundless. I looked up. Adam was looking around too, his expression tight and sad. "Adam?"

He looked at me then, his eyes were sad and a little ashamed. "Emily, I'm sorry," he said and shook his head. "I had to do it."

"Huh?" Confused? Annoyed? Puzzled? Yes, indeed, all of the above.

"I asked Adam to invite you here this evening," said a voice and I swung around to face a tall, blond man wearing a Barbour jacket and jeans.

"Er, Emily. This is my dad, Richard Farlow." Adam said from behind me.

Uh, huh. So Adam invites me out on a date and brings his dad? This was not good.

Farlow senior extended his hand and I shook it. "Call me Rick," he said. I nodded, looking between father and son. The similarities were striking – same tousled blond hair, same deep blue eyes, same aquiline nose and full lips, even the same cute smile. Rick, however, moved unlike anyone I'd ever seen before. His limbs and muscles seemed to shift with a horrible slick fluidity that was as fascinating as it was scary. "So you're the demon half-breed," he went on, watching me carefully.

"Dad..." Adam whispered, glancing warily at me.

I remembered Sariel's advice about Weres – courage and strength, courage and strength, I chanted to myself – so I managed not to flinch but my heart was racing and I was beginning to feel very afraid. I swallowed a lump in my throat. "So you're another wolf wannabe." I said in as strong a voice as I could muster.

Adam's astonished face turned to look at me with comical slowness. His eyes were wide in an I-can't-believe-you-just-did-that expression. I stared calmly back. Rick Farlow threw back his head and roared with laughter making me jump. What was this all about?

Well, It's sure not a date.

Great. *Are you going to say 'I told you so' now?*

I wasn't planning on it but since you mention it…

Never mind. *What's going on here?*

I'm not sure.

That's helpful. Not.

You're surrounded so my advice would be to stay put and not run screaming into the trees.

Great plan. *What do you mean I'm surrounded?*

Look around.

I swivelled my head to one side and then the other and gulped audibly. The clearing was now alive with people – eight males ranging in age from about fifteen to forty stood in a loose circle in the shadows of the trees. All eyes were on me and no one was smiling. Not a twig had snapped, not a leaf had rustled - there had been absolutely no sound whatsoever to announce their arrival. I turned back to Rick and Adam.

"So, what do you want?" I figured it would be best to be blunt.

"You have something belonging to us," Rick told me, walking forward slowly. I stood my ground and he stopped a few feet away from me, scraping the ground in front of him with a toe of his heavy walking boots. He looked up. "Do you know where it is?"

I sighed. "I don't even know *what* it is so knowing *where* it is would be more than a little tricky."

Rick grinned, laughter lines appeared at the side of his eyes and his lips. "I like you, Emily. You've got backbone and you're funny." He grinned again and then became serious, gesturing around the clearing. "Some of the pack don't agree with my approach here. They think the way to get the information is to *make* you tell us. I'm asking nicely but if I can't get you to play nice with me then I'll have to let them try." He stepped back a little, a look of fake concern on his face.

I looked around the clearing again, meeting the fierce eyes of the rest of the pack with as much backbone as I could pretend to have and trying to force myself to stay calm whilst all my brain could think was *Oh, crap. I'm gonna die. I am gonna die. And in an orchard! I'LL GET BUGS IN MY HAIR IF I FALL ONTO THE GROUND!*

Seriously? This is what you're concerned about? Bugs?

Not now, Sariel. I'm having a freak out.

Maybe you could ask them to describe the artefact.

Huh?

Just a suggestion.

I smiled at Rick. "I certainly appreciate the fact that you're giving me an opportunity to stay in one piece, Rick." He gave a slight nod and I sighed. "The problem is that I don't have the faintest idea what you're talking about." A few of the others began to murmur threateningly. Rick frowned and held up a hand. All noise ceased immediately. "Maybe if you could describe this thing you're looking for I would have a better idea of what it actually is." Rick blinked at me. "Just a suggestion." I finished.

Quit stealing all my best lines.

Shut up and concentrate.

Rick was nodding. "I don't see any harm in that. The artefact is a knife about so big," he spread his hands to about 30cm across. "The handle is made of bone and is carved into the face of a wolf. The blade is very sharp, golden in colour and shaped like a claw." He drew a crescent shape in the air with his finger.

I chewed on the inside of my cheek for a moment before it came to me. "Oh, the knife that David had for the summoning!" I smiled triumphantly. There were angry growls all around the clearing, shouts of "I told you she had it" and "She stole it from us." I frowned at them. Enough was enough. "Shut up and quit acting like animals. You're on two legs so behave." I turned back to Rick who was trying to decide whether to grin or be angry with me. "Look, David had it that night. I don't know where he got it."

"It was stolen from us. It's sacred to our pack." Rick said gently, Mister Diplomatic.

"Well, I don't have it but I think I know who to ask." I told him.

He looked around the clearing, narrowing his eyes. He made an exaggeratedly sad face. "They want it back now." I tilted my head to the side and studied him. The light was fading fast and the orchard was filling with shadows. Rick Farlow's eyes shimmered in the gloom. I was trying to read between the lines of his fake expressions but it was hard.

"I don't have it now, but I can try to get it for you," I told him slowly and distinctly.

His head dipped a little and his eyes gleamed at me from under his brows. "They want it now."

"I don't have it now." This was getting boring.

Rick made a sound deep in his throat, a deep animal growl that seemed to vibrate around me. The hairs on the back of my neck stood to attention at that truly inhuman sound. I took a step back but he moved so fast that all I saw was a blur. One second he was five steps in front of me, the next he had a hand around my neck and his face against mine. "We want it now," he snarled.

Whatever happened in the next few milliseconds was too fast for me to see – my windpipe was getting crushed and then I was on the ground, coughing and Rick Farlow was eight feet away bouncing off a tree. I looked up and Sariel held out a hand to help me up.

"You will not touch her again," he said in a soft voice that carried. There was agitation all around us as the Weres prowled angrily at the edge of the clearing. From the corner of my eye, I could see Adam moving in front of one of them, pressing a hand to his chest to keep him back. A young boy of maybe fifteen couldn't hold back any longer and ran forward, teeth bared and hands clawing for my shoulder. Sariel was on him before I even had time to draw a frightened breath and the boy was knocked back into the depths of the orchard. Sariel moved back in front of me, crouching low, his arms slightly outstretched.

"Call off your pack," he told Rick who held up a hand for calm and then inclined his head to the others. They melted into the trees, silent as shadows.

"It was never my intention to hurt her," Rick told him and his voice was calm again. "Just to scare her into giving us the information we needed."

"She doesn't have the knife," Sariel told him. "But I know who does and we can get it for you."

We can? I asked.

Probably.

I gulped.

Rick smiled. "You have one week and then I won't be able to keep them from hunting her."

"Are you making a threat?" Sariel asked. He sounded amused.

"No, I'm stating a fact." Rick's smile had gone. He took a step towards Sariel. "I know who you are," he hissed.

"So we don't need to worry about awkward introductions then," I could hear the smile in Sariel's voice. "Here. One week."

Rick nodded and Sariel turned his back on him, taking my arm and leading me back towards the factory. The date, it seemed, was over.

CHAPTER FIFTY-FOUR

Adam very sensibly stayed out of my way for the next two days – perhaps it had something to do with the fact that I glared at him every time I saw him or that he said hello to me twice and I totally blanked him (much to Annie and Dylan's amazement). Whatever the reason, he did the right thing and by Friday I was ready to be civil again so when he slipped onto the bench beside me at lunchtime I was able to paint on a smile and say hi.

"I thought we should talk," he said, picking little slivers of wood off the table.

"I think perhaps you should do the talking," I told him. He glanced up at me sharply. "You know I like you," I said, feeling my face flush with embarrassment, "And you used that to get me to a meeting with your...pack." "Shush," he said, glaring at me. "Keep it down." He looked around the playground but no one else was paying any attention to us.

I folded my arms and waited.

He sat back and sighed. "Ok, yes. I knew and yes, I knew you'd agree to meet me. No questions asked." I grimaced – no questions asked all right. I hadn't even been bothered that he was already going out with someone else. "My dad is the alpha so I have to do what he says – that's the law – so when he told me to set up a meeting, I had to do it."

"And you couldn't tell me that's what it was? You had to lie?" I punched him on the arm.

"Ow!" He rubbed his arm and looked at me in shock. "What was that for?"

"For being a cowardly, lying scumbag. That's what. Why didn't you just tell me the truth? I would still have gone."

"You might have told Asmodeus."

I laughed loudly and some kids turned to look at us. There were a lot of amazed faces when they realised who was sitting beside me and I knew it wouldn't be long before word got around. "I hate Asmodeus, Adam. It'll be a cold day in hell before I go to him for anything." I sighed. "Look, we're getting stared at so you'd better go before people start thinking you're crushing on a nerd."

Adam got up to go and them paused and sat down again. "Can I ask a question?" I nodded. "If I did ask you out for real what would you say?"

Oh, God. Now there was a question. My head was screaming at me to tell him to let a long hike over a short cliff but my heart was going all Jane Austen and swooning. I decided to be honest. "Today? I'd say no way in hell. Next week? I'd probably say yes."

"I better wait until next week then," Adam smiled that adorable lop-sided grin again and I felt my heart stutter and then go into overdrive as he slid back off the bench and loped towards the main door.

I was idly wondering if his lips would feel as soft as Sariel's when I realised that he still hadn't apologised.

Bloody hormones.

CHAPTER FIFTY-FIVE

I could sense Sariel's mood before I even woke up.

It was strange to feel an alien anger swirl in my gut, to catch snippets of his anxious thoughts in my head and to realise that my right hand was clenched into a tight fist because his was. Was this what he felt when I was projecting strongly? Wow.

What's the matter? I asked.

What?

You're angry and upset.

You can feel that?

Yeah. Kind of hard not to.

Sorry. It's just been a rough night and I…did you hear what I was thinking about? Was it my imagination or did he sound worried that I had?

Just bits and pieces. Nothing that made sense.

Hmmm. Look, I'm going to come and pick you up this morning and I need you to act like it's no big deal, like we'd arranged to go to Norwich this morning.

What for?

I dunno. Whatever you can think of.

I frowned. *You sound tired.*

Yeah. I could feel his chin drop to his chest and his exhaustion radiated through me.

Are you okay?

He chuckled. *Either I'm slipping with my guards or you're getting more attuned to me.*

Is that a bad thing?

Sariel sighed. *Yes and no. I'll pick you up around ten, ok?*

Okay.

I lay still for a moment, listening hard and trying to feel what he was feeling again but he was obviously working even harder to keep me out. I wasn't sure how I felt about that – 'strangely bereft' was the first thing that came to mind. I shook myself and sat up in bed. The alarm clock said that it was only six fifteen and I could hear Seth's contented snores from the other side of the room but I was wide awake now and wondering where we were going and why all the secrecy. Chewing on a fingernail, I tiptoed out of the room and headed for the shower.

CHAPTER FIFTY-SIX

S ariel arrived a few minutes before ten, just as Seth was surfacing from the depths of our room. Sariel grinned at him and snagged a toasted pancake from my plate before sitting down at the table. I glared at him – it had been the most buttery pancake – and contented myself with annoying my brother.

"What's with the hay-stack hair, Seth?" I pointed to the four inches of bed hair currently sticking straight up at the back of his head. Seth yawned and scratched under one of his arm pits. "Ewww. I swear if you don't wash that hand before grabbing some toast with it, I may hurl."

Seth made a tutting noise and lifted toast from the plate that mum had set down for him. He then took a huge bite of it with a flourish grinning at me. Yeuk. Males are disgusting.

I scooted into the living room and rummaged around in the clutter drawer until I found our ancient camera. I snapped a photo of the cosy kitchen scene and earned myself a chorus of "Hey!' and "Emily!"

"I had to, Seth. It's only fair that Amber should see the truth about you. Beneath that façade of male beauty that she's so enthralled with lurks a total Neanderthal complete with caveman hair and stinky armpits." I wiggled the camera at him. "Sariel's taking me to Norwich today so I can get it printed up while we're there."

"You're going to Norwich?" Mum looked questioningly at Sariel.

"Um, yeah. Didn't Emily tell you?" he mumbled through a slice of toast that he'd snaffled while I was playing photographer.

I groaned. "Sorry, mum. I mean to tell you on Wednesday but you were working late and then I totally forgot. I asked Sariel to take me to the Millennium Library at the Forum so I could get some stuff for my senior project at the Heritage centre." Sariel's eyebrows rose and he glanced between Seth and mum. Seth was munching on his toast, an elbow on the table to support his chin while he chewed because obviously he was still much too tired to keep his head up unsupported. The big baby. Mum was nodding thoughtfully.

"So what does the library in Norwich have that the one in Ipswich doesn't?" she asked.

"Well, I'm hoping to do my project on the Myles family and, although I can get a lot of background from Ipswich, the Millennium library has all the original documents relating to the family since Arthur Myles moved there in his last years." I smiled sweetly. "I'll just get my bag, Sariel."

Sariel nodded, grinning and, as I left the room I could hear mum telling him to look after me and make sure I didn't lose track of time. (I'm kind of notorious for being able to spend hours in libraries. Well, there are just too many darn fine books!)

We were on the road shortly before half past ten, taking a lot of B roads from Dean's Lynn through Harleston and then North towards Norwich.

"The A140 would be faster," I said as we twisted and turned down yet another back road.

"Yes, but it would also make us more visible." Sariel muttered.

I nodded and made a face. "This is all very secret service and, although I enjoy playing a Bond girl, when are you going to tell me what this is all about?"

Sariel glanced at me. "You make a good liar. Even I started to believe we were going to the library." He smiled.

"I'm a teenager, Sariel. We're wired to be good at making our parents believe our stories." I twisted in my seat to face him. "Don't think I don't know that you're trying to change the subject. I am queen of answer avoidance so you can't fool me. Now, where are we really going?"

Sariel grimaced and sucked in a breath. "We're going to get you tattooed."

I blinked, opened my mouth and then closed it again. Then I sat back and folded my arms. "You're not joking are you?" He shook his head. "Then I really hope you're ready to meet God again."

Sariel frowned and looked over at me. "Why?"

"'Cause if you really get me tattooed, my mum is going to kill you."

We parked near the Assembly House and I got an hour in the Millennium library, which wasn't nearly long enough but ensured that I had a lot of leaflets and printed information to take home and convince mum that I'd actually been where I said I was going (We're devious, us teens) and then we got back in the car and headed North again, out of the centre of the city.

"We never really talked about what happened last week," I said softly as we turned down a side street bristling with boarded up shops and terraced houses.

Sariel shrugged. "I knew we'd get around to it eventually." I could hear the smile in his voice.

"I'm sorry," I told him. "I should've listened to you."

He nodded. "Yep. You should have, but you need to figure things out for yourself, Emily." He patted my knee. "I'm learning."

I smiled at him. "I think he'll ask me out." I told him. "Adam, I mean. Oh, quit rolling your eyes."

"He lied to you, allowed you to think that he wanted to meet you and left you to be interrogated or tortured by his pack..."

"He didn't leave me, he stayed and he held back one of the ...guys who wanted to attack me."

"What a hero."

"Well, you were making fun all the time. You didn't sound like it was any big deal."

"And would it have helped if I'd told you that the pack was unstable and I thought the alpha, what was his name?"

"Rick."

"Yeah, Rick was going to crush your windpipe while your lover boy stood by and watched. Would that have made you feel better?"

I folded my arms and looked out of the window. "No, I guess not. Where are we going anyway?"

Sariel laughed. "Yeah, Queen of changing the subject, all right. We're going to meet a friend of mine."

"You have a friend who does tattoos?"

"You have friends who enjoy maths and physics; I have a friend who enjoys sticking needles into people." He shrugged.

"Sariel?"

"Hmmm?"

"I don't like needles." I sounded like a three year old.

He sighed. "Don't worry; I'll hold your hand." He patted my knee again and I couldn't help the smile that spread across my face. A few hours spent holding hands with Sariel didn't sound so bad, right?

CHAPTER FIFTY-SEVEN

"Is it ever going to stop?" I whined for maybe the billionth time, squeezing Sariel's hand a little harder. Behind me his friend, Danny (he of the needle and ink enjoyment stuff) sighed and grumbled about my pathetic pain threshold. "You ever stick some of your own needles into yourself?" I asked. "You should try it sometime. It bloody hurts!"

Sariel chuckled. "Do you ever stop complaining? It's like a constant stream of carping and bellyaching."

I scowled. "And how many tattoos have you had done, oh great one."

Sariel grinned over my head at Danny. "A few."

"Show me."

"Er, no."

"Why not? Because you're lying? Not very manly to admit you're too chicken to have them done in front of your sadist friend, is it?" I squirmed as Danny shifted in his seat and what felt like several gazillion needles punched into my back.

"Stay still," Danny complained, "Another hour maybe and you'll be done."

"Another hour?! Oh my God! I'll be dead in another hour." I wailed and looked up beseechingly at Sariel. "Why are we doing this again?"

Sariel sighed and endured another tight squeeze of my hand. "Like I said, it's for your protection."

"And how will a pretty picture protect me. Ow!"

"Stay still!" Danny's tone was less than impressed but quite frankly I didn't give a damn. He wasn't the one lying half naked on a table getting needles tipped with coloured ink stuck into him.

"It's not just a pretty picture, Em. The tattoo you're getting is of two very powerful symbols of protection which, when combined together, will defend you from…unwelcome advances."

I looked sharply up at him. "You know what he's planning then?"

Sariel nodded. "I knew since London. He's quite excited about it."

I narrowed my eyes. "So why do this now?"

He sighed and looked away for a moment. "I honestly didn't think he'd go through with it. He's sensed that you are, or could be, very powerful so I thought he'd protect you instead of…" He made a face. "Anyway, Rosie came to me last night. She thought I should know that Dennis and Nybbus have both put in claims. And so has Daeshan." He watched me carefully for my reaction.

"Eww, eww and double eww."

"Couldn't have put it better myself." We grinned at each other.

"So this tat will protect me from them?" I asked. Sariel nodded slowly. "Do I sense a 'but' coming?"

"Well, it will protect you up to a point – it will repel most demons but the strongest will be able to deal with it. It will be an inconvenience to them, will mess with their heads a bit, confuse them and give you time to…"

"Cut off their heads with a big sword?"

"Well, I was going to say run away. Feeling a bit violent?"

Danny chuckled behind me and I looked up at Sariel in shock. I'd forgotten that Danny was there. *Uh, oh. Are we gonna have to cut off Danny's head now?* Even in my head, my voice sounded a little too enthusiastic about that idea but Sariel laughed.

"No, it's okay. Danny's in the loop with all this stuff. We can trust him."

"How do you know?" I asked, turning a little to shout over my shoulder, "No offense."

"None taken," Danny told me. "I've been tattooing your boy here for longer than you can imagine, Miss. We were friends for a long time before that too; back to a time when to betray a friend were both dishonourable and a sin before God."

I wanted to look over my shoulder at Danny, to see if I could tell by the look on his face if he was joking with me or not but I contented myself with looking at Sariel instead. His smile at his friend was mellow with shared memories. I wanted to ask more about their friendship but the last little speech was the longest Danny had made since we'd arrived and I got the feeling that he wouldn't be too comfortable with twenty questions.

"So," I turned my attention back to Sariel. "You do have tattoos, then?" He nodded reluctantly. "So come on, show me."

"Er, I'd rather not." Sariel wriggled on his chair and I gripped his hand a little tighter.

Behind me Danny was sniggering. "Think he may be shy," he suggested.

I considered Sariel's uncomfortable expression. "Your tat isn't on your butt is it?"

Danny belly laughed as Sariel's eyes widened. "No it most certainly isn't." He protested.

"So, what's the problem?"

"Reckon he's worried that you'll see his perfect body and not be able to control yourself, Miss." Danny choked out.

I pushed myself up onto my elbows. "Is that it? You're worried I'm going to launch myself at you again?"

"Again?!" squeaked Danny, earning a glare from Sariel.

I raised an eyebrow. *Chicken.*

Flirt.

I'm in pain here, distract me before I hurl all over your Reeboks.

Sariel shrugged his hand from mine and stood up, sighing loudly. He took off his jacket and threw it onto one of the spare chairs in the tiny work room, then reached for the top buttons on his denim shirt. He paused. "Do you mind?"

I shook my head. "Not at all, carry on."

"Not while you're both watching."

"Oh for goodness sake!" I averted my eyes and looked around the room. Danny had the walls of his small shop covered from floor to ceiling with photographs and stencils of the tattoos that he did. There were flowers, pixies, fairies, dragons, crosses, scroll lettering and, of course, angels; some of which were in colour, some were sepia toned and a number were striking in black and white. One in particular caught my attention – it was a tiny angel sitting on a rocky outcrop. She had pale blue wings tipped with delicate fringes of silver. Her head was resting on her arms which were folded across the top of her legs in a pose of complete sorrow and desolation. I felt a lump in my throat as I looked at her. "Did you draw that one?" I asked, pointing to her.

"Yes, Miss." Danny's voice was soft.

"Is she a fallen?" I asked.

There was silence for a moment. "Aye, Miss. Her name is Uriel."

I was about to make some comment along the lines of 'Isn't Uriel male?' when my eyes flicked towards Sariel and I caught my breath. He was standing with his back to me, shirtless and, although I took in all the delicious tanned skin and broad shoulders, what really drew my eyes was the tattoo.

CHAPTER FIFTY-EIGHT

S ariel had wings tattooed onto his back. And not just any wings. His were dove grey with shimmering streaks of silver and deep violet here and there amongst the startlingly realistic filaments. They spread out from his spine, across the width of his shoulders and cascaded down each side, the tips disappearing into his jeans. I reached out to touch them, expecting to feel soft, silky feathers instead of hot skin. "They're beautiful," I said a little breathlessly.

"Yep. Took months to finish 'em," Danny told me, pride obvious in his voice. "Give us a twirl then. Show her the other side."

Sighing Sariel turned around and I raised an eyebrow, trying to keep my eyes on the rich array of symbols scrolling across his pectoral muscles and wrapping around his abdominals. The scripting was beautiful, the interlocking design of the Celtic runes and pictographs was incredibly detailed and the black ink on his tanned skin was certainly eye catching. It was difficult to concentrate on the tattoos 'though – I wasn't used to such an abundance of naked, fit male flesh within kissing distance..

"Er, what does that mean?" I asked to distract myself pointing to a small piece of writing just above his belly button.

"Amina y'Eloi," said Sariel. "It means 'Soldier of God' in my language."

I managed to meet his eyes. "You have a whole different language?" He nodded. "I thought it would be English, or maybe Latin." He grinned and turned to grab his shirt from the back of his chair. I watched in fascination as his deltoids and biceps flexed with the movement, tilting my head so I could watch his tattooed wings shift across his back as he stretched his shirt over his head. I wanted to reach out and touch the tattoo again to feel his skin shift under my fingers. I wondered fleetingly how far the tips of those wings extended down below his waistband.

Er, easy on the strong projection please.

Oh, um, sorry. Maybe you should teach me how to block? It would save me a lot of embarrassment.

"Will it be much longer?" I grumbled to Danny as Sariel re-dressed.

"About an hour."

"You said that about half an hour ago," I complained.

"Well then it'll be half an hour more. If you already knew then why did you ask?" He mumbled to himself and went over the same area three of four times just to make sure he was hurting me as much as possible (Well, okay, probably not but that's what it felt like).

Sariel was sitting back down in his chair, his shirt buttoned to just below the top button which did nothing to stop me thinking about what I now knew was underneath it. "Emily, please," he whispered.

I sighed. "So, teach me already."

He took my hand again and I jumped a little at the contact before forcing myself to relax. *Ancient bloke, fallen angel, not interested.*

What?

Never mind.

He shook his head. "Okay, relax and close your eyes. That's it, breathe deeply and concentrate on your breathing for a bit. Breath in, breath out. Feel the air in your lungs and the beat of your heart. Imagine your blood pumping around your body with each breath and each beat. Good. Now, let's think about your mind. You have to imagine it as a place, somewhere that you're comfortable."

My mind immediately went to Sariel's library but I forced myself away from it. I need somewhere of my own. I thought about my bedroom but Seth was there, our back garden? No, too many houses overlooking it.

"What if I can't think of anywhere?" I asked drowsily.

I could sense him rolling his eyes. "Okay, then imagine somewhere. You have a good imagination, Emily. Use it. Build yourself a place."

I thought about a house on a cliff overlooking the ocean. There was a beach snuggled into a cove to the west and room after room opened onto incredible views. Waves thundered against rocks far below or hissed and chased sand up the beach and I turned around on the wooden deck and went inside. It was warm and cozy and I giggled when I realized that the inside of my cliff home was 'Bag End' from 'Lord of the Rings' – lots of wood, circular doorways, books and maps scattered everywhere, a pot of tea on the range. It was perfect.

"Okay, I'm here. I'm in my place. It's…"

"You don't have to tell me anything about it, Emily. It's your place." Sariel told me. "Now. Remember how it makes you feel to be there?"

"Yes, safe, comfortable, warm."

"Perfect. Those feelings are your anchors, your safeguards and in your mind you can weave them into defenses. Imagine building a wall around your special place. The wall is made with strong bricks and you know how strong they should be – you want them to protect the place you've created, don't you?" I nodded and realized that my head had slipped down onto the day bed that Danny had made me lie down on. My left cheek was pressed into a small pillow and I could smell cinnamon and heather. "Tell me when the wall's built." Sariel whispered.

I sank into a strange dream of stacking bricks one on top of the other, cementing them together with glue given to me by Johnny Depp's Mad Hatter and tapping them into place with my granddad's hammer. The wall towered above me and surrounded my serene and Tardis-like hobbit house on three sides. The last side was open to the ocean but it felt safe on that side and so I left it as it was. "I'm done." I whispered, afraid of breaking the spell of peaceful contentment that I seemed to be under.

"Good," Sariel's voice seemed to be coming from far away. "Now, if you need to think about something that you don't want to share, or if you need protection from another's thoughts, you can hide behind the wall."

"How do I get here quickly?" I asked, sleepy and sluggish.

"You just have to imagine how it makes you feel to be there."

"And if I want to come out again?"

"You just imagine yourself on the other side of the wall."

I gave a little soft snort of laughter. He made it all sound so simple but surely you couldn't just think yourself over a...oh.

I was looking back at my wall, seeing it from the other side – it looked like a fortress.

I'm outside.

Good now try to get back in and I'll keep...

I was back and everything was quiet. I zipped back out again.

...so you can tell me if it works or not.

I giggled. *It works.*

Well done, Emily. You'll probably need to practice when you're awake too.

Huh?

I opened my eyes, blinking and looked around. Sariel and Danny were drinking coffee a few feet away. "Are you done?" I asked in surprise.

"Have been for about half an hour, Miss. Thought you'd be lodging here tonight by the way you were snoring." Danny laughed.

I glared at him and sat up slowly, rubbing my eyes and yawning. I tried to twist around to see my tattoo. Danny sighed and moved me across to the door where he'd hung a long mirror. He held another up in front of me and I was able to look into it and see my back. I gasped in delight. "Oh, wow! It's beautiful." I told him. Danny beamed at me.

At the small of my back I had a medium sized, upright pentagram in various shades of black and grey. In the very centre of it was a Celtic knot in colours of gold and brown, drawn with such intricacy and beauty that it took my breath away. Both symbols were connected by the intertwining green stems of five white roses.

"What does it all mean?" I asked Danny, softly, still staring into the mirror.

"The upright pentagram and the Celtic sigil are both powerful symbols of protection. The white roses are for secrecy, silence and the presence of the angels. The five of them symbolize the wonder of life and the ability to look past the obvious and see the truth. The number five is also linked to spirituality and the realization that sometimes the best trips are taken in the mind." He winked at me in the mirror and I turned to smile at him.

"Thank you, Danny. It's absolutely amazing." His grin widened.

"Okay, Emily. Once Danny puts a bandage on that we'll need to head for the coast or we won't make it today." Sariel slapped his friend on the back and gave him a proud and happy smile.

"The coast? Where are we going now?" I wailed.

Sariel shook his head wearily at me. "Well, if you want to get your pal Adam's knife back then we have to go and speak to Asmodeus."

I sat down dejectedly on the edge of the day bed. "Do we have to?"

"Quit being a baby."

"Slave driver."

"Drama queen."

I folded my arms and did what I do best in these situations – scowled.

CHAPTER FIFTY-NINE

D anny had covered my new tattoo with a sterile bandage which I had to keep on for a few hours. He'd also given me a small tube of antibacterial ointment to rub onto it and instructions not to 'pick the scabs' (yeuk) and not to 'get the damn thing too wet' until it was all healed which would take about 3 weeks.

I sat forward in the car seat, leaning my head on my folded arms while Sariel drove and we made calls on his mobile to Rosie, asking for an appointment with Asmodeus, and my mum, to tell her where we were going. I also made a call to Annie to tell her the goss – when I told her about getting a tattoo she squealed with delight and I could hear Dylan in the background asking "What? What's she saying? What's happened?" over and over.

Sariel drove the back roads back to Dean's Lynn and then took main roads through Ipswich and Colchester before turning back onto B roads for the last few miles to the mansion that Asmodeus called home.

We arrived shortly after 8 and Rosie was waiting for us at the front door. She was wearing a conservative gray suit with a frilly cream blouse and black heels. Her hair was pulled severely back from her face and swept up into an elegant chignon. Her green eyes followed the car into the sweeping drive in front of the house and she waited with her arms folded as we got out and walked up the steps to meet her.

"He's in the pool," she told us. "He seemed to be pleased that you were coming to see him." She glanced behind me.

"Seth's not here," I told her with a slightly smug grin. "Wait. This place has a pool?"

Rosie was staring at me, her nose wrinkling. "You're different," she told me, stalking up beside me. She sniffed. "Still smell like hot days in the sun and massage oil."

"What?!" I sniffed my own arm.

"There's definitely something…" she touched my arm and yelped, jumping back as 'though she'd been burned. Her eyes wide, she turned to Sariel. "What did you do?" She blanched beneath her make up. "He'll kill you."

I frowned at Sariel's impassive face. "What does she mean? Sariel?"

He smiled. "Let's go and catch him in his Speedos, shall we?"

I grimaced and made a retching noise. "Bleugh. Was that really necessary? I'll be having nightmare visions of that for weeks now!"

I followed Sariel into the main house and down the corridor past the kitchen. To the right was another door with stairs beyond it that led down into the basement. We went down and for a moment I just stood and gaped.

"Most people keep old paint tins and broken toys in their basements," I whispered. My voice echoed around the vast room which had been converted into a pool area complete with loungers, a small dining table for six, and a sauna. The main feature was, however, an azure blue pool which seemed to run the length of the house. The room was bright; with lights in every corner, up lighters under the water; and large, green, leafy, plants giving it a neat jungle feel.

Asmodeus was wrapped in a fluffy cream robe and lying on one of the loungers. His hair was damp and he was drinking from a small china cup whilst reading a newspaper. He raised the cup to us when he caught sight of Sariel striding towards him.

"Good evening. What a wonderful surprise. Will you join me in a coffee? Or perhaps you'd prefer a dip?" He smiled that smarmy, charming smile of his and I sighed, shaking my head and followed Sariel.

"Thank you, Sir, but we're here on business," Sariel told him as I caught up.

Asmodeus made a face – part surprise and part distaste. "Hmm. Should we adjourn to the table?" He waved a hand vaguely in the direction of the dining table beyond a low archway.

Sariel shook his head. "No, sir. We won't take up too much of your time. It's to do with the Weres."

Asmodeus narrowed his eyes and looked up at me. "I see. Sit then and tell me what's going on with your Were friends, Emily."

Sariel and I plonked ourselves down side by side on the nearest sun lounger. I wanted to ask Sariel how to go about telling him everything but I was very aware that using any form of secretive communication in front of Asmodeus was probably not a good idea. "Well, they seem to think that we stole something from them." I said at last.

Asmodeus raised and eyebrow and then chuckled. "They're always complaining about something. What have we apparently done to annoy them now?"

"The knife that David had for the summoning of Azrael, do you remember it?"

Asmodeus nodded.

"Well, the Weres say that it was stolen from them and they want it back."

He laughed again and took a sip of his coffee. "Do they indeed? And what if we don't have it?"

"They made a threat to hunt Emily if she was unable to obtain it for them," Sariel told him.

Asmodeus looked up at him sharply. "And I hope you took care of that threat most expediently."

Sariel shook his head. "The alpha's cub is in Emily's class and a friend of hers. He is no direct threat to her. He's, um, uninitiated." Sariel looked meaningfully at Asmodeus who scowled and nodded. "I thought it best to leave the decision about what to do in your hands, master." He bowed his head subserviently and I frowned.

Asmodeus studied me in silence for a few minutes, making me feel more and more uncomfortable. It was balmy in the pool room and I could feel sweat trickle down my back and under my bandage. I worried that my tattoo would run. I worried that Asmodeus was reading my mind without me realizing it. I worried about Rosie's remark to Sariel. Letting me get a tattoo wouldn't make him hugely popular with mum and if it affected Amadeus's little bidding war for me then he probably wouldn't be too impressed either. So why do it?

"We do have the knife," Asmodeus was saying. "It is safe." He stood up and began pacing. "I knew that it belonged to the Weres but quite how your young torturer managed to get his hands on it is a mystery. Perhaps one of the pack is a traitor?" Sariel made a face and Asmodeus nodded to him. "Unlikely, yes, but not impossible. What we have to consider is who gains from a feud between my house and the Weres. They're not as powerful or as influential." He went on pacing and muttering to himself.

"Or who gains from me being dead and you blaming the Weres," I said softly. Asmodeus and Sariel looked over at me. "Sorry, just thinking aloud."

Asmodeus' face was serious as he sat down on the edge of his lounger. "Azrael would never have been able to hurt you," he said thoughtfully.

I nodded. "But he might have hurt Adam."

Asmodeus lifted an eyebrow.

"The alpha's son who was also taken prisoner with Emily." Sariel reminded him.

"Yes, he might very well have used the cub if you hadn't thought to use your blood to keep him safe." His eyes searched mine. "I've never really understood how you knew to do that."

I kept my heart in my chest with difficulty – it was pounding hard enough to jump out and run off back to Dean's Lynn on its own. "I read a lot," I said lamely.

"Indeed." Asmodeus turned a knowing frown on Sariel who remained as impassive as always. "So the question then becomes; who would have benefitted from a feud between my house and the Weres due to the fact that we would've been blamed for the death of this cub?"

We sat in silence for a moment and I looked at the serious expressions on both Sariel and Asmodeus' faces. It seemed entirely obvious to me, what was confusing them? "Wouldn't the other houses benefit most?" I asked timidly.

Asmodeus looked at me. "Explain."

"Well, at the party everyone was playing nice but it seemed to me that there was a lot of competition under the surface. As you said, you have a lot of power and influence. You're also well protected." Asmodeus nodded and glanced at Sariel who was listening to me with an expression of pride on his normally closed features. "If even a few of your guards were busy elsewhere..."

"Like fighting the Weres," Sariel added and I nodded.

"...then your protection is lower and the way is open for someone to try and get to you or your family."

Asmodeus smiled wickedly and I shivered. It was easy to forget that he wasn't human sometimes; but when he showed his teeth and smiled like that, then you saw him for the predator that he really was. He stood up and tightened the belt of his robe. "I will give you the knife to return to your Were friends, Emily, on the understanding that they help us to find out who stole it from them. The perpetrator will be brought to justice and the penalty for their deceit will be swiftly dealt."

"Can't trust a demon, eh?" I mumbled and earned a raucous laugh from my father.

CHAPTER SIXTY

No matter how many arguments I tried, Asmodeus wouldn't take no for an answer – I was staying the night.

After fixing us both a light supper in the kitchen, Sariel led me into the family room at the back of the house where we dined on his speciality – cheese on toast – and watched TV, sitting together on the sofa and giggling at Cougar Town. I felt good, relaxed, chilled. I should have known that it was too good to last.

My room was on the first floor. It had an amazing four poster bed, an en-suite bathroom and a view towards the back of the house in the general direction of the sea. It was too dark to see much by the time Sariel saw me safely to my door but he explained that there was a pretty walled garden, a small tennis court and a sun deck at the back. I could explore in the morning.

"Where do you sleep?" I asked as Rosie deposited a selection of sleep-ware on my bed. "What's all that?"

"I sleep on the third floor," Sariel told me. "It's not too far away."

"I didn't know what you'd like since you seem to have weird taste in clothing so I brought a little of everything." Rosie explained. "Now, I'm off to bed. I have an early start in the morning. She glanced between Sariel and me, pulled the door closed and then seemed to think better of it and opened it again. "I expect you'll be wanting to get to bed yourself, Sariel." She said pointedly before leaving.

I rifled through the clothes on the bed. There was a chocolate brown baby doll set with cream lace edging and next-to-nothing lace panties, a long white cotton Victorian-looking nightgown with a high lace ruffle neck, a pink and white playboy t-shirt studded with diamante and a matching pair of shorts with 'sexy' across the back in fuchsia pink sequins.

"Wow. And she thinks my taste in clothes is questionable." Sariel laughed as I held the Victorian nightie up. It even had long sleeves and I would be tripping on the hem. "I suppose it was nice of her to help me out."

Sariel headed for the door and I resisted the urge to ask him to stay longer and keep me company. He turned at the door. "Feeling scared?" I nodded and lowered my eyes. Now I felt ridiculous and childish. "Why don't you practice going to your place?" He tapped his temple. "Sometimes I go to my garden when I can't sleep and it settles me."

I smiled at him. "I'll try it."

"Good. Oh, and there's a phone on the table. If you need me just dial '4' and I'll only be a few seconds. Ok?"

I nodded and, with a final smile, he left.

CHAPTER SIXTY-ONE

I woke screaming in agony.

Jumping from the bed I scampered into the en-suite and snapped on the light, whimpering. I examined myself in the mirror above the sink but not even a millimeter of my skin was marred by a cut, bruise or scar. Confused and slightly disoriented I went back into the bedroom and pulled back the curtains. It was still dark outside with the subtle lighting of the sky that promises dawn isn't far off.

I decided to get dressed and turned back towards the bed. The pain took me by surprise, lancing through my stomach and up towards my heart. My legs turned to jelly and I hit the floor hard. My mouth opened to scream but no sound would come out. I honestly thought I was dying. This was it. A heart attack in the bedroom of a demon's country manor - what a way to go.

The pain slipped slowly away and I was able to sit up a little, brushing sweat from my eyes and feeling it run down my back and my throat. Something in my arm snapped and I squealed in fear, lifting my arm up to inspect the damage. I searched every inch but there was nothing and, strangely, no pain. I pulled myself up onto the bed and pulled up my borrowed t-shirt. My flat stomach was clear. Huh?

I had felt something slice into my skin, had felt it rip up through my body and now there was nothing? I had heard something snap in my arm – a bone breaking – but there had been no pain and nothing was out of place. I wiggled my fingers in front of my face. Yep, all present and operational.

I lifted the phone and dialed Sariel's room. The phone rang and rang but no-one answered. I put down the receiver and sat staring at it for a few moments while fear settled between my shoulder blades and concern began to chew at my insides.

Pain zapped through my neck for a split second and I gasped. The agony was quickly dampened and then dissipated altogether. I frowned. I knew now what I was feeling. The pain was Sariel's and he must've been working hard to block it from me.

I pulled on my trainers and burst through the bedroom door, tripping over the seated form of Alexa. We rolled across the hall and I bounded to my feet, heading for the stairs. I made maybe two strides before Alexa caught my arm and hauled me back.

"Master says you must stay in your room," she said, her fingers digging into my upper arm.

"I'm going to Sariel's room." I told her, trying to shake her off. It was like tying to shake off a pit bull.

"Why?" she looked confused.

"Because I want to go jogging with him," I told her, figuring that telling her the truth would not be a good plan.

Alexa's china doll features creased into a frown. "At four in the morning?"

"Yeah, um, too much caffeine last night," I said with a grin.

Alexa released my arm, her eyes distrustful. "Then I will go with you. Master told me to stand guard but I guess I could walk or run guard too."

"Er, yeah. I guess you could." So she was coming with me. I didn't care, finding Sariel was all that mattered.

We took the stairs two at a time and she showed me which room belonged to Sariel. The door was unlocked and I clicked on the light.

The room was spacious with only a bed, wardrobe and small writing desk. The bed was still made and the room was tidy and clean. He hadn't slept here last night. I turned back towards the hall, uncertain about what to do. Invisible fingers tightened around my throat and a disembodied voice shrieked into my ear. I fought for breath and for a moment my vision swam showing me, not Sariel's room but a cavernous space lit by flickering lamps where a tall hooded figure leaned close to my face and tightened his grip on my wind pipe. Sariel fought to keep me out of his head, giving me a less than gentle push back to my own body. Alexa was watching me carefully, as though waiting for me to grow horns or have an alien explode from my belly. I grinned widely at her.

"Wow, he's up early, huh? Maybe he's waiting outside for me already," I suggested. Alexa rolled her eyes but followed me downstairs and through the silent house. We went out by the front door and I stood for a moment shivering in my borrowed t-shirt and shorts while I got my bearings and made a decision about which way to go.

I led Alexa around the side of the house and out past the deck. My heart was pounding or perhaps it was Sariel's heart that was hammering a thrash metal tempo, I was getting kind of confused about who was feeling what.

To my left was the tennis court, to my right a flagged path led to the walled garden and there was also a path straight ahead which was swallowed by trees at the edge of the property. I stopped, uncertain again. Three options and I had no idea which one to take – where did demons torture their victims? Wouldn't they go to hell for that? I mean, who wants blood and entrails all over your tennis court? I gagged on that image. The idea of seeing Sariel with blood dripping from his hollowed out abdomen was just a step too far. What should I do now?

I turned around a full 360 degrees but Asmodeus hadn't seen fit to help out with a glowing neon sign that specified the way to his torture chamber. Damn!

"So, are you guys going jogging on the beach or what?" Alexa asked. She blew a large bubble gum bubble which popped loudly in the still of the early morning. Hmmm. Alexa. Who better to ask the way to the demon's lair than another demon!

"Alexa, I wonder if I could ask you something," I said slowly turning to face her.

She chewed fiercely on her gum for a moment. "Okay."

"If I decided that I wanted to, I dunno, torture someone, where would be the best place to go for that?" I gave her a 'seriously interested' look and hoped for the best.

Alexa chewed and regarded me carefully. "Who would this be, this person you want to hurt?"

"Um." I racked my brains. "Well, you know the way my eighteenth will be a big, um, day? I was thinking that maybe my dad would allow me to have some fun with whoever wins the auction. Y'know ... afterwards."

"You mean after they've used you, you want to be able to inflict pain on them?" I nodded and she clapped her hands delightedly. "Can I watch?"

I gaped.

And then I recovered fast. "Yeah, sure. I mean, if I'm allowed."

She sighed. "Yes, Asmodeus usually prefers to do things like that himself."

"Absolutely. So where would be a good place?"

Alexa smiled, showing two rows of small but wicked looking white teeth. "Follow me. I know just the place."

CHAPTER SIXTY-TWO

There were forty-two steps set into the side of the cliff leading to the mouth of the cave. I counted them all to keep my mind off what we might find at the end and by the time we got there my leg muscles were in spasm and my sense of Sariel's feelings were growing stronger with each step. I could feel his broken bones knitting back into place, hear the snap of each finger that Asmodeus broke again and sense the huge effort of will that it took for Sariel to keep his pain from me. I felt weird, eerily calm even though my heart burned with fury. Asmodeus was hurting Sariel and before we'd even entered the cave I knew that I would try to kill him.

Sariel had known that finding a way to protect me would cost him suffering at Asmodeus' hands but he'd done it anyway because he cared. Whether he just thought I was a decent half human being, a friend or because he saw me as more than that wasn't important right then. The fact was that I cared about him and Asmodeus was hurting him because of me. That was more than I was willing to allow.

The cave was well above the water line but still damp and dark. There were torches every few feet and they cast flickering shadows all around us. Alexa strode purposefully beside me, her eyes shining and a contented smile on her face. I laboured under the weight of my anger and the knowledge of what Sariel was enduring. We walked for maybe ten minutes and then the passageway opened out into a large room that had been cut into the rock.

Sariel was lying on a rocky ledge in the middle of the room and I had to bite my fist to stop from crying out when I saw him. He was pale, like a statue of white marble, and streaked with his own blood. His hair was caked with it, his chest awash with it and his jeans were stained black with it. Asmodeus had been off to my right, choosing a new weapon. He came into my line of vision, polishing a small silver implement with a wickedly curved blade. He was so intent on how much more of my friend that he was going to carve up that he didn't hear us come in. Alexa opened her mouth to call to him and

I slapped my hand over it and shoved her back into the passage. She looked at me in shocked amazement. I kept my hand over her mouth and whispered to her urgently. "I won't tell him that you led me here if you leave now." She glanced into the room and then back at me. "Sit down outside my room. I'll say I got out through the bathroom window or something. You were never here. You never saw me come out." She shook her head fiercely. "Please, Alexa." I whimpered. She frowned and I could almost hear the cogs turning in her head as she tried to figure things out. Glancing back towards Asmodeus, she finally nodded and I carefully took my hand down, backed away and let her leave, then I retraced my steps.

Sariel's body was half raised in agony from the rocks that he was lying on. His neck stood out in cords and his mouth was wide in a soundless scream of despair as his head turned slowly to look my way. His eyes pleaded for help even as he shook his head and his mind pushed against mine. Asmodeus seemed to be trying to remove the muscles from his right leg with his hooked contraption.

I snapped.

There was a table to my right where Asmodeus had been standing earlier. It was cluttered with an assortment of knives and other instruments. The Were's knife was there too and it was this that I grabbed before I swung around, pelted across the blood soaked floor and jumped for Asmodeus. It all happened in slow motion. I had the time to see Sariel's startled eyes look into mine. To see him mouth 'No, Emily, Run.' And then I was on Asmodeus' back, leaning over his shoulder and driving the knife deep into his chest.

Blood sprayed in an arc as he spun us around, bellowing like a bull and reaching back for me. I clung on, pulling the knife free and striking again. He fell to his knees and I was jolted free, rolling across the ground, striking my shoulder and hip. I felt nothing. I was up in the blink of an eye and hurried to Sariel who was heaving himself from the rocks. I was still holding the knife and I glanced at it briefly, the sight of Asmodeus' blood on it made me catch my breath for a second and then I shoved it into the pocket of my sequined shorts.

"Don't be an idiot. Run, Emily. He'll kill you." Sariel spluttered.

"I'm not leaving without you," I told him, slipping my arms behind his shoulders and helping him to his feet. He grimaced and I felt the residue of his torment slide over me. "Quit trying to protect me. I know you're in pain, let me take some of it if that helps." I nagged.

Sariel sagged against me and coughed, spraying blood across the floor. "It's okay," he told me, catching sight of my anguished face. "I'm healing. It'll be okay."

We staggered our way to the edge of the room, rested briefly and then lurched down the passageway and out into the biting air. The trip to the top of all those steps seemed to take forever and I kept looking back, certain that Asmodeus was just behind us. He never came out of the cave.

"Keys," Sariel whispered. "Car keys in the kitchen. My phone in the cloakroom. Left pocket of my jacket."

"What?! We can stop at a payphone somewhere if you need to make a call."

He took a wheezing breath. "Please, Emily."

I nodded, more concerned now than ever and dropped him at the foot of the main steps. It took me almost three minutes to locate his car keys on a peg board in the kitchen and to drag his phone and jacket from the hall cloakroom. They were the longest three minutes of my life.

Sariel was slumped against the concrete steps when I came out. He struggled to sit up and I pulled and hauled him to his feet, anxious to be away from that house. We limped to the car and lurched inside.

"Can you drive?" He rasped.

"Er, well I sat in on one of Seth's lessons," I told him.

We looked at each other. "That'll have to do. I'll direct you and the traffic'll be light anyway."

"Where are we going?"

"Somewhere safe. Let's go. I have calls to make."

"Who do you need to call? You're bleeding and you have bones broken and, oh my God, you still have bruise marks from Asmodeus' fingers on your throat. We need to get you to a hospital." I touched the marks lightly, feeling faintly nauseous.

"I have to send someone to get your mum and Seth away from your house."

"Huh?"

He looked at me sadly. "You can't go home again, Emily."

CHAPTER SIXTY-THREE

I slid into the pew and gazed up towards the front of the small parish church. Jesus hung from a huge white cross, his face bathed in the afternoon sunshine shining through the stained glass windows. To his left a statue of the Madonna looked benevolently over the small congregation, her right hand extended as if in welcome.

We'd been moving around now for four days, changing cars when we had the opportunity, stealing clothes from washing lines, sleeping rough. Sariel said that mum and Seth were safe. They were confused, of course, worried for me and scared about what exactly was happening, but they were safe and for now that was enough. I would see them again soon. Asmodeus was alive but badly wounded – the Were knife, it seemed, worked especially well on demons. His anger went beyond nuclear and he had what amounted to an army looking for us.

I took a few deep breaths and tried to relax in the serene quiet but my gaze shifted around, looking for possible pursuers. I didn't think I would ever feel safe again.

Someone slid into the pew behind me and I stiffened, waiting for a knife to the throat or the cold steel of a gun at the base of my neck (the perils of an over-active imagination).

"I brought a friend," Sariel whispered.

I turned around in surprise and came face to face with a dark skinned man whose brown eyes twinkled with humour. "Emily," he said in a deep baritone. "It's a pleasure to meet you, finally. Sariel has told me a lot about you. My name is Danel."

I smiled at him and raised an eyebrow at Sariel who managed not to meet my eyes. "Pleased to meet you, Danel." I said softly.

He smiled, studying me intently. "I apologise for staring. You're just not what I expected."

"That's okay. I'm sure I'm quite a sight." I looked down at my 'borrowed' clothes and ran a hand through my filthy hair. Sariel managed to still have a glow of beauty about him whereas I just looked like a hobo.

"I was wondering if you'd like to come to my home and get cleaned up. I'm sure a hot shower and a good meal would go a long way towards making you feel a bit better. My wife purchased some clothes for you both – they're not exactly high fashion but they're clean." Danel turned to Sariel. "How long do you think you can stay?"

Sariel sighed. "I don't want to risk staying for two long, Dan. If they track us here then your family would be in danger."

I frowned. "I'm not going to his house if it's going to put him and his family in danger, Sariel."

Danel smiled gently at me and clapped a hand on Sariel's shoulder. "We have been waiting for the chance to be of service to you for a very long time, my old friend. And we have all taken precautions. They will not find you here. Stay tonight at least. I know Samyaza is keen to see you and to meet your Emily."

Sariel smiled. "I know, he is kindly providing passage to Italy for us."

"Italy?!" I snapped.

Sariel sighed and glanced at Danel who nodded in acknowledgement and made himself scarce. We watched him walk back down the aisle and leave the church before Sariel moved into the pew beside me. We sat in silence for a moment.

"You remember when you asked me about your ability?" he asked finally and I nodded. "I wasn't entirely honest with you." I opened my mouth to complain but he went on talking. "This ability is only shared between angels, Emily, and for a mortal to be given such a gift is highly unusual. In fact it is unheard of." I rubbed my temples. "What I believe is that this ability was gifted to you by one of the archangels. They are the only ones with the power to do this. Do you understand?"

I shook my head. "Are you saying that Asmodeus isn't my real dad? That my dad is an archangel?" I could hear a note of hope in my voice.

Sariel shook his head. "I can't change who your parents are, Emily. But at some stage you were gifted with this ability because they were able to foresee that you and I would meet."

"So, why did they ensure that we would be able to …communicate like this?"

He shook his head and rubbed his eyes wearily. "I don't know, Emily. I wish I did."

"Could it have been an accident?" I asked, trying to think it through. "I mean, what can a seventeen year old do that a posse of archangels can't?"

Sariel chuckled softly. "A 'posse' of archangels?"

I grinned. "Yeah. I mean, I've met you so I just can't imagine your home boys wearing flowing white robes and carrying harps."

"You think I make a bad angel?"

"Don't go getting your panties in a twist, I just meant that I reckon God's Special Forces have probably modernized by now."

"God's special forces? Yeah, I suppose that's what they are. So, how do you imagine them?"

"Well, the normal troops are all like boyz in the hood, y'know? Ready to rumble at the drop of a hat kind of dudes. Then you have your Marine Corps angels who might have to go into enemy territory so they're all kind of 'Buffy and Angel' types – dressing in black with the long leather dusters and stakes in their utility belts. Oh, and they'll have swords strapped to their backs like Blade. That'd be cool." Sariel raised an eyebrow but said nothing. He had a small smile on his lips 'though so I figured he was enjoying the image. "The archangels would be different 'though, I reckon they would all be like James Bond types – suits and exploding chewing gum." We giggled together and it was good to make him smile although it didn't last long. He lapsed into serious mode again.

Talk to me. I told him.

About what?

Whatever's bothering you. I don't like it when you block me out and you've been blocking really hard this past few days.

Sariel turned to look at me. "I've put you and your family in danger, Emily. I will never forgive myself for that."

I eyeballed him in astonishment. "What are you talking about?"

"I got lost in the...pain and I forgot to block it from you." *Or perhaps I wasn't strong enough to block it.* He shook his head. "That was unforgivable. You should never have had to go through that.

"No, Sariel. You should never have had to endure everything that Asmodeus did to you. Or Daeshan before that. You blocked what you could but, you said it yourself, we have a link and I was given a link to you for a reason. Maybe the reason is that I was to save you." It seemed a reasonable suggestion to me.

"At the cost of your life? Or Seth's? Or your mother's?" He shook his head again. "That cost is too high. I would never allow it."

Well, that got my back up immediately. "Oh, you would never allow it? Really? Hello?" I tapped him on the head. "Anyone in there? This is me you're talking to, pal. I will do what I want to do whether you 'allow' me to do it or not. You're not the boss of me. Besides, free will, remember?" I folded my arms and Sariel sighed. He leaned forward on the pew and put his face in his hands.

"I've ruined your life, Emily. I'm sorry." He sounded heartbroken and in that moment I fell in love with him all over again.

I put my hand on his shoulder. "Sariel. You are not responsible for me and my actions. That was your job when you worked for Asmodeus but you're free now. I am my own person and I make my own decisions about whose ass I kick and which of my friends I refuse to allow to be tortured. Okay?"

He sat back and looked at me for a long time. "You saved my life, Emily."

"Er, yeah." A thought occurred to me and I wriggled uncomfortably in the pew, ashamed that I hadn't thought of it before. "Look, Sariel. I don't want you to feel that you have to stick with me anymore, just 'cause of what I did. It was no big deal. I'd have done the same if it was Dylan or Annie getting their innards made into outards. So don't feel, um, beholden. Okay? You can go wherever you want to go and I'll be okay." I swallowed a sudden lump in my throat and was glad that I sounded a lot braver than I felt.

Sariel reached over and pulled me close for a hug. He smelled of damp clothes and warm skin and I wrapped my arm around his waist, afraid that this was where he left and I would never see him again.

I'm not leaving you, Emily. And not just because you saved my life. I have friends who can help us. Friends that you may be able to help as well.

What do you mean?

He sighed and stroked my hair. "I'm not certain, so I can't tell you but I know of some people who might know more than we do. Getting them together will be tricky but not impossible."

What about mum and Seth?

They're safe and we'll visit them before we leave for Italy.

Who's looking after them?

A friend. You'll meet her very soon and then you'll feel better.

How long will we be in Italy?

Not long.

I get plane sick. And boat sick. I felt tears threaten again. It was finally hitting me. I would never go home again.

Sariel released me and stood up. He glanced towards the cross, closed his eyes briefly and then turned his attention back to me. He held out a hand. "Come with me, Emily," he said softly. "Trust me."

I gulped, felling a hot tear slide down my cheek. I knew that if I went with him that there would be no going back. School would be over forever; I might never see Annie or Dylan again; mum, Seth and I would be hunted by Asmodeus for as long as we lived and I'd definitely never get a date with Adam if I ran off with a fallen archangel. And if I didn't go with him? I'd never know exactly who I was, my family would be under Asmodeus' thumb for as long as he found us entertaining, Adam still wouldn't be interested and I wouldn't be able to see Sariel anymore. Either choice would cause pain and problems. My nerd brain was still summing up the pros and cons but my heart was already way ahead of it in the decision-making process.

Taking a deep breath, I looked up at Sariel and took his hand.

ACKNOWLEDGMENTS

Big thanks to my friends Shauna, Bex, Debbie and Irene for all the reading of drafts and correcting of my horrendous mistakes.

And to my family for your support and enthusiasm; and for putting up with my daydreaming, burnt dinners and book-buying problems! Love you. Xx

I hope you enjoyed 'Demon's Daughter'

Look out for the next installment in Emily's story

– 'Demon's Revenge'.

Available soon!

Connect with me online.

Email me: mailto:aly3008ish@gamil.com

Facebook http://www.facebook.com/pages/Ashley-McCook/117584825012617

Twitter: http://twitter.com/@aly3008

Smashwords: http://www.smashwords.com/profile/view/ashleymccook

www.ingramcontent.com/pod-product-compliance
Lightning Source LLC
Chambersburg PA
CBHW031308170626
46807CB00001B/323